MORGAN AT GATEHAVEN

MORGAN
AT GATEHAVEN

Walter Miller

The Book Guild Ltd
Sussex, England

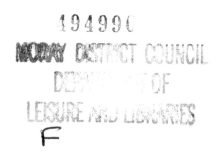
This book is a work of fiction. The characters and situations in this story are imaginary. No resemblance is intended between these characters and any real persons, either living or dead.

This book is sold subject to the condition that it shall not, by way of trade or otherwise, be lent re-sold, hired out, photocopied or held in any retrieval system or otherwise circulated without the publisher's prior consent in any form of binding or cover other than that in which this is published and without a similar condition including this condition being imposed on the subsequent purchaser.

The Book Guild Ltd
25 High Street,
Lewes, Sussex

First published 1994
© Walter Miller 1994
Set in Baskerville
Typesetting by Southern Reproductions (Sussex)
East Grinstead, Sussex
Printed in Great Britain by
Antony Rowe Ltd
Chippenham, Wiltshire.

A catalogue record for this book is
available from the British Library

ISBN 0 86332 912 8

CONTENTS

1

Arrivals

To the casual visitor, Gatehaven in the early 1970s would
not have seemed the kind of place that people would
write a book – or even write home – about. A small West
Country town, close to a thriving city, it was on the way to
nowhere in particular – the end of the line. That is of
course if it still had a line. Its single-track railway link to
the city had been closed some years earlier and its former
railway station, inexplicably refurbished not long before,
was now a supermarket. Approaching the town by road
the unwary would be guided by a sign to the 'Town
Centre'. This it was not, geographically, or in any other
sense. The single thoroughfare which strove in vain to
fulfil this function had barely outgrown its former
existence as a village street. Narrow and winding, it
consisted of a parade of small shops leading to a square
dominated by the parish church nestling traditionally
cheek by jowl with a village pub. The marks of past
religious dissent were also present in the shape of two
nonconformist chapels, both undistinguished buildings
which contrasted, by design at the time of their
construction no doubt, with the relative splendour of the
parish church. A little more surprising perhaps, given
the religious history of the region, was a cluster of
buildings half-hidden in a lane meandering away from

7

the square which housed a community of Catholic priests and nuns.

But first impressions, even with one or two small surprises, would yield few clues to the essential Gatehaven, which closer inspection might reveal. The shopping parade, for instance, showed an unusual preponderance of banks, building societies and estate agents. Many of the old shops had surrendered to the challenge of the railway station turned supermarket and their replacement by these newer enterprises yielded a clue to the existence of a wider Gatehaven which surrounded and almost swamped its village heart. Away from the village, Gatehaven had long ago turned its fairest face to the sea. But now, here on slopes which once ran green and wooded down to the beach, stood rank on rank of 'identikit' executive homes. Wiser planning practices had now halted this intrusion but the exodus from the city in earlier times had left its mark. Gatehaven now was home to two communities – 'villagers' and 'newcomers' – existing uneasily side by side and sharing, not without difficulty, its inadequate facilities.

Unlike other towns in the region, Gatehaven had few pretensions to being a seaside resort. Its beach was rocky and barren, stretching for about half a mile below the new estates on the slopes above. Between these and the beach, lapped by grey forbidding tides, was what passed for its promenade. This owed its existence more to sea defence considerations than to any aspirations to attract visitors. There was a cafeteria at one end and a public convenience at the other. Both, regardless of weather, were by some strange municipal edict open from May to September only, and afforded no comfort to either residents or occasional visitors at any other time of year. Between these monuments to community enterprise of yesteryear, the austere sweep of the promenade was broken only by a couple of storm shelters, their once-glazed panels now open to the elements and their rough benches pock-marked with the carvings of generations of young lovers. On a grey winter's day amid the swirling sea mist and the raucous accompaniment of the gulls, few coastlines could have seemed more inhospitable. To the romantic, however, there remained the vestige of a certain wild beauty about it, which owed little to the attentions of man.

Industry was hard to find. The old harbour had long been abandoned to the sea-birds and creeping vegetation and the rusting hulks of a few old fishing smacks were the sole testimony to its past. Farming continued roundabout but mechanization had displaced manual labour to such an extent that few of the 'villagers' were employed on the land any more. Their conversation still tended to revolve nostalgically around tides and seasons but they had drifted into a new kind of economy. Most of them had two jobs. The check-out girl at the supermarket would re-emerge by night as a barmaid; the traffic warden would acquire an off-duty resplendence as steward of the social club; the postman underwent a daily metamorphosis to reappear as a taxi-driver at pub closing-time. And so it went on. The 'villagers', deprived by progress – if progress it was – of their traditional livelihoods, had created a kind of economic stranglehold on the provision of services in the town, not only feeding off their own needs but battening too on those of the 'newcomers'. Not for the families of the latter were the part-time jobs beloved of bored wives and youngsters anxious to boost their pocket money. The 'closed shop' was total.

The distinction between 'villagers' and 'newcomers' was not confined to employment. Both dress and speech also marked them out. Except where the requirements of employment dictated otherwise, 'villagers' tended to affect the garb of the countryside – mud-caked gumboots, sleeveless leather jackets and shapeless hats, all of which had seen better days. Conversation was conducted – deliberately it seemed – in an exaggerated West Country burr with a blatant disregard for the cases and tenses of standard English usage. No doubt it owed more to symbolism than schooling.

'Newcomers' were markedly different. In the main they were commuter families, young husbands upwardly mobile in their city-based careers, driving there each morning smart-suited in their company cars, wives clogging the town's inadequate roads in inevitable second cars – usually small and far from new – to deposit children at school. Apart from these fleeting glimpses, they were rarely seen except on Saturdays. Then, clad in ubiquitous jeans and trainers and speaking in flat classless accents they would descend *en famille* on the supermarket in an orgy of stocking up. They invariably paid by cheque, leaving muttering queues of cash-carrying 'villagers' behind them at the check-out. Credit cards had been slow to penetrate the Gatehaven economy.

Leisure pursuits were a problem for 'newcomers' but not for 'villagers'. There was a once-a-week cinema show in the social club, but this was organized by 'villagers' for 'villagers'. The flat floor demanded craning necks, and the overlong interval for liquid refreshment and local gossip, not to mention the age and quality of the films, held little attraction for 'newcomers' accustomed to more sophisticated diversions. There had been an ill-fated attempt by some of them to remedy Gatehaven's social shortcomings by forming an amateur operatic society. This had been plagued from the outset by 'villager' control of the social club bookings and the local predilection for what were seen as less élitist pursuits such as bingo and barn dances. Eventually the venture collapsed amid a flood of relentlessly-spread rumours that it was a cover for a wife-swapping ring. The story had passed into Gatehaven folklore and was held by many to be true.

Little of Gatehaven's unique eccentricity, rooted in the social division between 'villagers' and 'newcomers', would have been apparent to the casual visitor. Nor was it to Morgan when he picked it out from his AA book as being convenient for his work in the city and yet situated beside the sea. This was the fulfilment of an old longing which had dogged him throughout ten years of land-locked claustrophobia in a South London suburb. He was a senior civil servant posted on promotion to the West Country, urbane and well-travelled. When he arrived in the dying days of 1972, with his wife and three children, after celebrating an uncomfortable Christmas on packing cases, his expectations of Gatehaven were modest. If he felt anything it was regret at the passing of the rail link. Good for rail, he would muse, but bad for transport. He was prone to the laconic comment.

Family reaction to their move to Gatehaven was mixed. His children, exploring the storm-lashed promenade the day after they arrived, returned home to pronounce that it was better than Greenwich Park. This was some compensation for Mrs Morgan's reaction. On her first sight of the village high street she upbraided him for bringing her to what she called 'Dodge City'. As for Morgan, his small tremors of excitement at being beside the sea were no measure at all of how Gatehaven would surprise and entrance him in the years to follow. He was about to participate in a series of events so bizarre that they would be indelibly etched on his memory.

2

Cheers

It was a few days after Morgan's arrival in Gatehaven. He made his way through the dark January evening – all rolling sea mist and rain which wasn't quite rain but just as dampening – towards the Catholic presbytery. He was in temporary disfavour with Mrs Morgan, who ruled her household with a rod of iron cast in pre-Vatican II zeal. At their first attendance at Mass the previous Sunday, Morgan, frustrated by an over-long sermon and impelled by a desire to reach the tobacconist's before it closed, had failed to report their arrival to the clergy. This was standard practice in the much-travelled existence of the Morgan family. Hence his pilgrimage to the presbytery.

Its grey bulk loomed through the dark. Morgan wiped the mist from his face and rang the bell marked 'Visitors'. The heavy door creaked open almost immediately to reveal a fat bespectacled man clad in baggy flannels, a string vest and braces.

'May I speak to Father Alphonsus?' said Morgan with due deference; the clergy and their acolytes demanded proper esteem in Morgan's social awareness.

'I am he,' boomed the fat man, biblically sonorous.

Morgan paused. His perception of the clergy was about to undergo a radical change.

'Well, my son?' said the priest a trifle impatiently.

Morgan recovered his composure and explained his mission.

'Not a moment too soon,' said Father Alphonsus. 'The others are out and I'm just off for my constitutional. Wait a tick and you can come along.'

He disappeared into the dimly-lit interior and returned almost at once, his string vest covered by a shapeless sweater and tugging on an old anorak. They set off together.

'Which way, Father?' said Morgan conscious of Mrs Morgan waiting at home for his return.

'There's only one way on nights like this,' replied Father Alphonsus. 'Some sustenance is what we could do with.'

'Oh,' said Morgan, lost for words.

In the gloom Morgan had failed to notice a large building set back from the road between the presbytery and the convent. As they approached he realized that it was a hotel. The drifting mist swirled around its flickering neon sign. This meant to convey 'Hotel Maritime' but the 't' in 'Hotel' had teetered to a crazy angle; at first glance it appeared to indicate 'Hovel Maritime'. Morgan could not suppress a chuckle.

'Surprised at the way I'm dressed?' said Father Alphonsus, misreading Morgan's amusement.

'Well,' began Morgan only to be interrupted.

'I don't like strangers in pubs to know I'm a priest,' said Father Alphonsus.

Morgan shrugged his shoulders; he was becoming used to surprises.

They entered the building. The hall retained some pretensions to grandeur. Straight ahead were double glass doors and above them a sign which said 'Ballroom' but there was no sign of activity in the darkened interior.

To the left was a door marked 'Cocktail Bar'.

'Not in there,' said Father Alphonsus, 'it's a penny a pint dearer.'

He veered to the right and pushed open a door marked 'Public Bar'. Morgan followed him into the room.

'Good evening Father,' said the pretty girl behind the bar, a sentiment echoed by at least a half-dozen of the patrons present.

So much for anonymity, thought Morgan. Meanwhile Father Alphonsus was responding to the greeting with something between a blessing and a wave.

God bless the house,' he muttered, and then addressing Morgan, 'mine's a pint of that one there – it's the best value here.'

Morgan suspected that he was present at some ritual occasion. A wry smile flickered over his face.

'Two pints of Father's,' he said and the barmaid delivered them without a word.

They sat at a table in the corner, hurriedly vacated by a customer at a nod from Father Alphonsus. The ritual continued. Father Alphonsus fished in his anorak pocket to produce a cigarette roller and tobacco. He proceeded laboriously to construct one of those mis-shapen tubes, strands of golden weed drooping from its ends, which bear a passing resemblance only to the conventional product.

'Got a light?' he said, banging various pockets in a seeming paroxysm of frustration.

Morgan obliged and was immediately enveloped in clouds of blue smoke. Father Alphonsus coughed his way through his first inhalations.

'Tell me about yourself,' he spluttered.

Morgan obliged.

'Very good, my son,' was the response, 'I'll make a few

notes. You'll be an asset to the parish.'

Morgan's essential particulars were swiftly scribbled on the back of a beer mat. A vision flashed across his mind of a parish register which consisted of a box of beer mats. His amusement must have been obvious.

'Think we're a funny lot here, do you?' said Father Alphonsus.

Morgan's polite denial never reached his lips.

'I suppose we are,' continued the priest, 'clergy, nuns, people – the lot.'

How true that was would become apparent to Morgan later.

He learned much about Gatehaven's idiosyncrasies that evening. Father Alphonsus spoke volubly as if he were holding court. There were, it seemed, four priests at the presbytery, all members of some obscure Eastern European order, whose predecessors had drifted into Gatehaven on a tide of missionary fervour following the Catholic emancipation of the last century.

'We Catholics have got it all here, you know,' commented Father Alphonsus. 'Church, hall, school – the trouble is, it's all a hundred years old.'

Morgan waited for the arrival of the begging bowl but it didn't come. Instead, Father Alphonsus turned his attentions to his fellow priests.

'None of the others want to stay,' he said. 'Two of them are desperate for the foreign missions and one wants to pack it all in and be a social worker. God in Heaven,' he added wearily, '*he* needs a social worker.'

Morgan struggled to recall if he had done all that Mrs Morgan had decreed. Oh God, no, he thought, there's the school. His youngest child was still of primary school age. With some difficulty he managed to interrupt Father Alphonsus's flow to enquire about schooling.

'You'll have to ask those bloody nuns about that,' said

15

the priest a trifle shortly.

Morgan reeled at the epithet. What on earth had the poor sisters done to deserve it? Enlightenment soon came. Father Alphonsus launched into yet another anecdote. His sister, it seemed, was a nun and he was obliged by some vestige of family loyalty to spend his annual holiday with her each year, an event which he regarded as a precursor to purgatory. Because of this all nuns were anathema to him. It was, thought Morgan, a strange attitude for a priest, but he was beginning to realize that with Father Alphonsus, like God, all things were possible.

Suddenly Father Alphonsus leapt from his chair.

'Time to water the horses,' he said, and made for the door. 'Mine's the same again,' he shouted *en route,* and the barmaid sprang into action. She had, of course, seen it all before, and two pints were on the bar almost before Morgan reached it.

'That'll be ten shillings exactly,' she said.

Morgan, resigning himself to the role of host, fished in his pocket for fifty pence.

In the few minutes that elapsed before the return of Father Alphonsus, Morgan took in the room. It appeared to have been furnished on some kind of a 'reach-me-down' basis, with chairs and bar stools topped with a faded ragged velour which had seen service in more auspicious surroundings – probably, mused Morgan, the cocktail bar. They contrasted oddly with the rough tables and emulsioned stone walls with their plain facia disturbed only by indistinct sepia prints of what Morgan assumed was old Gatehaven. The bar counter was empanelled in black and surrounded by a brass footrail above which innumerable scratches remained untreated. Morgan's eye flickered over the customers – about a dozen in all, all male, and clothed in the off-duty garb of 'villagers'. They were mostly gathered around the bar addressing the barmaid in a buzz of banter to which she riposted with evident relish. She was a pretty blonde girl, dressed in black and white as if making some concession to the status of the establishment. It did, after all, claim to be a 'hotel'. Morgan wondered where he had seen her before but at that point Father Alphonsus returned.

The 'watering of the horses' had clearly renewed his thirst.

'That's better,' he said, attacking the fresh pint with enthusiasm. Morgan struggled to match him mouthful by mouthful, stealing surreptitious glances at his watch. The bar clock had stopped at twenty past three – a.m. or p.m. Morgan could only guess. Father Alphonsus followed Morgan's glare.

'No need to worry about the time,' he chuckled, 'it's closing time by appointment here.'

His glass was now drained. He licked his lips and fiddled with it.

Morgan rose to his feet reluctantly. 'Another drink, Father?' he said.

'That's most kind, my son,' replied Father Alphonsus as he began another performance of his cigarette-making routine. 'Leave your lighter here while you get them,' he added.

Morgan produced his lighter, flicking the wheel as he did so. To his annoyance it failed to light. His momentary embarrassment was, however, abruptly ended by a shout of 'There you go Father' as something hurtled past his head. Father Alphonsus lunged to his right like a goalkeeper and disappeared beneath the table. A second or two later he re-emerged clutching a box of matches.

'Saved again,' he said.

Morgan made for the bar. As if by magic the drinks

17

were waiting as he got there. By now he was worrying about the wrath of Mrs Morgan. His simple errand to the presbytery was turning into what she would term a 'session' for which he had not obtained her prior acquiescence. A silent prayer crossed his mind. At that point fate, or maybe God, intervened. The telephone behind the bar spluttered into a shrill ring. The barmaid answered it.

'For you Father,' she called. 'It's Bridie.'

'Roger and out,' said Father as if responding to some carefully rehearsed military signal. 'Tell her I'm on my way.' He stared ruefully at his untouched pint. 'It'll be a sick call,' he said to Morgan. 'Bridie's the house-keeper.'

Morgan marvelled at the bush telegraph. Father Alphonsus lumbered towards the door struggling with the zip of his anorak.

'God bless,' he shouted at the room at large.

The barmaid intervened. 'Don't forget your groceries, Father,' she said, producing a large hamper from beneath the bar.

'Thank you Sally,' said Father, enveloping it in his arms as he shouldered-open the door and disappeared into the hall.

Suddenly Morgan remembered where he had seen Sally before. She was the check-out girl at the station-turned-supermarket.

The departure of Father Alphonsus brought a change in the atmosphere. Conversation at the bar dropped to a murmur and Morgan became conscious of inquisitive eyes turning sporadically in his direction. That they were speculating about him he had no doubt. He gulped his pint. Morgan was not the man to leave a drink half-finished and in the present company he felt it would be something of a loss of face. He rose to his feet.

'Excuse me,' he said, 'I'm afraid Father's left his drink.'

'That'll be OK,' responded Sally. 'I'll put it in the cooler till he gets back.'

Morgan felt he should have known.

'Well – er, good night,' he said, 'I'll be off.' What sounded like a muffled series of grunts accompanied his exit.

Morgan hurried home. He let himself in quietly, dutifully removing his damp shoes just inside the front door, nursing a hope that Mrs Morgan might have retired to bed. It was forlorn. She appeared at the living-room door, fixing him with a cool unflinching stare which in his mind he thought of as her 'evil eye'. It conveyed her disapproval to perfection. He opted for the truth. After all it was strange enough to rule out any assumption of invention on his part.

'My dear,' he said, 'we have joined a very strange parish.'

3

Reprise

Morgan's account of his evening at The Maritime had an unusual effect on Mrs Morgan. Far from provoking condemnation, which he had feared, it resulted in curiosity, so much so that a day or two later she announced their intention of paying a visit. Morgan was in two minds over this. His relief at her reaction was tempered by anxiety about her possible perception of the bar and its customers. Then a thought struck him. The cocktail bar of course, he mused, that's bound to be more her style.

After supper, when Morgan had recounted the events of his day, as he always did, they were ready to set off. The rain of the last few days had gone but it was cold with a hint of frost.

'It's not far,' said Morgan, 'we can walk it in a few minutes.'

'In that case,' replied Mrs Morgan, 'I'll need my umbrella.'

Morgan, at the front door, looked heavenward at the cold clear sky, bespeckled with a myriad of stars.

'Yes, my dear,' he said resignedly. Mrs Morgan was seldom without her umbrella.

Entering The Maritime, Morgan pushed open the door of the cocktail bar. He paused to absorb the scene; it

20

was not what he had expected. No chrome or glass or arty wall panels – instead his eyes lit on what seemed to be a replica of Olde England. Plastic beams, perfectly symmetrical, adorned the ceiling, horse brasses still lacquered shiny from manufacture, which had never graced a stallion, glinted prolifically from every corner of the room. Mock-oak trestles and wooden benches jostled around a log fire, the faint hiss of its gas connection betraying its artificiality. Propped against the square black upright which marked the corner of the bar was a notice-board which would not have been out of place in a church. It announced 'Today's Special' which, since it happened to be 'Ham, Egg and Chips' Morgan thought to be distinctly unspecial.

His momentary appreciation of the scene was interrupted by a dig in the ribs from Mrs Morgan.

'Where shall we sit then?' she asked.

Morgan gazed at the empty tables; most customers were at the bar. He pondered how people entering bars or restaurants always seemed to engage in debate about where to sit even when the entire room beckoned. Mrs Morgan settled the matter by making for a corner near the fire, peeling off her coat and gloves and stowing her umbrella beneath the table.

'It's very nice,' she commented. Morgan was non-committal.

'Your usual, my dear?' he asked, and went to the bar.

Here was another surprise. The barmaid was a small dark girl with raven hair swept back to a pigtail and secured by flowers on each side of her head. She was dressed in black in skin-tight breeches reminiscent of a matador, stopping at her calves to reveal shapely ankles teetering on high-heeled shiny shoes resplendent with gilt buckles. Around her neck an ornate crucifix swung like a pendulum over her plunging neckline. To Morgan she seemed about as far from the ambience of Gatehaven as one could contemplate. Her name, he gleaned from the bar-side chatter, was Dolores. He assumed, correctly as it turned out, that she was of Hispanic origin.

Morgan ordered a gin and tonic for Mrs Morgan and then a pint of what he recognized as 'Father's' for himself.

'Ees off!' responded Dolores. Morgan looked blank. Had he mis-heard, he wondered?

'Ees off. Barrel empty,' said Dolores with a hint of shrill impatience.

'Oh, sorry,' said Morgan in some confusion as he sensed ears around the bar following the exchange.

He ordered a pint from the next pump along, which turned out to be lager. This was not to his taste but he had no wish to prolong his embarrassment.

Seated with Mrs Morgan he surveyed the company at the bar. They were 'newcomers' – womenfolk perched on stools, legs crossed, playing with schooners of sherry, menfolk draped nonchalantly against the bar like giant stick insects sipping from half-pint mugs of lager but never grasping them by the handle. Jeans, tee-shirts and training shoes were heavily in vogue. The buzz of conversation revealed a preponderance of those slightly nasal drawls which in latter times seem to pass for universal English.

At this point enter mine host – or rather mine hostess, a lady for whom the phrase 'fair, fat and forty' might have been invented. She appeared to have been compressed into a black dress, seemingly to match the outfit of Dolores, but betrayed by somewhat more generous proportions. Gigantic gaudy earrings and a bouffant hairstyle in an unlikely shade of what seemed to be blue only served to enhance the vision. Once seen she could never be forgotten.

'Good evening all,' she greeted the room at large, swooping on the stick insects and their wives with evident *bonhomie*.

'All right, Ted, all right, Fiona, all right this one, that one and just about everyone,' was her opening salvo to the group around the bar.

They were all apparently all right as they responded in slightly ragged unison, 'All right, Sonia.'

The bar was now functioning in 'all right' mode. Suddenly Sonia spotted the Morgans, who were also 'all right' but, modestly, had not joined in the chorus. She bore down upon them, reaching for tinted frame spectacles which dangled from a chain about her neck.

'You're new here,' she said, evidently relishing an increase in trade.

'Yes,' replied Mrs Morgan. 'We've just moved here from London,' she added in a barely disguised tone of metropolitan superiority.

'From London, fancy that,' gushed Sonia, as if it was outer space. 'You'll be finding it a bit quiet here then.'

Morgan, from what he had seen and heard so far, was not so sure. Sonia snapped her fingers in the general direction of Dolores.

'Another round here and one of my specials,' she said.

'So kind,' said Mrs Morgan, and then as if to regain the initiative, 'I do like your dress.'

Liar, thought Morgan enjoying the opening gambits. Mrs Morgan was out to establish her presence.

Dolores minced her way to the table with the drinks. Morgan settled back to savour the encounter. Talk of shopping and families, pets and gardens swirled like a

23

tide around him. His role was to nod or shake his head at appropriate moments, a practice at which his long experience of Mrs Morgan had left him adept. Eventually he began to find it a trifle boring but relief was not too long in coming. The door burst open to reveal Sally from the public bar.

'Trouble Sonia,' she gasped, all hot and bothered. 'It's Jason – he's had one too many.'

Sonia heaved herself to her feet with the unsolicited aid of Morgan's shoulder.

'Excuse me,' she said and, hitching up her dress, sailed towards the door like a marauding battleship.

Morgan felt sorry for the unfortunate Jason.

'Well, my dear,' he said to Mrs Morgan, displaying his habitual disregard for statistics, 'how about the other half?'

'You've already had it,' she replied with superior perception.

Morgan capitulated and rose to his feet. Mrs Morgan gathered her belongings and led the way to the door. The denizens of the bar barely noticed their departure. In the hall Mrs Morgan stopped suddenly.

'What's in there?' she asked, stabbing her finger at the door of the public bar.

'Er – just another bar,' replied Morgan, 'spit and sawdust I s'pose.'

At that moment the bar door opened and Sonia appeared dragging a dishevelled young man by the ear. Morgan assumed that this was the hapless Jason.

Sonia propelled him unerringly towards the front door amid an exchange of language which could only be described as ripe. It ended with his unceremonious ejection accompanied by Sonia's shrill dread sentence, 'You're bloody well banned indefinitely,' she screamed.

She continued to stand at the front door, hands

aggressively on ample hips as she followed the progress of the now chastened Jason into the night.

'It seems very interesting in there,' said Mrs Morgan, 'shall we take a look?'

Morgan demurred. 'We've had our share for tonight dear,' he said, hoping to strike the same chord as Mrs Morgan a few moments earlier.

'Spoilsport,' replied Mrs Morgan, oblivious to Morgan's impeccable consistency, 'one more won't hurt you.'

In there it might, thought Morgan, but he thought better of continuing the argument. Mrs Morgan pushed open the door of the bar with her umbrella. Morgan made for the corner which he had occupied with Father Alphonsus.

'No – not there,' said Mrs Morgan, 'let's sit at the bar.'

There were two stools vacant amid the group of 'villagers' who seemed to be the same as on his previous visit. Morgan eyed them uneasily as the buzz of conversation gave way to a worrying hush. Scenes reminiscent of a Western B movie flashed through Morgan's mind. Sally, the barmaid broke the ice.

'Good evening, sir,' she said. 'Nice to see you again.'

'Good evening,' replied Morgan, somewhat relieved, 'a gin and tonic and a pint of er . . .'

'Father's,' interjected Sally.

'But it's not on,' said Morgan.

'It is now,' said Sally. 'Sonia had to change the barrel. There was nearly a revolution in here.'

'Well,' said Morgan, 'Father's will do fine.'

Conversation resumed among the 'villagers'. They seemed to be engaged in some kind of barter, the floor at their feet occupied by dead poultry, over which they were

25

haggling furiously. Sally moved up and down the bar attending to their liquid needs and winking at Morgan each time the tempo of sound rose as a bargain was struck. Occasionally she would engage Morgan in desultory conversation mainly about the weather. Morgan sensed she was trying to make him feel welcome, but Mrs Morgan she ignored totally. This, of course, was not to Mrs Morgan's liking and eventually her patience snapped.

'What have you got there?' she asked loudly in the general direction of the 'villagers'.

There was a momentary silence. Morgan awaited the response anxiously but when it came it was polite enough.

'What, this ma'am,' said one of them, holding up a plucked chicken by the legs. 'Straight from the market this morning – fresh as can be,' he went on.

'Are you sure?' said Mrs Morgan.

'Couldn't be surer,' was the reply. 'Wrung his neck myself on the way home.'

Mrs Morgan's nose wrinkled in distaste but she was not disposed to retreat from the encounter now.

'I'll take it,' she said, and to Morgan, 'pay the man, my dear.'

Morgan hesitated. 'But you don't know how much,' he said.

'Price is not the essence of this transaction,' said Mrs Morgan magisterially. 'Don't make a fool of me – pay him.'

Morgan edged down the bar and completed the transaction. It was a bargain. He realized that Mrs Morgan had achieved a minor triumph the like of which had so far eluded him.

'It was very cheap,' he whispered to her out of earshot of the vendor.

'No more than I expected,' she said, 'but what's more important is that they accept us here now.'

'Yes, I see your point,' said Morgan humbly.

At this point Sonia re-entered the room.

'What on earth are you doing in here?' she said to the Morgans as if nothing could be stranger.

'Just sampling the local colour,' replied Mrs Morgan, a trifle condescendingly in Morgan's view, but she hadn't done too badly so far so he bit his tongue.

'Oh I just thought the cocktail bar would be more your scene,' said Sonia with scant regard for the feelings of the rest of the customers.

'No, as a matter of fact, we like it here,' countered Mrs Morgan, 'and we've done quite nicely too, thanks to these gentlemen,' she added, pointing with one hand to the chicken and waving imperiously with the other towards the 'villagers'.

'Well – whatever turns you on,' said Sonia with a shrug of her shoulders. 'But that's not what I wanted to ask you,' she went on. She leaned on the bar and whispered to Mrs Morgan. 'You haven't any marriageable young men in your family by any chance, have you?' she asked. 'I've got to find a husband.'

'Have you?' said Mrs Morgan. 'I'd have thought you had one.'

More than one, thought Morgan.

'Not for me, silly,' said Sonia, 'It's Dolores. She's illegal – no work permit – and the only way I can keep her here is to get her married.'

'Oh, I see,' said Mrs Morgan in that tone which people use when they don't quite see. 'But we can't help – our son is far too young.'

'Worth a try I s'pose,' said Sonia. 'Keep your ears open for me won't you?'

Morgan could think of nothing less likely than Mrs

27

Morgan touting for a husband for Dolores. She was, however, equal to the occasion.

'Of course I will,' she said sweetly.

Sonia departed with an all-embracing wave to the customers, accompanied by the inevitable 'All right everybody'.

Morgan looked quizzically at Mrs Morgan.

Her face had reddened and she began, 'What a damned . . . .'

'Sh,' interrupted Morgan hurriedly, conscious of ears pricked around the bar. 'I thought it was funny,' he added.

'You mean it was a joke?' asked Mrs Morgan.

'No, not a joke – she was serious all right, but I found it funny,' he explained.

Mrs Morgan thought for a moment and smiled. 'I suppose you're right,' she said. 'Well, enough fun for tonight,' she added, 'let's be on our way.'

They gathered up their things, Morgan rather self-consciously holding the chicken. Mrs Morgan waved to the 'villagers'.

'Goodnight, gentlemen,' she said.

'Good night ma'am,' came a chorus of response.

'Good night, sir,' said Sally as if to console Morgan for his lesser role in the night's events.

'I like that place,' said Mrs Morgan, as they arrived back at the house. 'We'll make it our "local".'

Morgan grunted. He had not enjoyed the experience to quite the same extent.

'Yes, we'll go again soon,' went on Mrs Morgan, divesting herself of her coat. 'It was so unusual.'

'I'm sure we will,' said Morgan, wearily still holding the chicken. 'You've left your umbrella there.' That, at least, he thought was not unusual.

4

Neighbours

Shortly after their excursion to The Maritime the Morgans' induction to Gatehaven was to take a different direction. One evening, as Morgan settled down, children safely abed, to resume his day-long struggle with *The Times* crossword, the doorbell rang.

'I'll get it, dear,' he called to Mrs Morgan, suppressing his irritation at being disturbed on the verge of enlightenment with ten across.

He opened the door to find a small plain woman clad in tweeds who peered at him over heavy-framed spectacles.

'Marigold Speke-Johnson,' she said, as if no further explanation was called for.

'Yes,' said Morgan, his hand darting to his pocket, ready to seek relief with the smallest contribution he could decently concede to what he assumed to be some local worthy cause.

'We are your neighbours,' said Marigold.

Morgan looked beyond her to find nobody and concluded that the plurality suggested that he was in the presence of someone important in Gatehaven society.

'Er – please come in,' he said.

Marigold darted past him to confront Mrs Morgan emerging from the living-room, a prey to curiosity.

'Marigold Speke-Johnson, your neighbour,' repeated the visitor.

'How very nice of you to call,' gushed Mrs Morgan, impressed, it seemed to Morgan, by Marigold's dress and demeanour.

They sat in the living-room.

'We were just about to have a drink,' said Mrs Morgan.

Would that we were, thought Morgan.

'A small dry sherry for me,' said Marigold.

What else, thought Morgan?

'The same for me,' said Mrs Morgan, 'I adore sherry.'

Morgan suppressed a chuckle. She hated it.

Over drinks Marigold chattered incessantly. She appeared to be the repository of all local good causes. Morgan wondered sympathetically about Mr Speke-Johnson, but his entry to the conversation was not long-delayed.

'Oliver and I are having some people in for pre-lunch drinks on Sunday,' said Marigold. 'We would be delighted if you would join us.'

'How kind,' said Mrs Morgan. 'My husband has been anxious to make the acquaintance of Mr Speke-Johnson.'

This was news to Morgan, but he nodded obediently.

'Doctor!' said Marigold reprovingly, 'not Mister – Doctor.'

Mrs Morgan looked even more impressed.

'He's so busy, poor love,' went on Marigold. 'Came home exhausted this evening, had his hot milk, and went straight to bed.'

Morgan's recently assumed desire to meet Dr Speke-Johnson receded abruptly, but he tried to remain affable.

'Does he practise in Gatehaven?' he enquired, making a mental note to find another practitioner when his family required medical services.

'Oh he's not that kind of doctor,' said Marigold, 'he's a scientist in the city.'

For that relief – much thanks, thought Morgan.

Eventually Marigold departed. 'Must dash,' she said, 'have to feed the goats.'

'Of course,' replied Morgan, as though not to have goats to feed was inconceivable to civilized folk. He was glad to return to the bafflement of ten across.

Sunday came. Mrs Morgan had led the family out of Mass during the last hymn – a sacrilege if Morgan had suggested it – in order to be ready to visit the Speke-Johnsons. Morgan felt uncomfortable in his suit and tie on his day of rest but he had bowed to Mrs Morgan's anxiety to make a good impression. Mrs Morgan emerged from the bedroom attired in a floral dress and wide-brimmed hat.

'It's not a garden party,' said Morgan.

'I know that,' replied Mrs Morgan, 'but we mustn't let ourselves down. Will I need my umbrella?'

'It's only next door,' said Morgan, and off they went umbrella-less.

On the Speke-Johnsons' garden path a young goat scampered past them. Mrs Morgan started. Morgan looked down to find a liberal covering of goat droppings between them and the front door. Offering Mrs Morgan his arm, he attempted to assist her to guide her immaculate shoes past this unexpected hazard – alas with only partial success.

'Damn,' said Mrs Morgan as they reached the front door. 'I haven't got a tissue. Give me your hand-kerchief.'

'But,' began Morgan in protest, but thought better of

31

it.

Mrs Morgan lifted her dress and assumed an ungainly squatting position as she cleaned her shoes with Morgan's handkerchief.

'Don't ring the bell yet,' she hissed at Morgan, but it was too late. As if on cue the door swung open to reveal Marigold.

'Oh, my dear, is anything wrong?' she enquired.

'Not a thing,' said Mrs Morgan, with admirable aplomb, as she struggled to conceal Morgan's soiled handkerchief behind her back.

'Do come in then,' responded Marigold.

As they entered the house, Morgan felt Mrs Morgan's hand ramming the handkerchief into his trouser pocket. He pushed it further in only to feel a glutinous mess adhering to his fingers. It was not an auspicious start to the proceedings.

'Come and meet the Morgans,' announced Marigold to the assembled company as they entered the living-room.

Morgan's face fell as a phalanx of outstretched hands confronted him. Desperately trying to wipe his sticky fingers on the backside of his trousers under the flap of his jacket, he steered Mrs Morgan into the prime position for receiving handshakes, thus gaining a few vital seconds of damage limitation. She thought he was being polite. Her own discomfort had passed but this was to be merely a temporary relief.

As they passed down the ranks of outstretched hands, Morgan's own hand now clean if not quite sweet-smelling, he noticed that everyone was casually dressed. Mrs Morgan in her dress and hat brought to mind a royal personage graciously receiving homage from the peasantry. He caught her eye. There were signs of embarrassment but she was equal to the occasion.

'Excuse our dressing up,' she said to the room at large, 'we have to go on to lunch with some of my husband's colleagues.'

Morgan marvelled at her inventiveness.

With handshakes over, drinks were dispensed – small dry sherries inevitably. The names of the other guests had passed through Morgan's consciousness without stopping but he recognized one or two of the stick insects from the cocktail bar of The Maritime. Some were wearing tee-shirts emblazoned with the logo 'Gatehaven Preservation Society'. Morgan wondered quite what it was they were trying to preserve. After all, the railway was gone, the harbour was disused, and no doubt some of these very people had participated in the spoiling of the once green slopes above the beach. Nevertheless, he knew what was expected of him.

'That's very interesting,' he said, stabbing his finger at one of the tee-shirted bosoms.

'Why, yes,' said Marigold, 'are you into preservation?'

'Of course,' said Morgan with as much conviction as he could muster. 'Who isn't these days?'

'Well,' replied Marigold, warming to her theme, 'you must support our campaign to save the Victoria Regina post-box in the high street.'

Morgan found it difficult to maintain his show of enthusiasm. Post-boxes were to him distinctly uninspiring and boringly utilitarian. But he managed to conceal his thoughts. A change in the direction of the conversation was called for. He took the initiative.

'Where is Dr Speke-Johnson?' he enquired.

'Right here,' replied Marigold, and the doctor appeared from somewhere behind her right shoulder.

He was even smaller than Marigold, balding and bespectacled, and clad in one of the society tee-shirts which appeared to be rather too large for him. Morgan surmised that they were probably only made in two sizes, neither of which happened to correspond with the dimensions of Dr Speke-Johnson.

'In business, are you?' queried Dr Speke-Johnson, in what Morgan was beginning to recognize as a 'newcomer' drawl.

'No,' he replied, 'I'm a civil servant.'

Morgan was usually reticent about what he actually did, as if the Official Secrets Act was burning a hole in his back pocket.

The effect on Dr Speke-Johnson took Morgan aback.

'Oh dear,' said the doctor in tones reeking with scarcely concealed condescension. 'I would have thought a fellow like you would have been in the private sector.'

Morgan seethed inwardly. He decided to go on the offensive.

'And what do you do, may I ask?' he said with the merest hint of reciprocal dislike.

'Research,' said the doctor as if no further explanation was called for.

Morgan was unrelenting; his dander was up.

'Into what precisely?' he pressed.

'Er – garden products,' replied the doctor, his air of superiority beginning to wane.

'Slug pellets, actually,' interrupted Marigold and Dr Speke-Johnson transfixed her with a look that would have destroyed a multitude of slugs.

Morgan, conscious of his own long involvement in important affairs of state, had regained the ascendancy.

'How fascinating,' he said smugly.

Honour was satisfied.

None too soon for Morgan, Mrs Morgan signalled that it was time to go. They departed to a chorus of 'see you again soon', which Morgan devoutly prayed would not be true. Negotiating the goat droppings, successfully this time with the benefit of experience, they arrived at their own front door.

'Get the car out,' hissed Mrs Morgan conspiratorially.

'What for?' asked Morgan, genuinely puzzled.

'They will expect to see us going off for lunch,' said Mrs Morgan, still *sotte voce.*

'But we aren't,' said Morgan.

'Sh – keep your voice down and do as I say,' whispered Mrs Morgan. 'We will have to pretend. You can drive around the block and we can sneak in by the back door.'

The penny finally dropped with Morgan. Mrs Morgan's subterfuge over their dress had to be maintained if her dignity was to remain intact. He opened the garage and moved the car into the drive while Mrs Morgan went inside to tell the children that they would not be long. They drove past the Speke-Johnsons' garden gate. Mrs Morgan had been right. Marigold was at the window, waving.

Around the block Morgan stopped the car close to the rear gate to his garden. As they started to creep furtively towards the back of the house, the heavens opened.

'I knew I should have brought my umbrella,' moaned Mrs Morgan.

'Well,' replied Morgan, 'at least you've got your hat on.'

5

Friends

More by first impression than considered judgment, Morgan had chosen to live in a large rambling house close to the village. Mrs Morgan had been seduced by the detached splendour of the garden, as far removed as one could imagine from the terraced confinement of their town house in London. In the winter months following their arrival there was a soothing stillness about the lifeless lawn, the brown barrenness of flower and vegetable plots and the brooding empty greenhouse alongside. Morgan too was attracted to it. Neither of them thought too much about the explosion of growth which would accompany the spring and the hours of labour which would be needed to control it. That experience was to come.

As the winter gave way to the spring of 1973 it began. Most evenings and weekends they struggled, inexpertly, to master the garden's rampant growth. Morgan had devised a plan for distancing himself from what he now thought of as the 'unspeakable Speke-Johnsons'. The side of the garden adjacent to them was the responsibility of Mrs Morgan while he laboured a full forty yards distant on the other side. It was while cutting the privet hedge in this safe seclusion that he first encountered Arthur Potts. Initial contact was in the form of a disembodied voice.

'About time you cut this hedge between us,' it said.

Morgan snipped away at the overgrown hedge in front of him until he could see into the adjoining garden. The source of the voice was a large elderly man in the garb of a 'villager', weather-beaten with grizzled grey hair just visible beneath the uniform shapeless hat.

'How do you do?' said Morgan.

'Seen you about, lad,' said Arthur, 'and thought it was about time I got to know 'ee.'

'I'm pleased to meet you,' said Morgan, relieved to know he was not surrounded by neighbours of the Speke-Johnson variety.

Arthur, it turned out, had lived in Gatehaven all his life. Until about a year or so ago he had kept a greengrocery shop in the village, but advancing years and the challenge of the railway station turned supermarket had forced him into retirement. He was comfortably off with his state pension and the proceeds from the sale of the shop. Since the death of his wife and the departure of his children to the more sophisticated locale of the city, he had lived alone in the cottage next to Morgan's house, where he was born.

Through the summer of 1973 Morgan learned much from Arthur about gardening – and about Gatehaven. Mrs Morgan adhered to her side of the garden, maintaining her acquaintance with the Speke-Johnsons; this barely involved Morgan but for an occasional wave and greeting. Even this meagre contact was, however, on one occasion put in jeopardy by Morgan's cat which insisted on using the Speke-Johnsons' garden as a toilet. Mrs Morgan remonstrated with him over this but he managed to convince her of the futility of trying to control the habits of cats which invariably did as they, not their masters, wished. Short of having the animal put

37

down, he argued, occasional friction with the Speke-Johnsons would have to be endured. In his heart he applauded the cat's sagacity.

Mrs Morgan did not approve of Morgan's burgeoning friendship with Arthur. She considered him gruff and uncouth and prone to language which she described as 'salty'.

'Don't you get too thick with that fellow,' she would say to Morgan, 'he's not our type.'

But Morgan could be stubborn when the occasion required and she knew well how far she could go with him.

However, in the autumn of that year Mrs Morgan's forebodings about Morgan's friendship with Arthur appeared to acquire some substance. One evening on his return from work, she was waiting, eyes ablaze.

'I told you so,' she said, 'he's got a woman living there.'

'Who?' said Morgan naively, already aware of the answer.

'Your so-called friend next door,' she said. 'What are you going to do about it?'

Morgan's patience was sorely tried as he reproved her gently.

'It's not really our business,' he argued. 'Perhaps it's a relative visiting,' he proferred by way of explanation.

'Relative, my foot,' thundered Mrs Morgan. 'It's a girlfriend and she's living with him – in sin.' Suddenly, rushing to the window, she shrieked as if she had discovered proof positive. 'There – see for yourself.'

Morgan crossed to the window. He could just see in Arthur's garden a tall elegant woman hanging out some clothes to dry.

'Just look at those clothes,' said Mrs Morgan.

They were certainly not Arthur's – delicate fragments

of lacy underwear which Morgan's mind could only associate with glamorous ladies in lingerie departments. He opened the window to get a better view.

Arthur's voice suddenly boomed from the house. 'I'm ready for 'ee,' he said.

'Coming, honey,' said the woman, frizzing her hair, as women invariably seem to do at the last minute before an important assignation.

Morgan felt uneasy. Mrs Morgan was triumphant.

'And she's foreign,' she said.

Morgan too had detected a transatlantic twang in the woman's response. He continued to try and counsel neutrality.

'I still don't see what it's got to do with us,' he said.

Mrs Morgan bristled. 'What will the neighbours say?' she countered.

'I've no idea,' said Morgan, his mind boggling at the likely reaction of the Speke-Johnsons and their cronies. 'Time will tell,' he added lamely, for want of something more positive to say.

Time told very quickly indeed. Later that evening, as the Morgans sat in awkward stalemate over the affair, he with his crossword, she with her knitting, the doorbell rang. Morgan answered the door to find Arthur.

'Shan't come in,' he said, to Morgan's intense relief, 'just want to ask a favour. Got a friend come to live with me. She works in the city and would appreciate a lift of a morning with you.'

'Of course, Arthur,' said Morgan, outwardly calm but inwardly apprehensive. 'Eightish suit you all right?' he added.

'Lovely,' said Arthur. 'Knew you wouldn't let I down. See you mornin'.' And he stomped away.

Morgan returned to the living-room with a heavy heart.

'Who was it?' enquired Mrs Morgan.

He took a deep breath. 'Arthur,' he said. 'He wants me to give his friend a lift to work.'

He sat down casually and picked up his crossword as if to normalize the situation, but it was not to be.

'Friend?' said Mrs Morgan in a tone which boded ill for all concerned. 'Is that what he calls her?'

Morgan tried logic. 'Well, you wanted me to do something,' he argued. 'I can't if I ignore them – can I?'

It was a clever ploy, all the more so for being impromptu.

Mrs Morgan was half-persuaded by his ingenuity. 'Well, you had better let them know what we think about it all,' she countered, to justify her attitude.

'Naturally,' said Morgan, relieved that he had scored a point. But he wondered what he could possibly do to assuage Mrs Morgan and protect his friendship with Arthur. He was not looking forward to the next morning.

He did not sleep well and breakfast was a tense affair, but neither of them allowed the children to notice. When the time came to go Mrs Morgan accompanied him to the door.

'You're a bit bothered by this, love,' she said, squeezing his hand and kissing him with more than usual ardour.

Morgan was surprised but grateful. He should have known, however, that Mrs Morgan always came up trumps at a time of crisis. This was hardly that yet but Morgan felt in his bones that there were difficulties ahead.

Mrs Morgan tried to diffuse the situation again. 'Don't do anything I wouldn't do,' she said with a wink.

Morgan felt better.

He sat in the car, waiting. Promptly at eight Arthur appeared with the woman.

'This be Penny,' he said.

'Hi!' added Penny and got into the car.

She was attractive – tall, dark and slim in a well-cut business suit which should have stopped about the knee but which rode up in the car to reveal an expanse of sun-tanned thigh. His fleeting first impression was that she was sun-tanned all over – at least on the evidence of the bits that he could see.

'Let's go then,' she said, waving to Arthur.

As they drove off, a slight movement of the curtain, glimpsed from the corner of his eye, confirmed the watchful presence of Mrs Morgan.

The journey to the city was to take about twenty minutes. Morgan resolved to use the time to find out more about what he had now come to think of as the extraordinary affair of Arthur and Penny.

'Visiting from the States?' was his tentative opener.

'No,' said Penny. 'I'm Canadian actually but I'm based in Gatehaven for the time being.'

'I see,' said Morgan, not much the wiser. He tried again. 'Friend of Arthur's?' he enquired.

'You could say that,' was the reply.

Morgan had the feeling that she was amused by his probing.

'Actually, I'm his mistress,' she added.

Morgan gulped at the directness of the reply.

'Shocked you, have I?' said Penny, the suspicion of a smile playing about her lips.

'Well – surprised me anyway,' said Morgan, recovering his composure.

Penny sighed, seemingly in exasperation. 'It's really quite simple,' she said, 'and no great shakes. We met in a "singles" club in the city a few weeks ago. I was living in some grotty apartment and he offered me a home.'

Morgan could not imagine what Arthur was doing in a 'singles' club but he concluded that that was a question for Arthur rather than Penny.

'So, what do you think of me as your new neighbour?' went on Penny, now positively coquettish.

Morgan felt himself blushing. 'I'm sure we'll get on very well,' he said.

'I'm sure we will too,' said Penny huskily, hitching up her skirt to reveal yet more sun-tanned thigh.

Morgan averted his gaze, aborted his mission and lapsed into silence for the remainder of the journey. He was relieved when they reached his office. He felt as if he was perspiring slightly although it was not a warm day.

'Is this all right for you?' he enquired of Penny.

'Very,' she replied, smiling. Morgan was beginning to think that everything she said was a *double entendre.*

'How about going home?' he asked, as she got out of the car.

'That's very sweet of you,' she replied, 'but I have some shopping to do. I'll get a taxi.'

Morgan wondered how long Arthur's bank balance could cope with the cost of taxis from the city.

'See you tomorrow then, same time,' he said.

'Sure thing, sweetie,' she replied as she turned away.

Morgan watched her go. She was certainly an elegant woman. Not young, he mused, but much younger than Arthur – probably about my age. He snapped back into character. What am I thinking about, he said to himself. It was not a situation he was used to.

Morgan knew well what to expect when he returned home that evening. Mrs Morgan would be ominously expectant. He was not wrong.

42

'Well?' she said, as he hung up his coat.

'Not in front of the children,' replied Morgan unguardedly. The words had barely passed his lips when he realized his mistake. Mrs Morgan he guessed would now be expecting something really sensational.

'I see,' she said, but her eyes spoke volumes.

Morgan might have been mistaken but he sensed that she consumed her evening meal with more than usual speed. There was no mistake, however, about the rapidity with which the children were dispatched to their rooms to concentrate on their homework. The moment of truth had arrived.

Sitting in the living-room he recounted the events of the morning in measured tones, sparing any mention of Penny's manner towards him and his own reaction to it. Mrs Morgan's response was predictable.

'The dirty old man,' she spluttered.

'Lucky old beggar,' was the phrase which sprang to Morgan's mind but his reply was restrained.

'It takes all sorts, my dear,' he said.

Eventually Mrs Morgan's early indignation subsided and gave way to speculation.

'What on earth can she see in him?' she pondered.

'Well,' responded Morgan, as convincingly as he could, 'he's not badly off, with a nice home, and she wanted somewhere better to live, I suppose.'

Mrs Morgan was unconvinced.

'From the look of her she wants a bit more than that,' she said.

Morgan felt himself reddening.

Mrs Morgan looked up. 'Don't be so naive, dear,' she added.

As they continued to chat however, the change in Mrs Morgan's attitude became more pronounced. Curiosity was firmly in the ascendant. It was as if a page in some

43

Sunday tabloid, which she would never allow in the house, was being compiled in front of her eyes.

'I'd love to know what the real attraction of Arthur is,' she said, barely suppressing a giggle.

To Morgan's surprise he began to detect a hint of vicarious pleasure in her manner, and he knew what his next assignment was to be.

'I'll see what I can find out,' he said, 'but it's a damned tricky subject to raise.'

'You'll be equal to it, I'm sure,' said Mrs Morgan sweetly.

Morgan was not equal to it. Unknown to Mrs Morgan, his main problem was to repel Penny's flirtatious advances with as much grace as he could muster. This left little scope for inquisitive forays into Penny's relationship with Arthur about whom she was consistently reticent, preferring, it seemed, to taunt Morgan into indiscretion. His lack of progress led to Mrs Morgan becoming impatient and then bored with it all. Occasionally she would enquire after his 'girlfriend' with heavily-laden sarcasm, secure in her innate conviction that Morgan, though dear to her, was not the kind of man other women would get excited about. Events were, regrettably, to prove her wrong.

6

Crisis

As autumn shivered into winter Morgan noticed a change in Penny's attitude towards him. Her teasing on their daily journeys to and from the city had given way to long periods of silence; she seemed to have become morose and quite unlike the out-going person whose outrageous remarks had troubled him over the summer months. One morning close to Christmas Morgan's decent politeness led him unwarily into a new situation.

'Is anything wrong?' he enquired, not pondering the consequences of his question.

'Yes,' said Penny, surprisingly emphatically, 'I thought you'd never ask. I am bored – period.' Morgan was lost for words but Penny was not finished yet. 'All he ever does is take me to that bloody social club,' she went on.

'I thought it was very nice there,' said Morgan lamely. At that time his actual knowledge of the club was sketchy.

'If you like constant boozing and bingo,' said Penny ruefully. 'God – I'm dreading Christmas.'

Morgan sensed that she was expecting some response from him. After a few seconds thought, which seemed like an age to him, he bowed to the inevitable.

'Perhaps you would like to have a drink with us over the holiday,' he said hesitantly, half-hoping she would refuse. No such luck attended him.

'Now that would be something else, sweetie,' responded Penny, her voice recapturing some of her old ebullience.

All that day Morgan worried about Mrs Morgan's reaction to what he had done. By the time for going home he had convinced himself that it was ill-considered. Penny was full of it in the car returning to Gatehaven and any determination he might have had to retract the invitation was overwhelmed by her gratitude. In the event, Mrs Morgan's response was nowhere near as bad as he anticipated. She had been expecting a quiet Christmas – too quiet in fact even for her. The Speke-Johnsons – her link to Gatehaven society – were going away for the holiday and she had been recruited to look after the goats in their absence, a sacrifice which she regarded as a necessary penance to retain their patronage. Little else was planned. Her initial reaction to Morgan's news was predictable enough.

'What,' she spluttered. 'You must be mad.'

Morgan explained patiently the predicament in which he had found himself. He began to sense that her spontaneous outrage was not deeply felt and that, if truth were known, she might actually welcome the diversion he had unwittingly perpetrated. Her ultimate words were grudging but she had clearly accepted the situation.

'Well,' she said, 'you've done it now so I suppose we'll have to go through with it.'

Christmas came. Midnight Mass on the Eve followed by exchanges of presents over a drink before the children were packed off to bed exhausted. Christmas morning with Mrs Morgan hot and bothered in the kitchen preparing a gargantuan meal as she fortified herself with gin and tonic. The ritual meal ending in bloated contentment over brandy, Morgan with his cigar – a concession granted by Mrs Morgan on Sundays and Holy Days – and the children furiously pulling crackers. Later a sort of togetherness as Morgan and Mrs Morgan ploughed through a pile of dirty dishes, pleasantly at ease with each other. Finally the last act of tradition as they dozed through the admirable television sentiments of the monarch trying earnestly to reach the nation's heart.

Morgan awoke with a start in the darkened living-room. 'God – what time is it?' he said to himself, panic-stricken. Arthur and Penny were due for drinks in the evening. He made his way uncertainly to the kitchen, rubbing his eyes. Mrs Morgan was there, standing in an obviously self-congratulatory pose as she surveyed the table before her.

'My word,' said Morgan as he took in the array of snacks and sweetmeats.

But what was this? Among the delicacies were two wine glasses stuffed with cork-tipped cigarettes and topped with books of matches acquired by Morgan from various hotels in the course of his travels. Mrs Morgan followed his gaze. 'She does smoke, I imagine,' she said, 'among her other vices.'

'Er – I'm not sure,' said Morgan. 'I only see her in the car.' He tried to recall whether she had smoked in the car, but he wouldn't have told Mrs Morgan anyway. In terms of sin, Mrs Morgan held smoking to be mildly venial, but done in the car it was positively cardinal.

'Arthur smokes a pipe,' he added.

'Well I can't help him there,' she replied, 'he'll have to bring his own. Now give me a hand to get this lot to the living-room. They'll be here soon.'

Arthur and Penny arrived soon afterwards. Morgan's

first thought was that Penny's appearance did not augur well for the success of the evening. Her dress would not have disgraced a chorus line and revealed too much of her for Morgan's comfort. Mrs Morgan appeared unperturbed; no doubt it corresponded with her mind's image of Penny. She was, however, rather more perplexed when Arthur installed himself without ceremony in her favourite chair. Morgan thought she looked a trifle forlorn seated on the settee away from the handily-placed cupboard containing her knitting and supply of chocolates. The latter was a vice which Morgan held to be partially compensatory for his own predilection for a cigar and a drink.

Conversation and attendant drinking and smoking was restrained while the Morgan children were paraded to perform their party pieces before being dismissed to their rooms. At this point in the proceedings Penny breathed an audible sigh of relief, curled her legs under her like a coiled cat and gulped the remains of her 'regulation' dry sherry, which hitherto she had been decorously sipping.

'Another drink, my dear,' said Mrs Morgan in her 'impeccable hostess' style.

'Do you have any scotch?' enquired Penny.

'Of course,' replied Mrs Morgan, signalling Morgan with her eyes to fetch fresh glasses.

'I'll join 'ee,' interposed Arthur, stoking up his pipe with some villanous-looking metal instrument.

'So will I,' said Morgan, courageously jovial. 'Nothing like a good scotch to get the party going.'

'Quite,' said Mrs Morgan, taking the tiniest of sips from her dry sherry as if to shame the rest of them. Morgan knew it was a pose and that she would switch to her favourite gin and tonic at a suitable opportunity.

Over the next hour or so the two women dominated

the conversation. Mrs Morgan probed ever so politely and Penny, hands waving extravagantly in the air, repulsed her with generalities, while consuming prodigious quantities of scotch and attacking the wine-glasses of cigarettes with relish. To Morgan it seemed like a kind of gladiatorial contest which had all the signs of ending in a draw with both combatants exhausted. Arthur spluttered through several pipefuls of evil-smelling shag, but said little, taking his cue from Morgan. With two such daunting adversaries as Mrs Morgan and Penny in full flow there was little need for intervention by mere males. Eventually, with clouds of blue smoke twirling around the ceiling, Mrs Morgan abruptly terminated the engagement.

'Phew it's hot in here,' she exclaimed, rushing to open a window, seemingly oblivious to the time of the year and the temperature outside. The draught of cold air which followed aroused Arthur from his then near-somnolent state.

'Time for bed, m'dear,' he said to Penny, hauling himself from his chair and tapping out his pipe, half in the ashtray and half over the coffee table.

'Not yet, Arthur,' whined Penny petulantly, 'I'm enjoying myself.'

Morgan concluded that this had more to do with the scotch than her exchanges with Mrs Morgan. But Arthur insisted.

'No, it' high time to be abed,' he said, shuffling towards the door.

'No, no, no!' said Penny, uncoiling herself and stamping her foot to emphasize her dissent.

Arthur shrugged his shoulders. 'Please yourself, bitch,' he hissed and stomped off in the direction of the front door in high dudgeon.

Morgan closed the front door after Arthur and

returned to the living-room. Mrs Morgan was silent but the expression on her face conveyed her sense of self-satisfaction over the incident. Penny was giggling.

'He just wants his share – the dirty old man,' she said, 'let's all have another drink.'

'Why not,' said Morgan, attempting to put a finer gloss on the affair. 'It's Christmas after all.' The absence of seasonal goodwill in the recent exchanges seemed to have escaped him. He closed the offending window which had precipitated Arthur's outburst and departure and stared Mrs Morgan full in the eye. 'I think that has achieved its purpose,' he said.

She smiled what they both recognized as her secret smile; no answer was necessary and Morgan's mild reproof had been graciously accepted.

The new drink proved too much for Penny. Leaning over to extract the last cigarette from its wine glass, she tumbled from her chair in a heap of legs and bosoms trying to escape from her skimpy dress.

'Steady on,' said Morgan, but whether this remark was addressed to himself or to Penny was not clear. Mrs Morgan took control.

'My husband will see you home,' she said.

Morgan staggered uncertainly from the house with Penny like a dead weight on his arm. He too was feeling the effects of the scotch but a still small voice in his head warned him of the danger of taking too long over his errand. He propped Penny against Arthur's front door.

'For God's sake don't ring the bell,' she said. 'I don't want to wake that dirty bastard up now.'

She rummaged in her handbag eventually producing a key and Morgan opened the door quietly. He felt uncomfortably conspiratorial.

'Goodnight, darling,' cooed Penny. 'I've had a lovely

evening but now I'm too tired – even for you.'

Morgan concealed his half-felt relief in humour. 'Well, it was something else, sweetie,' he said in the best transatlantic accent he could muster.

'Sure was,' said Penny, kissing him gently on the cheek as she slid inside the door.

Morgan hurried back. Mrs Morgan had acted quickly; the living-room had been cleared of the debris of the evening and she was in the bathroom. He waited patiently outside until she swept past him to the bedroom. He took two aspirin in anticipation of the next morning's hangover – a reliable remedy which he had learnt in his bachelor days and never forgotten. Returning to the bedroom he found Mrs Morgan already in bed.

'Goodnight, darling,' she said. 'I enjoyed that.'

'I know you did,' replied Morgan, with just a hint of sarcasm. 'Perhaps we should do it more often,' he added speculatively.

'Not too often,' yawned Mrs Morgan.

Enough was enough, thought Morgan. 'Of course, my dear,' he said.

As sleep enveloped them neither could have imagined the sequel to the evening which was to come a little over a week later. It was late at night. Mrs Morgan had gone to bed. Morgan was alone in the living-room watching boxing on television – vicarious thuggery on his part in Mrs Morgan's opinion – when the doorbell rang insistently. It was Arthur, his trousers pulled on over his pyjamas, and looking very agitated.

'My God – help me. She's gone and done herself in,' he gasped.

'Who has?' asked Morgan, naively.

'Penny, of course – who else?' sobbed Arthur, trembling uncontrollably.

51

Morgan followed Arthur to his house. Penny was stretched out on the settee in her dressing-gown, unconscious if not worse. A half-empty bottle of whisky and an empty pill phial lay on the floor nearby. Morgan slapped her face gently and she stirred.

'She's not dead, Arthur – thank God,' he said. 'I'll fetch Mrs Morgan.'

His faith in Mrs Morgan at times of crisis was absolute. Returning to his house he roused her.

'What on earth is it,' she said testily.

Morgan explained and she threw on her dressing-gown and followed him to Arthur's house. Penny appeared to have regained consciousness and was gazing blankly in front of her through half-closed eyes while Arthur stood as if transfixed by the door. Mrs Morgan bent over her.

'Come along, my dear,' she said, putting her arm around Penny's shoulders.

At this point all hell erupted.

'It's him I want – not you,' shrieked Penny, pointing at Morgan. 'I've wanted him for months.'

With that she bounded from the settee pushing Mrs Morgan violently across the room. Morgan was in a quandary. To one side of him was Mrs Morgan in a heap on the floor ruefully rubbing her shoulder where Penny's blow had struck; to the other was Penny, now on her feet, eyes blazing, her dressing-gown gaping open to reveal her nakedness. Morgan concluded that Penny posed the more immediate threat to good order. He propelled her gently back to the settee into which she collapsed giggling.

'That's more like it,' she simpered, sliding her arms about Morgan's neck.

He glanced anxiously over his shoulder at Mrs Morgan and dexterously re-arranged Penny's dressing-gown to cover the worst excesses of her nudity. Mrs Morgan recovered her composure.

'Call an ambulance,' she barked at Arthur.

'What the bloody hell for?' interjected Penny. 'I'm just a bit tipsy.'

'Do as I say,' said Mrs Morgan in a tone which Morgan knew would brook no dissent. Arthur disappeared into the hall to the telephone.

It seemed an age until the ambulance arrived. Fortunately Penny had once more lapsed into a semi-coma and lay on the settee, arms and legs akimbo, still burbling expressions of longing for Morgan; both he and Mrs Morgan pretended not to hear them. Morgan stood near her, Mrs Morgan at his elbow, ready to prevent another eruption. Arthur had subsided into an armchair, his head buried in his hands.

As the doorbell rang to signal the arrival of the ambulance, Mrs Morgan prodded Morgan in the back.

'Stay and watch her,' she whispered, and went into the hall to explain the situation to the ambulance crew. Two of them came into the room to examine the whisky bottle and the phial.

'Can she walk?' enquired one of them of Morgan.

'I doubt it,' he replied.

'It's a chair job then,' said the ambulanceman, and he and his colleague disappeared to return swiftly with a collapsible wheel-chair. Gently Morgan and one of the ambulancemen lifted the now supine Penny into the chair. He was waiting for another paroxysm but none came; nevertheless he felt some warning was called for.

'I'm afraid she can be violent,' he said.

'I see,' said the ambulanceman, 'in that case better safe than sorry,' and he proceeded to strap Penny into the chair with webbing bands.

They wheeled her safely to the ambulance.

'I'll go with her,' suddenly announced Mrs Morgan, as if anxious to get back into the action. 'Get my heavy coat from the hall,' she added to Morgan. Morgan ran to get the coat and helped her on with it.

'What about Penny?' he asked, conscious of her lack of clothing.

'She'll be all right,' said the ambulanceman. 'We've plenty of blankets in the van.'

Mrs Morgan followed into the ambulance.

'You drive behind to bring me back,' she said to Morgan.

'City Infirmary – OK?' said the ambulanceman climbing into his cab as his colleague joined Mrs Morgan in the back with Penny. The ambulance sped off into the night.

7

Aftermath

Morgan surveyed the scene. The settee's crumpled cushions and the whisky bottle and phial, still on the floor, were all that remained of the drama that had passed. Arthur was still slumped in the chair, head in hands, shoulders shaking as he sobbed silently. He put his arm around Arthur's shoulders.

'Come along,' he said, 'we'd better follow on.'

'I can't,' sobbed Arthur, 'I just can't.'

Morgan felt the weight of responsibility descending on him once more.

'All right Arthur,' he said wearily, 'you get to bed and I'll see you in the morning.'

He drove at speed to the city, hoping to catch up with the ambulance but to no avail. At the hospital more time was lost as he looked for somewhere to park. 'Why are hospital car parks always full?' he grumbled to himself. It was a full forty-five minutes after leaving Gatehaven that he walked into the waiting-room of the casualty department.

Mrs Morgan was sitting there, huddled in her coat amid an assortment of bloody limbs and heads, no doubt resulting from nights out on the town to be regretted on the morrow.

'Thank God you're here,' she said, her voice as

woebegone as her appearance. 'What a time I've had.'

Morgan put his arms around her. 'Can we go?' he enquired.

'Yes,' said Mrs Morgan, 'they're keeping her in overnight. They wanted to know her next of kin but I could only give them Arthur.'

In the car going home she told Morgan of her ordeal. In the ambulance on the way to the hospital Penny had become violent again, even breaking one of the webbing bands strapping her to the chair.

'Dear God, what language,' said Mrs Morgan, 'she used words I've never heard before.'

Fortunately, the ambulanceman with her was a burly man and had managed to restrain Penny by sitting on her legs while Mrs Morgan clung desperately to the chair. At the hospital doctors and nurses had carried Penny, kicking and screaming, through the waiting-room to a treatment room. Mrs Morgan had been told to wait.

'But that's not all,' went on Mrs Morgan. Penny had wanted the toilet but had refused to let a nurse accompany her and once again Mrs Morgan had been pressed into service. 'That was the worst five minutes of my life,' she said. 'Vomiting, wetting over the floor, saying the most terrible things to me.' Morgan tried hard to imagine the claustrophobic hell of the toilet cubicle. They reached home.

'What you need, dear,' said Morgan, 'is a nice cup of tea.'

To Mrs Morgan not only was a cup of tea always 'nice' but it was also a palliative for calming the most desperate of situations.

'Thank you, darling,' she said and subsided into her chair.

Morgan made the tea.

'Don't bother yourself any more tonight,' he said. 'I'll

sort things out in the morning. Drink your tea and get a good night's sleep.'

'What's left of it,' replied Mrs Morgan ruefully but she was in no state to argue. By the time Morgan had washed the tea-cups and put out the cat she was in bed and asleep.

The next day was a Saturday and the Morgans slept late. Both were ill-served by the disturbance to their routine of the night before. Morgan was first up and brought Mrs Morgan a light breakfast in bed. It wasn't much – cereal, orange juice and toast – but his cooking prowess was a family joke and Mrs Morgan appreciated the gesture.

'You're so good to me,' she said softly. Morgan's spirits rose at this unaccustomed accolade. He was expecting some attribution of blame for the previous night's affair. But then Mrs Morgan added with a hint of anxiety. 'You didn't really have anything to do with the woman, did you?'

Morgan felt firmness was called for. 'In God's name I didn't,' he said stoutly, but his heart was troubled by the question. 'You know I wouldn't,' he added, coming swiftly to the conclusion that his failure to transfer thoughts of Penny into reality amounted to absolution. 'I'd better get dressed and go and see Arthur,' he went on. 'Are you well enough to see to the children?'

'Of course,' said Mrs Morgan, her confidence seemingly restored by his denials. 'You go and sort things out.'

Morgan dressed and went to Arthur's house. He wondered whether Penny had returned and what they would say to each other in the cold light of morning. He needn't have worried. Arthur opened the door.

'She's gone,' he said. 'Came home early this morning in a taxi, packed her bags and left.'

Morgan sensed Arthur's relief. 'Well that settles that, Arthur,' he said.

'Not quite,' replied Arthur. 'I owe you one. Come and have a drink with me at the club tonight.'

Morgan was slightly taken aback. He knew that very few, if any, 'newcomers' had penetrated this bastion of the 'villagers' who exercised absolute control over the waiting-list for admissions.

'But I'm not a member, Arthur,' he said.

'No matter,' said Arthur, 'I'm a committee-man. I'll get 'ee in.'

Morgan was impressed. He knew enough about the social structure of Gatehaven to realise that a committee-man was in local terms approaching a peer of the realm on the ladder of eminence.

'Well that's very decent of you, Arthur,' he replied, 'see you this evening then.'

He made his way back to report to Mrs Morgan. 'She's gone – for good,' he announced.

Mrs Morgan, back to form, pronounced a final valediction. 'That's that, then,' she said. 'I never understood what she saw in you anyway.'

They were never to see Penny again.

As they cleared away breakfast, Morgan pondered on how he could break the news of his evening assignment with Arthur. In his judgment it was not the outcome that Mrs Morgan was expecting or, indeed, was likely to favour. He opted for subtle preparation.

'You take it easy today, my dear,' he said, 'I'll dust around the house and do the shopping.'

Mrs Morgan looked bemused. 'Is there anything else you want to tell me?' she questioned.

Morgan's ploy had failed at the first hurdle. There was nothing for it now but to tell the truth.

'Not really,' he said, as casually as he could, 'it's just

that Arthur wants me to have a drink with him tonight.'

Mrs Morgan's silence seemed ominous to Morgan as he stood at the sink expecting the worst. Finally her verdict came.

'That seems a fair reward for the dusting and shopping,' she said, 'you'd better get on with your chores.'

Morgan's relief showed.

'I'm not quite the ogre you make me out to be,' said Mrs Morgan, her eyes twinkling.

Morgan and Arthur hurried through the cold night to the social club. It was a two-storey building situated behind the shops in the village, as if aspiring to the isolation of a masonic temple. Access was via a narrow pathway between two shops, difficult to find for a stranger. As they reached the pathway Arthur spoke.

'Watch out for the dog-shit,' he said.

Morgan picked his way gingerly along the path to be confronted by a neon sign which announced 'Gatehaven Sports and Social Club (Affiliated)'. Affiliated to what was not clear. He followed Arthur into the building to find his way barred by a man whom he recognized immediately as the village traffic warden. His yellow and black uniform had now given way to a dark blue blazer, its lapels crumpling under a plethora of enamel badges. Morgan could see that they represented a variety of club, trade union and political insignia with the little red flag of the Labour Party occupying pride of place at the top.

'It's all right, Sid,' said Arthur. 'Introductory guest,' as if he were uttering some kind of password. It worked.

'Go through then, Arthur,' said Sid, stepping aside.

They passed through swing doors to a large room of which the whole of one side was given over to a bar. Close to the door was an area devoted to darts, no fewer than

59

three boards. Centrally placed were two full-sized billiard tables, all this Morgan surmised to justify the inclusion of the word 'Sports' in the name of the establishment. Beyond the tables was a sitting area furnished roughly with old high-backed wooden settles and tables. Beside it, inevitably, were two gambling machines, all flashing lights and occasional shattering crashes as stacks of tokens tumbled into the pay-out trays. Apart from the billiard tables the lighting was poor and misted by a haze of tobacco smoke which hung in a pall just below the low ceiling. Spread around the room, engaged in its various pursuits, or propping up the bar, were about thirty 'villagers' - all men and, for the most part, dressed in what Morgan had come to recognize as their off-duty garb. Not so Arthur, who had removed his overcoat to reveal a blazer, tie and grey slacks which Morgan assumed was a mark of a committee-man. Morgan, removing his overcoat, felt over-dressed in his grey suit, but he felt comforted by the thought that as Arthur's guest he would, no doubt, be spared any ribald comments.

'This way,' said Arthur, making for the settles at the end of the room, 'we'll sit in the quiet area.'

'What - you mean there?' queried Morgan, as he absorbed the hubbub of conversation, the crack of cues on balls and the intermittent crash of the gambling-machine pay-outs.

'That's right,' said Arthur, 'sit down and I'll get 'ee a drink.'

Morgan eased himself into one of the high-backed settles behind a rough table, taking care not to scag his trousers on its splintered side. Following Arthur's example, he slung his overcoat over the back of the settle; there were no coatstands in evidence. He smiled nervously at the other occupants of the 'quiet area' but nothing was said. They all appeared to be totally absorbed in some game involving playing-cards and matchsticks with which Morgan was unfamiliar.

Arthur returned with two pint mugs brimming over with a light orange-coloured liquid.

'Thought you'd like to try the local brew,' he said, sitting down and attacking one of the mugs with obvious relish.

'Of course,' replied Morgan politely as he eyed his own mug nervously.

'Go on – drink 'ee up,' urged Arthur, 'it's only scrumpy, full of goodness and half the price of beer.'

Morgan took a sip; it was not unpleasant but with a hint of sweetness which suggested extreme potency. He began to wonder how Penny had reacted to the place but enlightenment was not long in coming.

'This bar be just for the men,' said Arthur, 'ladies m'un go upstairs. I'll show 'ee in a minute.'

Morgan took a longer look at the other occupants of the bar and was surprised when his gaze fell on Father Alphonsus. He was spread across one of the billiard-tables, his left leg pointing horizontally away from it as he concentrated on his shot. He too was in his off-duty clothing with one of his rolled cigarettes dangling from his mouth. Morgan's gaze moved to the notice on the wall which warned all and sundry that smoking was forbidden over the tables. Admonitions of this kind, surmised Morgan, did not seem to apply to Father Alphonsus. A burst of clapping followed his shot and he stood back from the table as if to receive the acclamation of the onlookers. Waving to Morgan he jabbed a thumb in the air in a gesture of victory. Arthur broke in Morgan's thoughts.

'Drink up,' he said, 'I'll show 'ee where the ladies go.'

61

Morgan looked ruefully at his barely-touched pint and Arthur's drained glass.

'Take it easy, Arthur,' he said, 'this stuff's strong.'

Arthur smiled enigmatically.

'Get on with you,' he said, 'it's nought but a lad's drink.'

Morgan was far from sure as he emptied his glass rather faster than he would have wished. They then made their way back to the hallway, where Sid was still at his post like a sentinel.

'Upstairs now then, Arthur,' he called as they turned into a narrow flight of stairs.

At the top of the stairs was a door marked 'Lounge'. Entering the room Morgan was astonished at the contrast with downstairs. Most of the space was taken up by comfortable semi-circular settees and matching arm-chairs grouped around shining glass-topped tables all resting on a deep pile carpet. A neat bar, its standing area fenced off by ornate trellis-work and well-tended potted plants occupied one corner. At the far end of the room was a small dance floor overlooked by a well-equipped stage. The walls were clad in an expensive-looking brocade covering broken here and there by tasteful water-colours enhanced by subdued lighting.

'Best appointed bar in Gatehaven,' said Arthur proudly. 'Puts Maritime to shame.' Morgan agreed.

'But there's no one here, Arthur,' he commented, wondering if it was quite the sort of place that the 'villagers' would patronize.

'Will be soon,' replied Arthur, 'tonight's "singalong" night. Then there's a turn or two at Sunday lunchtime and bingo every Wednesday.'

'It is well-patronized then?' commented Morgan. 'Are we allowed to stay for the "singalong"?'

'Allowed – yes,' said Arthur, 'staying – no. Not my cup

of tea – or pint of scrumpy – if you get my drift.'

They returned to the downstairs bar. Nothing had changed as if it and its patrons were caught in some kind of time warp. Morgan made for the bar.

'I'll get this one,' he said.

'No you won't,' insisted Arthur, 'rules of club. Besides I owe it to you.'

Morgan returned to the 'quiet area' while Arthur obtained two more pints of scrumpy. When he sat down he began to fidget with his pipe.

'Anything wrong, Arthur?' queried Morgan.

'Well,' said Arthur, 'I'm not very good at this sort of thing but I wanted to let you know how grateful I am for what you and Missus did for me last night.'

The thought passed through Morgan's mind that this was the longest speech that Arthur had made in his whole life and carefully rehearsed at that.

'Anyone would have done the same, Arthur,' he said kindly.

'You reckon,' said Arthur. 'Not most of them "newcomers".'

Morgan could sense Arthur's innate hostility to 'newcomers'; he had not encountered this in him before.

'Oh, I don't find them too bad,' he said, forgetting momentarily that he was one of them. 'After all,' he added, 'Penny was a newcomer and you did like her.'

'Not as she turned out,' said Arthur, 'anyway, that's all over now and I don't want to talk about her any more.'

Morgan persisted. He knew that Mrs Morgan's tolerance of his evening with Arthur would not extend to abating her curiosity about Penny.

'How on earth did you get mixed up with her, Arthur?' he said.

'Well,' said Arthur grudgingly, 'I s'pose you're entitled to some kind of explanation. Did she tell you about the singles bar in town?'

'Yes,' replied Morgan, 'but surely that's not your kind of place.'

'It is when you're lonely,' said Arthur.

'Lonely – you?' replied Morgan, 'but you know loads of people in Gatehaven.'

'Not that kind of lonely,' said Arthur, a trifle impatiently, 'you know what I mean. If I took up with some local woman it would be the talk of the village and I'd probably end up getting married again.'

'You wouldn't want that then?' queried Morgan.

'Not on your nelly,' said Arthur, 'all I wanted was a bit of the other.'

'Well,' commented Morgan, 'you needn't have brought her to live with you.'

'No,' agreed Arthur, 'but she spun me this yarn about her grotty digs and I fell for it. I knew she'd go in the end when she had a better offer – but not in the way it turned out. Anyway,' he went on, 'that's enough of her. I reckon you'll have to tell Missus but don't let it go any farther.'

Morgan sensed that, in Arthur's mind, the Penny episode was now over and that further questioning would prove fruitless. But the evening was to hold one more surprise.

'I wanted to thank 'ee properly,' said Arthur, fumbling in his pocket for two small red cards, which he handed to Morgan. 'You and the missus are club members now.'

'But, Arthur,' said Morgan, 'there's a long waiting-list, isn't there?'

'Yes,' replied Arthur, 'and you've just jumped it.'

Morgan was impressed. He knew enough about the 'villager' and 'newcomer' divide to realize what a great compliment Arthur had paid him.

'Thank you, Arthur,' he said, 'we will both appreciate this enormously.' He wondered if that was a fair representation of Mrs Morgan's likely reaction but it seemed the right thing to say. 'I can buy you a drink now, Arthur,' he added proudly.

Morgan arrived home. Mrs Morgan was waiting in the living-room, busy with her knitting.

'Well?' was all she said.

Morgan knew what that meant but he attempted to distract her by showing her the membership cards. She was not impressed.

'Fat lot of use we'll make of them,' she said.

'Well,' said Morgan, still flushed with pride at his achievement, 'they do have concerts and there's a lovely lounge bar. Oh, and there's bingo on Wednesdays.'

A sudden change came over Mrs Morgan.

'Bingo eh! – I do like bingo,' she exclaimed.

'You've never played it as far as I know,' said Morgan, crassly not recognizing the breakthrough.

'Well, you don't know everything about me,' replied Mrs Morgan. 'I played it at sea when my parents took me to the States for a holiday when I was single. My life didn't start when I married you, you know.'

Morgan fell silent. He was always slightly uncomfortable over Mrs Morgan's more advantaged upbringing.

She had made up her mind.

'We'll give it a try soon,' she announced.

'What – me too?' said Morgan.

'Of course,' was the reply. 'You don't expect me to enter that place alone, do you?'

'No, my dear,' said Morgan dutifully, scarcely able to adjust to the direction the evening's events had taken.

'Well, that's settled then,' said Mrs Morgan. 'Now tell me all about Penny.'

65

8

Clubbing

Mrs Morgan did not mention the club for some weeks. Throughout this time Morgan was in a dilemma. He could not make up his mind whether her intention to attend a bingo session would turn out to be good or bad for his own aspirations to make full use of his unexpected membership. He realized that if she had totally rejected Arthur's gesture his continued visits to the place, particularly in Arthur's company, could be a source of domestic friction. But what if she paid a visit and didn't like it? Could not that also spell the end of the adventure? He resolved eventually to test the water.

'My dear,' he said one morning at breakfast – he reasoned that this was the time of day that she was most open to suggestion – 'when do you intend to play bingo?'

The reply surprised him.

'Whenever you're ready,' she said, 'I've been waiting for you to ask me.'

Morgan suspected that this was a ploy to fix the blame on him as the prime mover if the proposed visit turned out to be a disaster, but he had to go on now.

'Well, tomorrow's Wednesday,' he said, 'how about it?'

The die was cast. When Morgan arrived home from

66

work the following evening Mrs Morgan was already dressed in casual clothes – or what she regarded as casual clothes. In her case this consisted of an old skirt, a loose tee-shirt and flat shoes. Morgan failed miserably to divine her motive.

'You'll be changing after supper,' he said innocently.

'No,' she replied. 'I don't want to be too conspicuous. Remember the Speke-Johnsons' party?'

Morgan bowed to her logic.

Arriving at the narrow footpath which led to the club he grasped her arm tightly as he remembered Arthur's warning about the dog droppings on his first visit.

'What is it?' asked Mrs Morgan.

'Remember the Speke-Johnsons' garden path,' he said, following her theme.

'They don't have goats here too, do they?' she asked, startled.

'Not goats – dogs,' replied Morgan, 'but a mess by any other name would smell as foul,' he added, pretentiously borrowing from the Bard.

'Humph!' exclaimed Mrs Morgan in disgust, but whether at the state of the path or Morgan's feeble humour was not clear.

Successfully negotiating the darkened path, they entered the club. Sid, the steward, was in his accustomed place, guarding the entry to the bars.

'Membership cards,' he said brusquely, looking the Morgans up and down.

Morgan proudly produced his little red card. Mrs Morgan fumbled in her handbag for what seemed an age while Sid rocked from one foot to the other as if scenting a kill.

'Damn,' said Mrs Morgan, 'I must have left it in my other bag.'

Not an unusual occurrence, thought Morgan as he contemplated running back to the house for it. Suddenly Sid relented.

'Aren't you a friend of Arthur Potts?' he enquired of Morgan.

'Well, yes,' replied Morgan.

Sid fixed them sternly in his gaze.

'I'll overlook the card this time,' he said, 'but be careful in future. Someone else on the door might not be so obliging.'

Mrs Morgan snapped her handbag shut and set off in the direction of the men's bar. Sid leapt to stop her.

'Not in there, ma'am,' he said and, turning her by the shoulders, propelled her towards the stairs which led to the lounge. Morgan went to follow behind only to have Sid leaping into action again.

'Not you sir,' he said, 'not without a tie.'

Morgan permitted himself a brief reproving glance at Mrs Morgan but she was standing motionless, her back towards them, as if they and the problem had nothing to do with her.

Sid sighed one of those 'What is the world coming to' sighs.

'Look,' he said resignedly, 'I've got a tie in the drawer which someone left here. You can borrow that for tonight.'

He disappeared into his cubicle and returned with a garish creation which looked as if it had started life in some far-off tropical resort. Reluctantly Morgan put it on and followed Mrs Morgan up the stairs. He could have sworn that he saw her shoulders twitch in uncontrolled laughter over his predicament.

Opening the door to the lounge was a shock. It was crowded with women all attired in what Morgan might describe as their 'best frocks'. A wave of conversation broke over them as they peered through the smoke-laden air in search of any empty seats. Morgan looked vainly for space near a man but there were few, if any, present. Suddenly he noticed a small bird-like woman, iron-grey hair severely gathered into a bun on top of her head, waving vigorously at them from the corner of the room. She looked vaguely familiar.

'It's Bridie, the priest's housekeeper,' said Morgan. 'I think she's got some seats for us.'

They made their way to the corner where Bridie had indeed saved two seats by covering them with her coat.

'I heard you might be coming,' she said. How she had heard such a thing was a complete mystery to Morgan but he knew enough about the Gatehaven 'bush telegraph' not to question her assumption. Bridie took over the task of organizing them.

'You go and get the bingo tickets,' she said to Morgan, 'I'll explain the rules to Missus.'

Morgan squeezed past the packed tables to where two large ladies sat near the stage dispensing the tickets. They seemed to be revelling in the importance of their role as a small queue formed obediently in front of them to obtain their tickets. He reached the front and one lady eyed him closely.

'Don't know 'ee. Is it OAP or ordinary?' she asked. Morgan hesitated. 'Come on,' said the ticket-lady, 'it's cheaper for OAPs. Can't wait all night.'

'Oh – er, ordinary,' replied Morgan and held out his hand for the tickets.

The ticket-lady looked exasperated. 'How many then?' she asked.

'Oh, two,' said Morgan.

'Two what – ones, twos, threes or what?' came the reply.

Morgan was becoming aware of some muttering in the queue behind him; he was evidently disrupting the normally fast dispensation of tickets.

'I'd better take threes,' he said.

The second ticket-lady entered the action. 'That'll be six bob,' she said, 'and don't forget your draw tickets.'

Morgan paid his money and returned to his table, clutching an assortment of bingo and raffle tickets only to find another *contretemps* had erupted.

Standing in front of Mrs Morgan, legs menacingly apart, hands on hips and glaring was a formidably-built lady, equally florid in dress and complexion. As Morgan approached she bellowed, '*You* are sitting in my seat.'

Mrs Morgan returned her stare unflinchingly. 'I beg your pardon,' she said, but made no move.

The formidably-built lady bristled. 'I always sit in that seat,' she thundered.

The hubbub of conversation on nearby tables dropped to an ominous hush. Morgan wondered what he should do but as he pondered momentarily Bridie intervened.

'But you're not entitled,' she said quietly in measured tones, 'just look at the notice.'

The eyes of all concerned switched to a large notice on the wall beside the stage – 'No Reserving Of Seats At Bingo Sessions – By Order Of The Committee', it said.

The formidably-built lady was undeterred. 'But my husband is on the committee,' she shrieked, 'I'll call him. He'll soon sort this out.' Turning to the room at large she yelled, 'Bert – come here. I want you.' Bert appeared from somewhere to the rear of the stage, blue-blazered and with an imposing array of lapel badges. 'This person has taken my seat,' said the formidably-built lady, and folded her arms in joyous anticipation of the outcome.

Bert, however, was more circumspect. 'Gone to the toilet 'ad 'ee?' he queried, feeling his way into the situation, and no doubt hoping for a positive response from his beleaguered spouse.

Alas, she failed to follow his lead. 'Don't be daft,' was the reply. 'I've just arrived but you know I always sit there. Tell her to move.'

Bert was now in something of a quandary. Domestic bliss was clearly in jeopardy but how could he – a committee-man – flaunt the very rules he had helped to make. Morgan felt sorry for him. Suddenly the voice of the people made itself heard.

'Rules is rules, Bert,' shouted an anonymous commentator from the other side of the room, quickly accompanied by a chorus of ''ear 'ears'. Bert looked anxiously at his spouse and raised his arms in a gesture of resignation. Morgan glimpsed what looked like real fear in his eyes. The formidably-built lady stomped off, disgust apparent in her every movement. It was safe for Morgan to resume his seat.

'I've been waiting a long time for that,' said Bridie with a smirk.

'But didn't you know that she always sat here?' asked Mrs Morgan.

'Of course I did,' replied Bridie, 'but I can't stand her and when you came in first I couldn't resist the temptation. Nobody else likes the stuck-up bitch anyway – you could see that.'

Mrs Morgan sat back in heroic style as if preening herself for striking a blow in the common cause.

'So you didn't know we were coming?' asked Morgan, thinking back to their entrance.

Bridie just smiled enigmatically.

Morgan sorted out the bingo and raffle tickets.

'Haven't they given you too many?' asked Mrs Morgan. 'I seem to have three for each game.'

'That's all right,' said Bridie, 'look I have six. Keep the columns in line and you'll have no bother marking them off.'

'I don't know about that,' said Mrs Morgan, prophetically as things were to turn out.

Morgan felt as if he had been there for hours and the action hadn't even started yet. But there was not long to wait. Bert stepped onto the stage looking none the worse for whatever chastening had befallen him. Clearly not even the wrath of his spouse could interfere with his weekly hour of glory. He flicked a switch under a large transparent box and as if by magic a host of coloured numbered balls sprang from somewhere to jostle for an exit into his right hand through a tube in the top of the box.

'Eyes down for your first house,' he shouted – far too loudly – into a hand microphone which he took from behind his back. Total silence descended on the room. 'One pound for any line and five pounds for the full house,' he boomed. The silence was punctuated by a series of oohs which quickly faded as he extracted the first ball. 'And your first number – all the twos, two little ducks,' said Bert.

The numbers came and went in total silence until a shriek of 'Line!' rent the air. The hubbub of chatter returned as Bert vainly pleaded for silence while one of his colleagues checked the numbers of the winning line. Morgan could hardly hear them being called back but Bert, hand cocked to ear, was obviously more attuned to the experience. 'Line correct,' he announced, 'and now to your next number for the full house.' The ritual was repeated for the full house and four times more for 'line' and 'house' before the interval arrived. Morgan came close to success once or twice but Mrs Morgan seemed to get nowhere. He took to trying to watch her card – surreptitiously of course – as well as his own but drifting clouds of cigarette smoke were beginning to make his eyes water and the dual effort proved beyond him. In between each house Bridie would light a cigarette and cough her way through an explanation to Mrs Morgan of the finer points of the game. The jackpot Morgan found particularly fascinating.

'That number on the notice over there,' she explained, 'do you see it – forty-seven – means that if you get a house in forty-seven numbers or less you get forty-seven pounds. That's why they announce the numbers called at the end of each house. It goes up a number and a pound each week until someone wins it and then they start again at forty-five.'

'It seems very complicated to me,' said Mrs Morgan modestly, but Morgan knew she was impressed by Bridie's grasp of the subject.

At the interval Morgan rose to get some drinks from the bar. As he did so Mrs Morgan kicked him under the table and jerked her head in the direction of Bridie. Morgan got the message.

'Would you like a drink, Bridie?' he asked.

'I don't mind if I do,' replied Bridie. 'Martini and lemonade – a double – if I may. You only get a thimbleful in these bar measures,' she added apologetically.

When Morgan returned with the drinks the raffle was in progress. Suddenly Mrs Morgan leapt to her feet waving her tickets.

'Here,' she cried.

Bert, who, of course, was presiding over the raffle, looked at her across the room with a distinctly painful expression on his face, as if he could not believe this further humiliation that was about to be heaped on him. Without a word of the usual cheery congratulation he picked up a garden gnome from the array of prizes beside him, strode to the table and plonked it, without ceremony, in front of Mrs Morgan.

'Thank you so much,' she said sweetly to his retreating back.

Morgan was finding the second half of the evening repetitive and boring. As the numbers were barked out, and chatter gave way to silence, and *vice versa*, over and over again, he began to yearn for what he now envizaged as the comparative peace of the men's bar. Even the so-called 'quiet corner' now took on the aura of a haven of refuge. His eyes were streaming and his nose twitching from the layers of cigarette smoke which drifted like wreaths around the room. His discomfort was aggravated by his proximity to Bridie, smoking between each house and proceeding to mark her numbers with the cigarette firmly in her mouth, only to be removed to accommodate a bout of coughing. At long last a signal of relief.

'And now for your last house of the evening,' bawled Bert into the microphone.

Morgan yawned, took up his pencil and began to go through the motions of marking his card. Past the 'line' and wearily on to the 'full house' he persevered when suddenly one of his occasional glances at Mrs Morgan's card disturbed his own drowsy progress. It was complete – a genuine full house.

'House,' shouted Morgan excitedly, cutting Bert off short in the process of announcing the next number.

'Two fat . . .', was, it seemed to Morgan, as far as he got.

The effect on the room of Morgan's shout was electric. Not only did the chatter restart but a wild stampede for the door began amid the pulling on of coats and hurried goodbyes shouted to all and sundry. Bert's acolyte approached to check the card.

'Last number out – two fat ladies,' said Bert.

The acolyte looked at Mrs Morgan's card, then at the Morgans, and then, tut-tutting at Bert, 'Not on the card, Bert,' he said.

Bert could hardly disguise his look of triumph as he stared at Mrs Morgan.

'House a bogey,' he announced pontifically.

The stampede for the door went into startling reverse as everyone waited, half-prepared for the exit, for the game to resume. A few numbers later a call of 'house' from across the room put the stampede back into gear. The session was over.

Mrs Morgan looked sternly at Morgan. 'What a fool you made of yourself,' she said.

'Me?' replied Morgan. 'Why didn't you call on the last number out?'

'Because,' said Mrs Morgan, 'I was trying to watch your card as well with you yawning so much. But I knew it was no use calling once I'd missed it. Seems to me you don't understand the rules.'

Since he had not had the benefit of Bridie's inter-house commentaries Morgan could do little but agree.

Goodbyes were said to Bridie and they made their way to the door. Bert was standing there smirking; for him honour had been retrieved.

'I do like your tie,' he said sarcastically to Morgan, no doubt emboldened by his success and anxious to demonstrate to his spouse that he had avenged her earlier embarrassment.

Morgan grunted, removed the offending garment, and handed it to Sid who had just emerged from his cubicle

75

in the hallway.

On the way home Morgan decided to ascertain Mrs Morgan's verdict on the evening.

'I don't suppose you'll be wanting to go there again,' he said by way of an opening gambit. Her reply surprised him.

'I haven't had such an hilarious time in years,' she said, 'we'll have to go regularly now.'

'We?' questioned Morgan.

Although he was keen to make the most of his unexpected membership of the club he had concluded by half-way through the bingo session that regular attendance at that event would be too high a price to pay for the privilege. Mrs Morgan read his thoughts.

'Oh, all right,' she said with a chuckle, 'I know it's not your scene. But you can take me in and buy me a drink and then go to the men's bar until it's time to go home. You'll probably find Arthur in there anyway.'

Morgan sighed with relief. He felt good. It seemed to him to be a case of mission accomplished.

9

Pilgrimage

During the summer of 1974 the Morgans' life moved into a comfortable routine – weekly visits to the club for bingo, with Morgan ensconced in waiting in the men's bar, Friday nights at The Maritime, usually in the cocktail bar but with occasional forays into the public bar for Mrs Morgan to renew her previous contact with the 'villagers' and their produce, coffee mornings with the Speke-Johnson crowd from which Morgan gratefully absented himself on account of work, and much hard but satisfying labour in the garden. This cycle of normality was broken only by the family's annual holiday, touring Morgan's beloved Europe, when he vied with his two elder children to see who could make themselves the better understood in fractured French and German.

It was on their return from holiday in mid-August that they learned about the parish pilgrimage to Knock in Western Ireland, to be led by Father Alphonsus.

'We shall all go,' announced Mrs Morgan, 'it will be a great spiritual experience.'

Morgan, with his deeper appreciation of the credentials of the organizer, had his doubts about that. His lack of enthusiasm was shared, for different reasons, by his two elder children. Now well into their late teens, they were undergoing the first strains of rebellion against

77

the Catholic orthodoxy imposed on them from childhood by Mrs Morgan. The younger child was still under the pervasive influence of the sisters at the primary school and posed no such problem.

Morgan was deputed by Mrs Morgan to persuade the revolutionaries. He did his best but their resistance was unshakeable. Coupled with blandishments about looking after the younger child while parents had time to themselves – even if it was only for four days – it was enough to convert Morgan to their point of view. In the end Mrs Morgan acquiesced too but not without misgivings about leaving the younger child. She was a consummate mother but not too single-minded not to savour the thought of a rare break away with Morgan, perhaps recapturing some of the ambience of their courtship and early marriage before the children came along and imposed their dominance on the household. The next Sunday after Mass two places were booked on the pilgrimage for Morgan and wife.

The venture was scheduled to start by coach early on a Saturday morning. From about the previous Wednesday, Mrs Morgan had started a comprehensive assault on the packing. This was always a source of irritation to Morgan, whose frequent travels in the course of his work had made him adept at packing a suitcase at the last minute and rarely leaving with anything missing. He contented himself with his usual comment: 'We are not planning the D-Day landings,' but as usual it had little effect. Clothes, toiletries and assorted gadgets appropriate to a longer and more distant voyage were all included, accompanied by Mrs Morgan's standard rejoinder. 'You never know,' she said.

Saturday arrived and the Morgans made their way to the pick-up point near the church, Morgan struggling manfully with the over-heavy suitcase. Father Alphonsus was there to welcome them, his sober clerical suit contrasting oddly with what appeared to be a Panama hat sporting a brightly coloured band around the brim. His *ensemble* was completed by dark sunglasses; it seemed he was in holiday mood.

'Going to the moon?' he asked, eyeing Morgan's suitcase.

'You never know,' replied Morgan, permitting himself a whimsical glance at Mrs Morgan.

With suitcase stowed away in the luggage compartment, they climbed aboard the coach to a chorus of 'Hi's and 'Hello's from those already there. Morgan surveyed his fellow pilgrims. They were a motley crew – 'villagers' in their Sunday-best gathered in self-conscious silence at the rear and 'newcomers' mostly in leisure gear to the front. The Morgans took their place tactfully in mid-coach. Among the 'villagers' Morgan recognized several hard-drinking frequenters of the men's bar at the club whom he had not previously associated with matters religious. Mrs Morgan, meanwhile, was waving and chattering to some of the 'newcomers' whom he knew to be equally regular patrons of the cocktail bar of The Maritime. He began to think that the pilgrimage would turn out to be more of a social than a devotional venture. What happened next only served to confirm his suspicions.

With a shout of 'all right everybody' Sonia clambered breathlessly aboard the coach, bursting out of tight blue jeans. She was followed by Dolores, clad in her matador outfit and sheepishly grasping the hand of a young man shuffling almost reluctantly alongside her. Morgan could have sworn that it was the unfortunate Jason, he who had been unceremoniously ejected from The Maritime by Sonia on the occasion of their first visit. Sonia collapsed into the seat in front of the Morgans with an escape of breath which sounded like a deflating balloon. Dolores and the young man slid into the seat across the aisle and dissolved into a passionate embrace.

'Now, you two,' said Sonia, 'remember where you are.'

Father Alphonsus stood imperiously at the front of the coach, complete with clipboard, and proceeded to call the roll.

'Three missing,' he said, scratching his head. Then suddenly, 'It's those bloody nuns,' he exclaimed, and leapt from the coach, his hand to his eyes in a manner reminiscent of Nelson, to peer down the road.

Sure enough, three nuns, one with a walking-stick, were making their way slowly towards the coach.

'C'mon, girls,' he shouted with scant regard for reverence and, abandoning his prejudices, strode down the road to help them with their luggage.

With the nuns safely embarked, Father Alphonsus launched into an introductory talk about the journey, punctuated by 'Ooh's as he extolled the delights of the places they were to visit. It was first to Liverpool to catch the night ferry to Dublin, and then on to Glendalough – 'the meeting of the waters' – before reaching Galway where a hotel had been booked for them for the Sunday night. On Monday morning they would go on to Knock and then to Athlone for a second night in a hotel, before returning to Dublin for the ferry back to Liverpool.

'How long will we spend at Knock?' enquired one of the younger nuns – somewhat rashly in Morgan's view.

Father Alphonsus reddened. 'Long enough, sister, long enough,' he said, 'you'll get a few decades of the rosary in.'

'It sounds lovely,' said Mrs Morgan, bravely intruding on the muttering of the nuns.

80

Morgan was not so sure. His earlier suspicions were strengthening.

'All set then,' said Father Alphonsus, 'take it away, driver.'

As the coach lumbered through Gatehaven's narrow streets towards the distant motorway the pilgrims formed into little groups to converse. Sonia buttonholed the Morgans.

'That's him,' she said, pointing at Dolores and her escort, 'they're getting married in October. I'll see you get an invitation.'

'But isn't that Jason – the lad you banned from The Maritime?' queried Morgan.

'Right first time,' replied Sonia, 'he's been after her body for months but I've made sure the only way he'll get it is by marrying her and doing us all a favour. He's out of work too so a little job at the pub will encourage him no end.'

'Well I never,' said Mrs Morgan, 'what does Dolores think about it?'

'She'll do as I say if she knows what's good for her,' replied Sonia.

'I can imagine,' said Morgan.

When they reached the motorway, Father Alphonsus broke in on the hum of conversation.

'Time for a sing-song,' he said, inserting a tape into the PR gadgetry beside the driver. After some seconds of crackling, what sounded like a public house singer/pianist began a rendering of *Ten Green Bottles*. Father Alphonsus joined in lustily, waving his arms and exhorting everyone to follow him. Mrs Morgan led the way in a reedy soprano and gradually a ragged *ensemble* of on and off-key voices rose in self-conscious accompaniment. All went well until confusion entered the performance somewhere between the seventh and the fourth green bottle, a gap which the tape jumped with a loud crack. With various factions singing about differing numbers of green bottles, Father Alphonsus leapt to his feet and spread his arms sharply wide to put an end to the cacophony.

'Wait one,' he shouted, as the din subsided, and fiddling with the fast-forward control, contrived to restore a semblance of harmony somewhere in the middle of *Nellie Dean*. 'That'll do nicely,' he said, and the relieved pilgrims resumed their performance.

Less than an hour had passed when a bout of whispering and gesticulating among the nuns signalled the start of a fresh disturbance. Father Alphonsus approached them and entered into agitated conversation *sotto voce*. After a while he made his way back to his place by the driver.

'I'm afraid we shall have to have an unscheduled comfort-stop at the next service-station,' he announced tersely, his face flushed with irritation.

Clearly his meticulous journey-plan had not allowed for this eventuality. At the next service-station the nun with the walking-stick was assisted slowly from the coach by one of her companions. A few moments elapsed before several other pilgrims rose sheepishly to their feet and made their way to the door of the coach, studiously avoiding eye contact with Father Alphonsus. He remained firmly in his place, rocking with obvious impatience from one foot to the other, his face registering an unspoken 'Tut tut'. Suddenly he shot down the aisle to where the Morgans were sitting.

'I knew it was a mistake to bring them on a trip like this,' he exclaimed none too quietly, 'but what can a man do? Mention the word pilgrimage and they're off to pack their bags.'

The Morgans, believing discretion to be the better part

of valour on this occasion, declined to comment.

With the return of the comfort-seekers the journey resumed. Singing became more and more sporadic as the pilgrims began to doze their way along the interminable boredom of the motorway. By late afternoon the coach was threading its way through some of the more depressing urban decay of Liverpool towards the ferry terminal. The pilgrims revived and excitement rose as the ship came into view. The queue of vehicles waiting to board was quite short and it was not long before the coach was manœuvring into the yawning chasm of the car deck. Pilgrims scrambled to retrieve luggage from the overhead racks.

'Overnight baggage only,' said Father Alphonsus, 'the rest stays with the coach.'

One or two expressed some consternation at this but their leader was unyielding.

'All you need is a toothbrush,' he said, 'buy one on the boat if you've packed it away.'

Morgan could have sworn he was looking expectantly at the nuns. Eventually, amid some muttering, he led them up the narrow steps from the cavernous clanking discomfort of the car deck to the relative calm of the ship's reception area.

The pilgrims stood in a group while Father Alphonsus busied himself at the reception desk. It was one of those awkward hiatuses in the course of a journey which tend to induce in some people feelings of frustration. Mrs Morgan was one such. As Father Alphonsus returned, clutching a wad of blue tickets, she could contain herself no longer.

'Where,' she said, 'is my cabin?'

'Cabin?' replied Father Alphonsus. 'The only cabin on this ship is the captain's and I don't suppose he's sharing it with us lot.'

Not strictly true, thought Morgan, but effective.

Mrs Morgan persisted. 'Where then, Father, are we expected to sleep?' she enquired.

'In a *couchette*, of course,' was the reply. 'What do you expect for forty quid and two hotel stops?'

Mrs Morgan was not pleased.

'A *couchette*?' she said in a tone which suggested that she thought it was something vaguely to do with a French bordello. Morgan intervened.

'It's a reclining chair with a blanket and pillow, my dear,' he said, 'very comfortable too, I'm told.'

Father Alphonsus handed out the *couchette* tickets and led the way to a lounge where they claimed their seats and arranged their blankets, pillows and overnight bags while they waited for sailing. Mrs Morgan sat uneasily in her place, clutching her handbag and umbrella. Soon a series of creaks, clanks and vibrations signalled the moment of departure.

'That's it,' said Morgan, 'we're off.'

After about a half-hour the swaying movement of the deck under their feet and the growing insistent throb of the ship's engines confirmed their entry to the open sea. Through the salt-stained window Morgan could see the receding shore-line dip out of vision and reappear in a regular sequence which grew sickeningly longer and longer. It was not, he mused, going to be a comfortable night. Some of the pilgrims gathered themselves up from the *couchettes* and lurched hesitantly towards the lounge exit. A few returned shortly afterwards, pale-faced, and wiping their lips, victims to an early onslaught of *mal de mer*. Others, including Father Alphonsus, did not return and Morgan guessed that the ship's bar was now open. Dutifully he concentrated his attention on Mrs Morgan.

'Let me make you comfortable for the night, my dear,'

he said, starting to arrange her pillow and blanket.

'Night?' said Mrs Morgan, sitting bolt upright, 'but it's not even dark yet. I couldn't possibly sleep like this anyway.'

Morgan concluded that some kind of tranquillizing agent was called for.

'We could go to the bar,' he said hopefully.

Mrs Morgan thought for a moment.

'Well, I suppose it's better than sitting here for hours,' she replied.

As Morgan had suspected, Father Alphonsus was occupying the bar, surrounded by Sonia, Dolores, Jason and a mixed group of 'villagers' and 'newcomers'. He was surprised at the latter grouping but assumed that the Gatehaven 'divide' did not apply in foreign parts. It just takes a little adversity, he concluded, to produce strange companions. Morgan ordered drinks from the bar, whisky for him and gin for Mrs Morgan – large ones – surreptitiously disguising the measures with a liberal application of mixers, and they joined the group around Father Alphonsus. His ploy worked well. As evening faded to night through the bar window, and Father Alphonsus droned on, sermon fashion, about the delights of the Emerald Isle while Sonia struggled to prevent Dolores and Jason becoming more and more embarrassingly amorous, Mrs Morgan fell silent. Morgan guessed she was relaxed but he contrived to ply her with a second large libation, again skilfully disguising the measure. It was not long before he noticed her eyelids drooping.

'Gracious, look at the time,' he exclaimed.

Mrs Morgan started and began to rise unsteadily to her feet. Morgan grasped her firmly under the arm and to a chorus of 'Goodnight's and 'Sleep well's, they made their way back to the lounge.

'I think I've had one too many,' said Mrs Morgan as she fended off the wall of the companion-way *en route.*

'Nonsense,' replied Morgan stoutly, 'it's just the motion of the ship.'

Back in the lounge Mrs Morgan sank gratefully into the *couchette* she had despised but a short time before.

'Wouldn't you like to visit the bathroom before you settle down?' asked Morgan. Mrs Morgan gazed at him bleary-eyed. 'I think it would be wise,' he added.

Getting the now soporific Mrs Morgan and her bag of toiletries to the bathroom, avoiding outstretched limbs and luggage was a formidable task, but Morgan strove manfully to achieve it without succumbing himself to the effects of the whisky and the rolling of the ship. He decided that it would be prudent to wait outside for her. It seemed like an age as he braved the curious stares of assorted ladies who came and went. Eventually she emerged.

'Do you know,' she said, 'that place is full of women counting their money.'

Morgan did not answer. He could only guess at the nature of some of the shipboard activities and Mrs Morgan was too close to sleep to pursue her curiosity. Hopefully, thought Morgan, she would have forgotten all about it by the morning.

As Morgan had anticipated, it was a troubled night, punctuated by snores, groans and dashes to the toilet by the suffering pilgrims, plagued by the rolling and lurching of the vessel and the unrelenting throb of its engines. The arrival of morning was accompanied by an uncomfortable awareness of stiff limbs and aching heads. Everyone looked woebegone, with the exception of Father Alphonsus who bounced into life with unnatural exuberance.

'Don't bother about breakfast,' he shouted, 'we'll get it

on the road.'

His advice was superfluous. The last thing on their minds was food.

After queueing for the bathroom, mostly in a state of shocked silence, they filed back to the car deck and the coach to await disembarkation. The ship had now docked but they still had to endure the usual inexplicable delay which always seems to attend ferry landings. Eventually the coach rolled off the ship into the gentle light of early morning and crawled along the quayside towards the dock gates and a misty Dublin. Morgan summoned up a display of scarcely-felt enthusiasm.

'We're off,' he shouted with a single forced clap of his hands.

Mrs Morgan fixed him with her 'evil eye' expression. 'If you say that once more,' she hissed, 'I'll . . . I'll . . . I'll . . . .'

Morgan was astonished. She was never known to be lost for words. True to form, the aberration was momentary.

'I'll hit you with my umbrella,' she said.

10

Journeying

As the coach trundled through Dublin's not so smooth thoroughfares and out towards the Wicklow Mountains, the shattered pilgrims began to revive. Interest in the passing scenery manifested itself in jabbing fingers and shouts of 'Look at that!' But the revival was short-lived. What they had seen as mist lying over Dublin as they had left the ferry turned out to be a fine rain of the kind which seems to be peculiar to Ireland. It clung to the windows of the coach, bit by bit, obscuring their vision, aggravated by hot breath condensing on the inside to confine them blindly in a white cocoon, its blankness broken only by the driver's windscreen swept by its wiper. Even he was forced to make frantic sweeping movements with a bright yellow cloth to aid his steering. The creeping sense of claustrophobia which ensued was inadvertently heightened by Father Alphonsus, sitting conspicuously under a 'No Smoking' sign, constructing and igniting his 'hand-rollers' at regular intervals. Nobody dared to rebuke him.

It was hardly surprising that the enforced boredom precipitated thoughts of breakfast. Save for a few sandwiches on the previous day's coach journey, most had not eaten since they set out. Very few, it seemed, had possessed the stomach to avail themselves of the restaurant on the ferry. One of the 'newcomers' had the temerity to address the matter.

'What about some breakfast, Father?' he asked.

Father Alphonsus stubbed out his cigarette on the floor of the coach in a slow and deliberate movement. Morgan guessed he was making time to compose his answer. At last he turned to face his expectant flock.

'All in good time, my dear people,' he said, 'but have you forgotten what day it is?'

Everyone apparently had. The rigours of the journey so far had played havoc with their sense of time.

'It is, my dear people, Sunday,' he went on, 'and the first item on today's programme is Mass. We shall be stopping in about an hour at eight o'clock for that and then' – he paused and his chest swelled with pride – 'I have arranged for cooked breakfast in a parish hall next to the church.'

'Ooh, how lovely,' exclaimed Mrs Morgan and a chorus of approving noises rang around the coach.

Father Alphonsus allowed a triumphant smirk to cross his face. He had got his priorities right: even the nuns could find no fault.

As the hour ticked away the pilgrims fell silent, savouring the thought of food. Now that pre-occupation with *mal de mer,* and for some hangovers, was beginning to fade, appetites were growing fast. The time for the promised stop was drawing near when Morgan detected some agitation on the part of Father Alphonsus. He was in constant discussion with the driver, borrowing his bright yellow cloth to wipe his side of the windscreen, and pointing animatedly at each signpost or landmark. As the coach slowed down he was heard to say, 'This has got to be the place.' A shadow of suspicion about his navigational competence crossed Morgan's mind.

They emerged from the coach buttoning their coats

against the fine rain. Confronting them was a small stone church standing in isolation in the middle of a graveyard. No other buildings were visible – not even a parish hall – in the short length of road on either side before it disappeared into the mist and rain. Father Alphonsus pushed open the door of the church almost knocking over an elderly priest, attired in Mass vestments, who had come to greet them.

'Good morning, Father,' said Father Alphonsus, 'party from Gatehaven in England *en route* to Knock.'

The priest looked puzzled.

'Sure and you've a long way to go, Father,' he said, 'but I'm just about to start Mass and you'll be wanting to assist no doubt.'

He led Father Alphonsus away to a small sacristy while the pilgrims crammed into the little church. There were barely a dozen people present and the influx of another fifty or so from the coach was a signal for much head-turning and muttering. Father Alphonsus preceded the elderly priest to the altar, dressed in a hastily borrowed alb which reached only to his calves and threatened to burst somewhere around his chest. As the elderly priest began to drone through Mass he busied himself like a fidgety altar boy, finally sitting cross-legged on the altar steps for the sermon. This was delivered by the priest in a slow monotone, merely recapitulating the day's gospel which, but a few moments before he had ceremonially intoned. Father Alphonsus began to show signs of impatience as time ticked by, alternatively looking at his watch and then to heaven, as if praying for divine intervention.

Finally the priest returned to the altar to begin the canon of the Mass. Father Alphonsus sprang suddenly to a spot beside him to con-celebrate as if he had suddenly remembered his own daily obligation to offer the Holy

Sacrifice. Not surprisingly, however, given the apparent remoteness of his parish, con-celebration appeared to be a custom with which the elderly priest was less than familiar and synchronizing with Father Alphonsus's rapid delivery proved almost too much for him. Morgan could not suppress an involuntary chuckle, only to be returned to proper decorum by a sharp dig in the ribs from Mrs Morgan.

The distribution of Holy Communion only served to increase Morgan's growing suspicion that something was awry with Father Alphonsus's planning. There were not enough wafers and each communicant received no more than a sliver. Clearly, thought Morgan, they could not have been expected at this church.

Verification of the situation soon came. After Mass, with the pilgrims standing uneasily outside in the rain, Father Alphonsus emerged looking unusually sheepish.

'There has been some misunderstanding,' he announced – carefully, noted Morgan, omitting to attribute any responsibility to himself – 'breakfast is off.'

Morgan felt sorry for him, as he stood like a stag at bay facing a mounting rumble of dissatisfaction from the famished pilgrims. He needn't have. Father Alphonsus was nothing if not resilient.

'But – not to worry,' he went on, 'we shall execute Plan B.'

There followed an expectant hush.

'According to my reckoning,' he said – Morgan groaned inwardly – 'there's a Traveller's Rest a few miles on where we can get something.'

To Morgan's great surprise, there was and they did – plates of crusty fresh-baked bread and succulent ham at twenty pence a head. It was a satisfying, if somewhat hurried, repast as Father Alphonsus exhorted them to re-board the coach even as they ate. His navigational errors, it seemed, had left his schedule in some disarray. This was exacerbated while inevitable visits to the toilet were fitted in, but eventually they were rolling through green hills on their way to Glendalough. One of the 'newcomers' leaned confidentially over to Morgan.

'I reckon he took us to the wrong church,' he whispered.

'My feelings exactly,' replied Morgan.

Approaching Glendalough, Father Alphonsus waxed lyrical about the beauty of the place and how fortunate that he had been able to arrange for them to stop there. Alas, all this was to little avail. Glendalough was shrouded in mist and very, very damp. Most of the pilgrims exhibited a marked reluctance to leave the coach. Mrs Morgan – who, of course, was armed with her umbrella – finally persuaded a few hardy souls to follow her into the mist, which swallowed them up about ten yards from the coach. They re-emerged about ten minutes later, wet and bedraggled. Mrs Morgan was the last to re-board.

'I don't know what's the matter with you all,' she said, 'it's only Irish rain.'

Nobody bothered to ask her what she meant and the not entirely happy band of pilgrims made themselves comfortable for the next stage of their journey – on towards Galway.

As Morgan might have expected, this was not to be without incident. They were hardly under way when their dozing was interrupted by a screeching of brakes as the coach came to an obviously unscheduled stop. Condensation was hurriedly wiped from windows as they strained to see what had now befallen them. To say the least, it was an unusual sight. The entire width of the road ahead of them was occupied by untidily parked cars; there was no way through. Father Alphonsus gazed at the scene in disbelief until his eyes scanned to the roadside and fell upon a church.

'Got it in one,' he shouted triumphantly, 'they must all be at Mass.'

He leapt from the coach and stalked off in the direction of the church. He returned after a few minutes, his face wreathed in smiles.

'A very understanding priest,' he said, 'he'll let them all out during the sermon to move the cars. It'll only be a tick.'

Just as he had predicted, a short time later a crowd of men emerged from the church and amid much crashing of gears, squealing of brakes and sounding of horns cleared a path for the coach. Father Alphonsus waved happily to them as they moved off as if it was some sort of jolly jape that he had planned for the pilgrims' entertainment.

'Yes – a very understanding priest,' he murmured, ostensibly to himself, but audibly to the front section of the coach. The friendly 'newcomer' leaned over to Morgan again.

'I'm not surprised,' he sniggered, 'I bet it's the one who was supposed to feed us. They'll all be getting a free breakfast in there.'

If Father Alphonsus's planning had been suspect hitherto, he redeemed himself at Galway. The coach pulled into an imposing hotel, set back from the road in its own grounds. Morgan wondered if it would turn out to be the right one but he was being less than kind on this occasion. It was, and soon they were all installed in comfortable rooms, showered and changed, and feeling relieved. As if to complement their new-found ease the rain had stopped. That evening, after an excellent dinner, voraciously consumed, Morgan suggested to Mrs

Morgan a leisurely night-cap in the hotel bar and she agreed. This turned out to be a mistake.

Father Alphonsus was sitting in the bar ringed by what Morgan recognized as the harder-drinking elements from the club and The Maritime, including Sonia, Dolores and Jason. There was no escaping him.

'Come and join us,' he shouted to the Morgans as they entered.

He was extolling the virtues of some bar on the Galway seafront which he claimed was but a short walk away, and suggesting they all went there in a party.

'To visit Galway and miss this bar,' he said pontifically, 'is like going to Rome and ignoring St Peter's.'

Most of his audience needed no encouragement to join him. Morgan felt slightly uneasy and started to demur, only to be over-ruled, surprisingly, by Mrs Morgan.

'It's very early for going to bed,' she said, 'and we could all do with a bit of light relief after today.'

Father Alphonsus gave her a look which suggested that he could not see what was wrong about the day but he obviously had no time for recriminations.

'That's the spirit,' he said. 'Now this is what we do. Go to the rooms for a few minutes and then slip out the front door in twos and threes. We meet around the corner to the right.'

'Why the secrecy, Father?' enquired Mrs Morgan innocently.

He looked up at the ceiling and clasped his hands in an attitude of prayer.

'Nuns, woman, nuns,' he said.

The Morgans crept down the hotel stairs and out into the street. Around the corner, most of the conspirators were already assembled, including, to Morgan's surprise, the youngest of the three nuns. He looked

94

questioningly at Father Alphonsus who rushed over to him and whispered in his ear.

'She's all right,' he hissed, 'not been in the order long enough to have had all the fun knocked out of her.'

Inevitably, the short walk to the bar, which they had been led to expect, turned out to be a long one. Mrs Morgan's initial enthusiasm for the venture was beginning to wane when Father Alphonsus pointed excitedly to a dimly lit doorway.

'That's the place,' he said, and they shuffled after him through the narrow doorway.

The bar seemed to Morgan to be a smaller-scale version of the men's bar at the club, but very much noisier. This was accounted for by the presence in one corner, perched on some wooden boxes forming a rudimentary stage, of a fiddler and an accordionist, all full beards and gaily coloured kerchiefs, who were belting out a succession of Irish airs with gusto. Most of the patrons were waving mugs of stout and joining enthusiastically in the singing, marking the end of each number with a chorus of requests for their own particular favourites. The atmosphere was lively and infectious and soon the Gatehaven party were joining in the revelry. Father Alphonsus had organized a 'kitty' and saw to it that the men, and some of the women, were supplied with copious quantities of stout. Mrs Morgan and some of the other women opted for gin and tonic, which he insisted on excluding from the 'kitty', leaving Morgan and a few others ruefully to bear the cost. The young nun was restricted to orange juice, but to Morgan's astonishment she seemed to become more carried away with the occasion than anyone else. It was she who inadvertently brought the evening to a close a few hours later when she climbed onto a table, hitched up her habit and attempted a jig. Even for Father

Alphonsus, this was too much. Hauling her unceremoniously from the table he spread his arms wide in his habitual gesture of closure.

'That's it, folks,' he said, 'we're off to the holy shrine in the morning.'

Morgan was surprised that he had remembered. Mrs Morgan baulked at the walk back to the hotel.

'We'll have to get a taxi,' she said.

Surprisingly there was a whole rank of them parked in the street outside the bar, evidence, so Morgan thought, of the eventual inability of most of the patrons to get home under their own power. The Morgans' taxi set off at great speed. Morgan had no idea which way they were going, and Mrs Morgan, anaesthetized by gin and tonic, didn't appear to care, provided she did not have to walk. Suddenly Morgan panicked as the speeding vehicle turned abruptly into a one-way street – the wrong way.

'Driver,' he shouted through a gap in the glass partition, 'you're going the wrong way up a one-way street.'

The driver turned his head with a fine disregard for the road ahead, and slid back the partition.

'Sure, and who'd be coming down it at this time of night?' he said.

Morgan clung nervously to the crash bar in front of him; Mrs Morgan appeared to notice nothing amiss.

Due no doubt to this bit of unorthodox routing, they were very quickly back at the hotel. But they were not the first to return. As they crept along the landing to their room, Morgan noticed the young nun standing meekly in front of one of her elder companions, apparently undergoing some kind of inquisition. A sense of foreboding about the morning invaded his thoughts.

But it was an entirely different crisis that first exercised their minds on the following morning. Mrs Morgan rose to find her ankles alarmingly swollen and that she was reduced to getting about in a painful hobble.

'I haven't had ankles like this since I was pregnant,' she moaned, as she inched her way down the stairs to breakfast.

'You're not, are you?' asked Morgan, racking his brains to try and remember when this unforeseen eventuality might have been precipitated. Mrs Morgan was more precise.

'Chance would have been a fine thing,' she replied, 'it must be due to all the travelling.'

At breakfast the other crisis that Morgan had been expecting began to take shape. Father Alphonsus was seated with the nuns deep in conversation. They could not be overheard, but to Morgan all the signs seemed to point to an inquest into the events of the previous evening. At the end of breakfast, a somewhat chastened-looking Father Alphonsus asked them to collect their belongings and make their way to the coach. As Mrs Morgan boarded, one of the elder nuns noticed her hobbling.

'Whatever is the matter, my dear?' she asked kindly.

'Oh, it's nothing,' replied Mrs Morgan bravely, 'it's just that the travelling doesn't seem to agree with my ankles.'

'I know just the remedy for that,' said the nun, proceeding to rummage in her hold-all. She brought out two large paper bags and a ball of string. 'Put your feet in these and say a prayer,' she said.

Back to the hold-all for a pair of scissors and in a trice Mrs Morgan's feet were encased in brown paper secured with string around her calves. Morgan looked on, faintly amused. Was he about to witness some kind of minor miracle, he wondered? The nun caught sight of his slightly mocking expression.

'Don't you doubt,' she said, 'it'll work. I've been on too many long pilgrimages not to have seen this before.'

Never one like this, thought Morgan.

The journey to Knock was a subdued affair. No singing now, just muted conversation. Strangely, the pilgrims had divided into different groupings – those who had participated in Father Alphonsus's peccadilloes, 'newcomers' and 'villagers' alike, and those who hadn't. The renegade nun had been restored to the latter but the Morgans found themselves sitting somewhat uncomfortably in the former. Contact between the two groups was a trifle strained. Morgan's group was showing signs of travel-weariness aggravated, no doubt, by the effects of the previous night's carousing, but the other group took advantage of the improving weather to sightsee from the windows, as the coach sped across the rugged plains of Mayo. Morgan yawned and settled back in his seat. He was bemused by the apparent collapse of the Gatehaven 'divide' and he wondered how long it would last.

The imminence of their arrival at Knock was heralded by a strange sound, which at first hearing seemed like the buzzing of a swarm of bees. Morgan strained to listen as it came nearer. Suddenly it made sense. Hundreds of voices were reciting the rosary in sing-song unison. Led by the more alert group, the Gatehaven pilgrims took up the chant. Soon vision supplemented hearing as they could make out the crowds parading around the exterior of the weather-beaten old church. Father Alphonsus suddenly resumed his leadership duties.

'Here's what's going to happen,' he said, 'the authorities here have kindly allowed us to have a parish Mass at the shrine, but we must keep to our allotted time.

We are due on in about fifteen minutes for a half-hour slot. Then we'll see how things go.'

'What do you mean, Father – see how things go?' asked the elderly nun with the walking-stick, looking menacingly as if she might be tempted to use it on him. Morgan had never seen him look quite so discomfited.

'Er – we will have to see how much time we can hang around,' he said, his face reddening.

'I see,' said the nun in a tone which contrived to be both venomous and ominous.

As the coach came to a halt, Mrs Morgan removed the brown paper from her ankles.

'Any better?' called out the nun who had ministered to her.

'Much better, thanks,' replied Mrs Morgan.

'They don't look any better to me,' whispered Morgan.

'They aren't,' she replied, 'but you can't be rude to a nun.'

'Try telling that to Father,' said Morgan, mischievously.

From the coach they were ushered to the gable end of the old church where a large glass construction, rather like a giant fish-tank, enclosed three marble life-sized statues of the Virgin flanked by St Joseph and St John.

'Into the shrine,' said Father Alphonsus, hustling them along and looking at his watch, 'we're already behind time.'

As they crowded into the glass enclosure, he disappeared into a small room to the side, soon to return vested ready for Mass. He launched into the liturgy without further ado. As Mass progressed his tempo increased and his ceremonial gestures were punctuated with frequent glances at his watch. Only he, looking over the heads of the kneeling worshippers, could see curious faces pressed against the glass as the next party of pilgrims gathered for their half-hour spell at the shrine. In about twenty-five minutes it was all over and the Gatehaven pilgrims struggled to make their way out against the tide of new entrants. Standing outside Father Alphonsus called them to order.

'There's the new basilica,' he said, with a sweep of his arm, 'the village is that way for those who want some refreshment and don't forget your holy water before you go. There are some bottles in the coach if you've forgotten them.'

He pointed to a low wall beside the car park into which was embedded a line of taps.

'Ah, but how long have we got, Father?' asked the nun with the walking-stick.

She seemed to Morgan to have usurped some of Father Alphonsus's authority over the conduct of affairs. He was not wrong.

'Yes – I was coming to that, sister,' he said a shade hesitantly. Everyone waited expectantly. 'Back at the coach in two hours.'

Morgan gasped at the length of time allowed. Whatever plans Father Alphonsus had had for passing the time to their next overnight stop at Athlone had clearly been abandoned – probably, thought Morgan, at his breakfast encounter with the nuns. There was no doubt that he had finally capitulated to them.

The pilgrims dispersed. Morgan assisted Mrs Morgan on a slow and painful walk around the basilica where they bought some souvenirs. After a while, they made their way to the old church, past the crowds chanting the rosary outside, to the entrance at the opposite end to the shrine. They went in and sat down. Strangely, it was dark and empty, contrasting totally with the scenes outside and around the modern basilica. A welcome feeling of peace came over Morgan as he just sat and absorbed the atmosphere of the place, reflecting on the events of the day. Morgan was a devout but undemonstrative Catholic, and visions and miracles had hitherto had no place in his ordered approach to worship. Prior to coming to Knock he might well have concluded that the phenomena associated with the place could have been an unusual electric storm mistaken by some drunken peasants for a vision. But sitting quietly in the old church, his natural scepticism seemed to fall away. His mind ranged over images of countless pilgrims flocking from far and wide to this poverty-stricken village in a barren land, their faith flowering in the rain and the mist. He began to think that he too might now have walked on holy ground. Mrs Morgan interrupted his reverie. She, it seemed, was prey to no such pious thoughts.

'What I would like,' she said, 'is a nice cup of tea.'

They walked slowly down to the village for tea. Mrs Morgan's ankles continued to trouble her and she was glad when the time came to go back to the coach. They were a little early and Mrs Morgan began to fidget with the paper bags, tying them securely to her ankles. Morgan, almost involuntarily, fished in his pocket for the small phial of holy water he had obtained at the shrine.

'Here,' he said, 'I have a strange feeling that this might do you more good.'

11

Homecoming

As with most homeward journeys, the return from Knock seemed to be quicker than the going. It was not, of course, attended – at least so far as the Morgans were concerned – by any of Father Alphonsus's diversions, geographic or social. At Athlone he had booked the party into another comfortable hotel, but any lingering thoughts he might have entertained about a night on the town were skilfully anticipated by the nuns. After dinner they positioned themselves strategically in the hotel lobby at a vantage point which gave an unrestricted view of the front door and the hotel bar. It seemed as if they were daring him to pass. The Morgans bravely ran this gauntlet to seek a quiet nightcap in the bar, this time, however, unmolested by blandishments to greater derring-do in other places. A few of the other pilgrims drifted in but there was no sign of Father Alphonsus or his drinking coterie from Galway. Morgan suspected that there might just be the possibility of a conspiracy to wait until the nuns – accustomed to early bedtimes – succumbed to sleep, but he and Mrs Morgan did not wait to find out. They retired early and, if truth were told, discovered some of the romantic togetherness which their children had argued as a compelling reason for leaving them behind. They awoke happy and relaxed.

Out of the mouths of babes, thought Morgan, as he brushed his teeth with more than usual vigour.

Following an uneventful drive to Dublin that morning, they boarded the ferry – this time for a day crossing. It was calm and dry and the traumas of the outward journey were not to be repeated. On the coach back to Gatehaven Mrs Morgan noticed that her ankles were better.

'Worth knowing – that paper bag trick,' she commented.

Morgan smiled inwardly. He believed that a quite different remedial agent had been at work but he would not trivialize it by claiming success in the matter of Mrs Morgan's ankles, so he said nothing. Later in the journey, as they approached Gatehaven, he noticed that the 'newcomers' and 'villagers' had returned to their respective camps; the 'divide' had reasserted itself. Only to be expected, he thought.

They reached the house late at night. All was quiet and the children were in bed and they crept in so as not to disturb them. Mrs Morgan made straight for the kitchen to examine the cooker – a constant source of concern to her when hands other than her own had been on it. Morgan intervened and guided her to the living-room.

'All in good time in the morning,' he said, 'let's finish off the trip with a quiet drink together.'

Mrs Morgan conceded a fleeting blush; the romance of the previous night had not totally evaporated. They sat on the settee for a while, holding hands and sipping their drinks. But it had been a long day and sleep was the victor in the end. Soon they made their way to bed, yawning.

'Thank you, darling,' said Mrs Morgan, as they kissed goodnight. 'It's been a wonderful few days.'

'Very uplifting,' replied Morgan. And he meant it.

Morgan had arranged to have the next day off from work and they had intended to sleep late. But it was not to be. Their bedroom was subject to an early siege by excited children anxious for presents. When these turned out to be Knock rosaries the excitement waned and they went off to get their own breakfast. It was still school holidays and they were off to the city for the day. Eventually they left and a relative calm returned to the household.

After breakfast Mrs Morgan organized the cleaning rota. After four days' absence, with the house at the mercy of the children, there was much, so she said, to be done. Morgan, clad self-consciously in a pinafore, was despatched to dust and vacuum-clean the living-room. He made a bold show of removing what he saw as non-existent dust and cleaning apparently unsoiled carpets. She turned her attention to the cooker.

'Look at the grease on it,' she called to Morgan.

He went to look but his unpractised eye and male disinterest could see little amiss.

'That'll soon come off,' he said, striving diplomatically both to placate his spouse and exonerate his off-spring.

'Humph,' said Mrs Morgan, no doubt divining his intention.

By lunchtime she was satisfied. She pillaged the refrigerator to scrape together a small salad from what the children had left, and announced her intention of going to the supermarket in the afternoon to restock. Morgan's duties were, however, not quite discharged.

'While I'm gone,' she said, 'you can put some cleaning crystals down the bath drain and flush it out with hot water. I'll have a nice hot bath when I come back.'

Morgan followed his orders to the letter, even to the

extent of getting a magnifying glass to decipher the miniscule user instructions on the label of the crystals bottle. Flush thoroughly with boiling water, it said, and put two tablespoonfuls of crystals down the drain before flushing again. What could be simpler, he thought.

He first sensed that something was wrong when the second flush of boiling water stubbornly refused to disappear down the plughole. Back to the bottle label, he thought, arming himself once again with the magnifying glass. He verified that his procedure had been right, but then, to his consternation, he noticed a further splurge of miniscule printing at the bottom of the label. Leave for a while, preferably overnight, it said. With Mrs Morgan's return imminent, savouring no doubt her nice hot bath, he could sense the onset of a domestic upheaval.

He reviewed his options. The best thing, he concluded, would be to wait and hope. In the meantime, to restore some credibility with Mrs Morgan, he resolved to continue the 'homecoming' check-up by going into the garden to inspect her cherished flower-beds for any damage which might have been sustained during their absence. Damage to the flower-beds there was none but further damage to household serenity was imminent. While he was temporarily distracted in the garden, Mrs Morgan returned, anxious for her bath. Morgan re-entered the house to find Mrs Morgan, clad only in her brassière and pants, emerging from the bedroom *en route* to the bathroom. In other circumstances, the sight of a near-nude Mrs Morgan might have prompted Morgan's thoughts in a more gratifying direction. But this, he concluded ruefully, was not going to be one of those occasions. All he could manage was a lame restraining hand.

'My dear,' he said, 'I'm afraid we've struck a bit of a snag.'

'A snag,' said Mrs Morgan, in tones stentorian – almost theatrical. 'Whatever do you mean?'

Morgan explained the predicament only to meet with her not unexpected response.

'You can't have done it right,' she said.

Morgan protested. Mrs Morgan squinted at the crystals bottle, spurning the aid of the magnifying glass.

'Well,' she said at last, 'it always clears away quickly when I do it.'

It would, thought Morgan.

'What do you propose to do now?' she went on.

Morgan searched his mind for inspiration. Eventually it came.

'I'll poke some wire down it,' he said.

In the boot of his car he always kept an old wire coat hanger ever since someone had told him that it was useful for binding up a sagging exhaust pipe in an emergency. He went out to the car and unravelled it to produce a long strand of wire.

'This'll do it,' he said on his return. 'It never fails.'

What evidence he had for that show of confidence was not clear.

'Get on with it, then,' said Mrs Morgan. 'I still want my bath.'

Morgan knelt beside the bath prodding the wire gingerly down the plughole. He was aware of Mrs Morgan's menacing presence at his elbow.

'Don't scratch the bath,' she hissed.

God forbid, thought Morgan.

All was to no avail. Morgan decided to attack the problem from the other direction. He went outside to the outlet. It was raining and in the time he took to bend and manoeuvre the wire into the exterior pipe he was soaked. Success eluded him and he went back into the house wet and dispirited.

It was then that Mrs Morgan resumed command of the operation. She was standing – still unclothed – at the bathroom door, rather like one imagines Boadicea, thought Morgan.

'This is what we'll do,' she said. 'You keep on pouring boiling water down while I start getting things ready for supper.'

'That won't work,' protested Morgan, 'it'll only fill the bath up. We'll have to get a plumber.'

'Nothing you've done seems to work,' she replied. 'Plumber my foot,' she went on. 'I know what I'm doing.'

She went into the bedroom and reappeared, not in her clothes, but in her dressing-gown. Evidently she was not about to concede the impossibility of getting her bath before supper.

Morgan reluctantly began to ferry kettles of boiling water from the kitchen to the bathroom. As he had predicted, all that happened was that the bath filled up with water. Finally, his drenching from the rain exacerbated by exposure to clouds of steam, his patience ran out.

'I'm sorry, dear,' he said, 'I'll have to call a plumber.'

But even as he made his way wearily to the telephone, there was a loud gurgling noise from the bathroom; he rushed to look. The drain was free. Mrs Morgan's reaction was not unexpected.

'I told you so,' she said, 'that's how it was supposed to work all along. Now you keep an eye on the potatoes while I have my bath.'

She sailed triumphantly past him into the bathroom. Morgan knew that the balance of domestic authority had tilted sharply in her direction.

But the Morgans' unpredictable bathroom had not yet finished wreaking havoc on the planned tranquillity of the homecoming. Morgan's tending of the potatoes was suddenly interrupted by a loud banging on the bathroom door.

'I can't get out,' shouted Mrs Morgan.

'Just turn the key, dear,' said Morgan naively.

'Don't be silly,' was the anguished response, 'it won't turn and I can't get it out.' Incongruously the old 'actress and bishop' joke flashed through Morgan's mind, but this was clearly no time for flippancy.

'Do something, please,' said Mrs Morgan, increasingly more anxious.

'Don't panic, dear,' he said, 'I'll have you out in a jiff.'

He hunted for a screwdriver and proceeded to poke it through the keyhole in an attempt to dislodge the offending key, alas with no success. Mrs Morgan was becoming ever more agitated and, unusually for her, close to tears. Morgan knew that quick and decisive action was called for.

'Open the window,' he shouted, 'I'll be there in a tick.'

He rushed to the garage and fetched his extending ladder. Mrs Morgan had opened the bathroom window and he climbed gingerly up to it, carefully negotiating each rain-swept rung. He peered into the room. She was sitting, wrapped in a towel, on the toilet seat, her head in her hands.

'Thank God you've come,' she moaned.

Morgan levered himself awkwardly through the narrow casement window.

'Don't get mud all over the place,' said Mrs Morgan, her normal concern reasserting itself. Morgan marvelled at the mind of woman. She interrupted his momentary musing.

'What do we do now?' she enquired.

Morgan pondered. He hadn't really stopped to think before rushing to the side of his beleaguered spouse via ladder and window. Now it occurred to him that all he might have achieved was to put himself in the same predicament. Mrs Morgan stared at him in sudden disbelief.

'You're not going to make me climb down that ladder,' she said fearfully.

Morgan gathered his thoughts.

'Of course not, dear,' he said trying to make his tone belie his thoughts, 'we'll have the door open in a trice.'

He grasped the key. A silent prayer to the Virgin of Knock flickered across his mind. Mustering his strength, he twisted the key firmly. Dear God, his thoughts continued, don't let it snap. Providence attended him, and with a sharp jolt it sprang into the open position.

'There you are,' he said, 'all it needed was a little brute force.'

She put her arms around him and rested her head on his shoulder. Morgan began to feel better. The frustrations and humiliation of the past few hours faded into insignificance. He had recovered his standing with Mrs Morgan; he felt like the man of the house again.

That evening, Morgan savoured the return to normality. After all, through the good sense and perseverance of the nuns, the pilgrimage to Knock had been saved from total disaster, no doubt leading to an embarrassing inquest afterwards; even romance had flowered with Mrs Morgan on the way back, and Morgan suspected, might do so again following his triumph with the bathroom key. At very least, and despite the traumas of the first day home, the marital balance was on an even keel.

He sat with his crossword, Mrs Morgan with her knitting, the cat completing the domestic scene stretched out in utter relaxation on the settee. The children were in their rooms assaulting their ears with music which Mrs Morgan would not tolerate in the living-room. All was peace – but not for long! Suddenly Morgan started as he glimpsed what looked like a ball of fur hurtle past his chair towards the far end of the room.

'Good heavens,' he cried, 'there's a mouse in here.'

Mrs Morgan athletically drew her legs under her on the chair with a sharp intake of breath. Morgan looked to the cat.

'C'mon, Emma, – for that was the name given to her as a kitten by Mrs Morgan, rather twee in Morgan's opinion – 'c'mon, Emma,' he said, 'go for it!'

Emma raised her head wearily from its resting place between her paws, fixed Morgan with a green-eyed unblinking stare, and yawned. But that was all.

'Never mind the cat,' shrieked Mrs Morgan, 'you get it.'

Morgan's prowess as a mouse-catcher had never previously been tested. It soon became evident that it was not his *forte*. He rolled up a newspaper and crawled around the floor. Each time his tiny adversary appeared from behind a piece of furniture he lunged desperately at it with a total absence of contact. The cat watched him, unmoved and apparently uninterested in assisting.

'I shall never refer to that animal as "tiger" again,' said Morgan, breathlessly.

By now, disturbed by the commotion, the children had come into the room. They made some attempt to help, peering into corners, but they could scarcely hide their amusement at their father's desperate efforts. With his offspring sniggering and his wife cowering in her chair, Morgan felt ridiculous. He had to do something. Suddenly, enlightenment came.

'I know,' he said, 'I'll pop next door to Arthur – he'll know what to do.'

Arthur came back with him to the house. 'Where be the little varmint?' he asked as Morgan ushered him into the living-room.

'There he goes,' shouted one of the children, pointing to the skirting board close to Mrs Morgan's chair.

Arthur peered at the battle zone. ''E be nothing but a little vole come in from the garden,' he said, 'get Pussy out of the way.'

'For all the good she is,' commented Mrs Morgan ruefully, 'she might as well be.'

Emma, still looking bemused by the entire proceedings was duly despatched into outer darkness.

'Now,' said Arthur, rubbing his hands together, 'we mun catch him alive and return him to the wild.'

This surprised Morgan who, hitherto, had not looked upon mice as an endangered species, but he concluded that Arthur's caring approach had something to do with the Countryman's Code. Arthur, growing in self-importance, gave his instructions.

'Fetch me some books, an empty milk bottle and six small pieces of cheese,' he said, 'but – repeat but – do not handle the cheese or 'e'll smell 'ee on it.'

Morgan was impressed. He had an irreverent vision of another and greater miracle-worker performing long ago in Palestine. The books, bottle and cheese were placed carefully at Arthur's feet. Kneeling on the floor, Arthur placed the books one on top of the other to form a series of small steps with the top one level with the lip of the milk bottle. Taking out a penknife, he carefully skewered each piece of cheese and placed one on each book and the last one in the bottom of the milk bottle.

'That'll do it,' he said, 'you'll have 'im alive in the bottom of bottle by morning and then you mun let 'im loose in garden.'

'Thank you, Arthur,' said Morgan, much impressed by this display of rustic ingenuity.

'No sweat,' replied Arthur, 'now shut up the room 'til mornin'.' And off he went.

The Morgans retired to their respective bedrooms, leaving the unfortunate Emma to spend the night on the tiles.

Next morning Morgan rose early, anxious to dispose of the vole before he went off to work. He crept into the darkened living-room and switched on the light. Nothing! The cheese remained in the same pristine state as the night before and there was no sign of the intruder. He scratched his head; his confidence in Arthur was badly shaken. Wearily he went into the kitchen to begin preparations for breakfast. Suddenly he noticed what looked like small particles of chocolate scattered over the worktops and draining board. The awful truth dawned on him.

'God – it's in here,' he said aloud, 'how on earth could that have happened?'

Mrs Morgan was summoned.

'I am definitely not putting up with this,' she exclaimed.

Quickly she cleaned up the mess and prepared breakfast. They all sat down to eat, looking uneasily around the room, straining eyes and ears to detect the presence of their unwelcome guest. With the meal finished, Mrs Morgan cleared away.

'Now we'll do it my way,' she announced, opening the back door and calling Emma. 'Out of the room everyone,' she went on, depositing the cat in the middle of the floor and shooing them into the hall. She closed the door firmly.

'Aren't you going to feed Emma?' queried one of the children.

'She'll feed all right if she starts to behave like a proper cat,' replied Mrs Morgan, grim-faced.

Morgan sensed that the children were none too happy with Mrs Morgan's intended solution.

'May I make a suggestion?' he asked, 'why not leave the back door open and give the poor little creature a chance to escape?'

Mrs Morgan gave him a withering look; evidently she did not share his new-found concern for wildlife.

'I want it caught – dead or alive,' she said.

'Please, Mum,' chorused the children, 'give it a chance.'

Their advocacy was always more successful than Morgan's. Going back into the kitchen, she opened the back door wide. The cat, standing pitifully by her empty food dish, gave her a puzzled stare as she slammed shut the door to the hallway. Morgan picked up his briefcase and opened the front door.

'I wonder how it got out of the living-room,' he mused aloud.

His gaze fell on his youngest child, as she stood before him, finger to mouth, in an attitude of guilt.

'I did go and have a look in the middle of the night, Daddy,' she said tearfully.

He looked furtively around the hallway. Mrs Morgan had gone into the living-room, no doubt to dispose of Arthur's abortive trap.

'Shush,' he whispered, 'don't let your mother hear you.'

Still furtive, he crept back to the kitchen door and opened it a fraction. Emma the cat, having abandoned the prospect of any kind of breakfast, was asleep on the table.

During the day, thoughts of domestic difficulties were expunged from Morgan's mind by the exigencies of work. But on his drive home they came crowding back. He found it incredible that the intrusion of such a small defenceless creature could wreak such havoc on his household. But, sadly it was true. He had sensed at breakfast that none of the family felt easy in the knowledge of its presence. There was also, of course, the matter of hygiene. Mrs Morgan, quite rightly, would not tolerate the soiling of her kitchen for very long. He would have to resolve the matter that evening. But how? He certainly did not share Mrs Morgan's revival of faith in the cat, and Arthur's elaborate procedure for catching the intruder alive seemed less and less appealing to him. The option of the old-fashioned mouse-trap seemed to be the last resort. Oh damn, he thought, the shops will be shut by now. He arrived home with his mind still in turmoil.

As things turned out, his worries were groundless. He entered the house to find Mrs Morgan in the hallway in her triumphant stance, hands on hips, and a faint smile playing around the corners of her mouth. There was no need to ask.

'You've caught it then,' said Morgan.

'And killed it,' replied Mrs Morgan. 'I suppose you and Arthur will find that barbaric.'

Morgan, for one, did not. His brief flirtation with the Countryman's Code had been overwhelmed by his desire to see serenity and calm restored to his home.

'Not at all, dear,' he said, 'how did you manage it?'

'With difficulty,' replied Mrs Morgan, ruefully holding up a bandaged finger, 'those old-fashioned traps can be dangerous.'

'Particularly to voles,' commented Morgan, humour

restored by relief.

Later that evening Morgan reflected on the extraordinary week that they had spent. The ups and down of the trip to Ireland seemed a long way away now, their memory dimmed by the bizarre series of incidents which had attended their homecoming. He was looking forward now to easing back into the comfortable routine of life prior to the pilgrimage. He should have known better. This was Gatehaven where normality rarely seemed to endure for very long.

12

Nuptials

The invitation to the wedding of Dolores and Jason arrived during the following week. Mrs Morgan threw what Morgan always thought of as a 'wobbly'.

'Oh, how lovely,' she cried, 'but I haven't got a thing to wear.'

Morgan was sceptical. He thought about the ever-decreasing share of wardrobe space allotted to him over the years and decided that a mild protest was called for.

'But you've got plenty of clothes,' he said.

'None that people haven't seen me in before,' was the reply, almost defeating logic.

Morgan persisted. 'But it's hardly the social event of the season,' he argued.

'It is for them,' replied Mrs Morgan.

Morgan doubted whether what Mrs Morgan would be wearing would be of paramount importance to the happy couple, but he conceded the futility of further protest. The following Saturday they set off for the city to buy her a new *ensemble*.

Arriving in the city, Morgan parked the car in the office car park. He was always slightly uneasy about this. Public feeling about car parking availability in the city centre continually ran high and his, admittedly rare, use of this small perquisite preyed a little on his conscience, no doubt adding to his innate reluctance to embark on shopping expeditions in the company of Mrs Morgan. He was not an entirely happy man as they made their way to the shops and into the 'Ladies Wear' section of one of the larger department stores.

'You wait here,' said Mrs Morgan, 'I shan't be long.'

All Morgan's experience attested to the probable inaccuracy of that particular statement and he resigned himself to a long sojourn. He did what he always did, wandering about between the rails of feminine apparel trying not to look as if he was a potential shoplifter, never straying too far from the spot where he had left Mrs Morgan in case – just in case – her unlikely prompt return might find him missing. It was during this aimless perambulation, trying as ever to control his growing impatience, that he found himself to be the subject of curious glances from passing ladies. Calamity! Unwittingly he had wandered into a section of the shop floor devoted to ladies' lingerie. As far as the eye could see he was surrounded by flimsy lacy bits of near-nothing. This won't do at all, he thought. Suspicion of shoplifting he could bear but peeping perversion was something else. He hurried back to where he had left Mrs Morgan, there to be greeted by one of the shop assistants.

'Mr Morgan?' she asked. Morgan nodded. 'Your wife would like you to come and see her outfit,' she went on.

Morgan recognized this as a familiar part of the shopping ritual. He followed the assistant through the ranks of hanging dresses and suits to a small changing room where Mrs Morgan stood resplendent in her new outfit.

'What do you think?' she asked, pirouetting self-consciously.

Now Morgan didn't really think anything; sometimes he wondered if it mattered what he thought. But he knew what was expected of him and he was anxious not to run the risk of Mrs Morgan starting a fresh fitting with a different *ensemble* and prolonging his agony.

'Very nice, my dear,' he said, tongue in cheek. 'I can't remember seeing anything to suit you better.'

He always said that: she never seemed to be aware of his little deceit.

'In that case I'll take it,' said Mrs Morgan to the hovering assistant. Triumphed again, thought Morgan. With the purchase packaged, they walked towards the exit.

'Well, that wasn't too bad,' said Mrs Morgan. 'I've got a lovely suit with matching accessories.'

Morgan, relieved at his relatively early deliverance from the agony of waiting, permitted himself a small shaft of humour.

'Including a matching umbrella, no doubt,' he said.

Mrs Morgan was dismissive. 'I am not counting on it being wet,' she riposted imperiously.

Oh well, that's that then, thought Morgan.

On the day of the wedding, they awoke to lowering skies and torrential rain. Morgan conquered his desire to crow and concentrated his attention on the task in hand – how to get Mrs Morgan to the church dry and resplendent in her new clothes. There was, of course, plenty of time to plan this operation; Mrs Morgan's preparations were inevitably to take longer than the event for which they were the reason. Finally, she pronounced herself ready, and after the usual mandatory expressions of approval from Morgan and the children, she stood at the front door, ready to go.

Meanwhile, Morgan had made his plans. Not without some jeopardy to his own sartorial elegance, he had manœuvred the car to within a few feet of the front door, narrowly avoiding damage to flower-beds and fences in the process. He spanned the small space between the front door and the open door of the car with a large golfing-type umbrella, emblazoned with the name of a French hotel, which he had acquired in rather dubious circumstances on one of his more memorable occupational travels – but that's another story! Urged on by the children, Mrs Morgan launched herself from the front door to the car, slamming the car door firmly behind her. This was not something that Morgan had planned. Her loud 'Damn' was clearly audible as she was hit by a fusillade of raindrops from the lining of the door when she thought she was safely in the dry of her seat. When Morgan had braved the elements to reach the driver's door on the opposite side, she was dabbing her new *ensemble* with a tissue.

'What's the matter with that damned door?' she asked ruefully, 'I'm soaked.'

'Nothing,' replied Morgan, 'they all do that if you slam them in the rain. Hadn't you noticed before?'

There was no reply. Mrs Morgan was not, of course, prone to admissions of error.

There was still one more obstacle to overcome. The time taken by Mrs Morgan to get ready meant that they would be hard pressed to reach the church before the bride. They did, but not without incident. The inadequate church car park was already full and Morgan was forced to park in the street about fifty yards from the church door. Mrs Morgan stepped into the rain while Morgan, oblivious to his own discomfort, fumbled desperately to lock the car and hoist the umbrella. This done, they hurried to the church in less than elegant style. Mrs Morgan jerked along in a staccato movement, her high heels clip-clopping in synchronized accompaniment to the swing of her handbag. Morgan bounded along, side-on beside her, in steps which resembled those of a basketball player looking for an opening, as he manipulated the umbrella to save her from the ravages of the storm. This was ungainly but effective, but it was not to be Morgan's day. At the church door he shook out the umbrella vigorously but carelessly undoing most of the good work he had accomplished along the street. Mrs Morgan was far from pleased but there was worse to come. Inside the church she attempted to genuflect in the aisle, not realizing that her new skirt was of the pencil-slim variety and not designed for this kind of movement. As she wobbled alarmingly on one knee, total disaster was averted only by Morgan's hastily proferred arm. Even this was at a cost. He dropped the umbrella with a loud clatter, and every head turned as they crept embarrassed into a pew near the back. Ah well, thought Morgan philosophically, at least everyone knows we're here.

He surveyed the scene. The church was near to full mainly with 'newcomers', many of them patrons of the cocktail bar and their families. Sonia was just visible to him near the front, unmissable in a hat which seemed to have been designed around a fruit bowl. When she moved her head, Jason came into view in front of her, nervously fingering the back of his stiff white collar – not, it would seem, an article of apparel which he was accustomed to wearing. The altar and sanctuary were festooned with flowers and plants giving a fair likeness, so it seemed to Morgan, of a fairy grotto. As the organ crashed into the Bridal Entrance, Father Alphonsus emerged from the vegetation, flanked by two small altar boys, angelic in white albs. This angelic illusion was not destined to last for long. As Dolores made her slow and dignified entrance, on the arm of one of the cocktail bar 'regulars', and followed demurely by Sally the check-out girl-cum-barmaid, evidently enlisted as a bridesmaid, a near disaster occurred. Father Alphonsus collided with one of the flower pots which cluttered the altar steps and all but lost his balance. A buzz of scarcely concealed laughter ran through the congregation which rose to an embarrassing climax when one of the white-albed angels belied his appearance by joining in the sniggering and received, for his impertinence, a well directed clout around the ear from the discomfited priest. Father Alphonsus struggled to retrieve his dignity, spreading his arms wide in his familiar gesture for requiring silence.

'Before we begin,' he said, 'I have an announcement to make. In deference to the bride the nuptial Mass today will be in Latin.'

Fair enough, thought Morgan. After all, Dolores was not renowned for her command of English and she was old enough to remember when Mass was always celebrated in that way. His tolerance, however, was not shared by one of the 'newcomers' in the row in front of him.

'Well, that's that,' said the man, 'we're not a lot of bloody Italians,' and he marched out followed by his family.

There was an initial gasp from the congregation followed by a stunned silence. If looks could kill, the steely stare of Father Alphonsus at the retreating back of the dissenter would have been lethal. Morgan wondered what else could go wrong.

Fortunately, nothing did if one discounted a momentary aberration by Father Alphonsus when he sought to quell the activities of numerous amateur flashlight photographers during his sonorous progress through the Latin Mass.

'*Dominus vobiscum,*' he intoned at one point followed suddenly and incongruously by 'and keep all that snapping for later. I'll tell you when.'

That apart, things proceeded more or less as they were intended, and soon Dolores was retracing her path down the aisle, this time of course on the arm of Jason. She was a vision of loveliness, her exotic dark good looks thrown into sharp relief by the sheer white of her bridal gown. Not so Jason. His nervous fidgeting with his collar had contrived to pull his tie to one side and allow one wing of his collar to escape the restraint of his coat lapel and point towards the ceiling as if it were some kind of price tag. Attention to Jason's dishevelment was soon distracted, however, by the appearance of Sonia marching behind the bridal pair to lead the congregation from the church. She was at her most garish in an assortment of bright colours, the fruit-bowl hat perched dangerously on her bouffant blue hairstyle. She was, of course, as she probably intended, centre-stage and nobody moved as she made her way to the church door and disappeared from view. This was the signal for a stampede as most of the guests spilled into the aisle elbowing past the more pious few who were reverently attempting to genuflect and cross themselves before leaving the church. Morgan, anxious to spare his spouse any further indignity, grasped her arm and held her firmly back in her seat until the crush had passed. When eventually they emerged from the church, Sonia was in full flow organizing a photo session on the lawn outside. The rain had stopped and the sun was peeping through the clouds. Mrs Morgan winked at Morgan. She had, after all, been partly vindicated.

Inevitably, the wedding reception was to be at The Maritime. Morgan suggested that they should walk the short distance to the hotel from the church, but Mrs Morgan quibbled. She did not actually mention the possibility of further rainfall but Morgan guessed that her confidence in her ability to divine the weather was not quite absolute, so to the car they went. Entering the hotel they were given a glass of sherry by a smartly attired waitress and waved in the direction of the ballroom. Here stood a large notice which announced 'Ballroom Closed – Private Function'. Morgan could not actually remember the ballroom ever being open – certainly he had never entered it before. To his surprise it was a long narrow cavernous room with a bar at one end and a tiny dance floor in the centre beside an equally small stage. He speculated that in a previous existence it had probably done duty as a bowling alley.

With the guests seated the wedding breakfast began, preceded by a hastily muttered grace from Father Alphonsus. It was, Morgan thought, standard fare for the occasion – tomato soup, ham salad and a gooey trifle concoction, all washed down with glasses of *vin de table* sporting a taste which only served to confirm its dubious vintage. Then came the speeches – from the best man, a friend of Jason's, from the cocktail bar 'regular' who had given Dolores away, and finally from Jason. All were clearly unaccustomed to public speaking, a fact which each announced – superflously – as he began. Morgan began to experience feelings of boredom and thoughts about how soon they could decently depart were exercising his mind when things took an unexpected turn.

Sonia heaved herself to her feet.

'All right everyone?' she asked. What else, thought Morgan? 'Now, ladies and gentlemen,' she went on, 'that's the formal bit over. Did you all enjoy the wine, by the way?' Everyone 'Oohed' obediently if not entirely truthfully. 'Now as I was saying, that's all over and we can enjoy ourselves a bit. There's a cash bar open for as long as you want' – business as usual, thought Morgan – 'and we've been very fortunate to secure the services of a very good group. Once they're set up I want to see you all having a go.'

The group turned out to be a duo – a man and a woman in check shirts and jeans who disrupted the proceedings for the next ten minutes or so lugging large black boxes and coils of wiring across the floor to the small stage. Meanwhile, Father Alphonsus had led the rush to the bar at the far end of the room. Morgan, eager to erase the taste of the *vin de table* from his palate, joined in and obtained a gin and tonic for Mrs Morgan and a large whisky for himself. The hubbub of conversation was brought to a sudden halt by a series of loud chords on a guitar from the male partner in the duo. Everyone waited expectantly for the entertainment to begin, but what excitement there was turned out to be premature.

'Carry on talking,' said the guitarist, in a broad 'villager' accent, 'just tunin' up. Won't be long.'

Conversation resumed. It was mainly confined, of course, to comments about the beautiful appearance of the bride, which were true, and the excellence of the meal, which were not. Soon the duo were ready.

'Here we go, folks,' said the guitarist, his foot tapping and his accent subtly changing to mid-Atlantic.

They launched into a refrain which Morgan vaguely recognised as having something to do with a railway in the American Mid-West. The guitarist contorted himself as if he was engaged in a wrestling match with his instrument while his partner delivered the lyrics in an agonised high pitch which seemed to have little to do with the instrumental accompaniment.

Sonia was not satisfied. 'Excuse me, please,' she said –

more of a command than a request – 'that's no way to start a wedding party. We've got to have a waltz for the bride and groom.'

The duo stopped abruptly somewhere along the line to Kansas City.

'We don't do waltzes,' said the guitarist.

Sonia's expression would have demolished a lesser man but no doubt this was not the first time that his repertoire had been called into question.

'Well I do,' she went on, grabbing the hand microphone from the startled female vocalist. 'All together now, folks,' she cried, and she proceeded to belt out 'The Anniversary Waltz' with a gusto which went some way to compensate for its lack of tunefulness. Once the guests, after some initial hesitation, had joined in, she released the microphone and dragged Jason and Dolores on to the dance floor.

'Off you go,' she exhorted them, 'solo first, then we'll all join in.'

The bridal solo was not an unqualified success. Jason, it seemed, didn't do waltzes either. Sonia was undaunted. Seeing him stumbling embarrassingly around the floor, she acted quickly. Donning her dreadful tinted frame spectacles she scanned the room for people mature enough to remember how to waltz, darting here and there to press them into service. The Morgans fell early victims to one of her predatory swoops. On the dance floor Mrs Morgan grasped Morgan tightly.

'Ooh, I like it,' she said, 'I can't remember when we last danced together.'

The communal rendering of 'The Anniversary Waltz' came to an untidy end as various factions began to deliver their diverse and competing recollections of the lyrics and the duo took over again. Their performance was memorable only for the unrelenting monotony of its tempo and their unique talent for making each song sound the same. But drink and the occasion worked its wonders. Couples took to the dance floor to display a bewildering variety of styles, mostly versions of the 'stand off and jig a bit on the spot' mode of the times. Others, however, mainly the older guests, were actually touching each other as they tried to adapt a not-so-slow foxtrot to the unhelpful accompaniment of the duo. Mrs Morgan was one such, her appetite whetted by her participation in the waltz. Morgan found it hard going. The pencil-slim skirt kept Mrs Morgan's movements to a minimum which translated poorly into the rhythmic requirements of the dance and he was hard-pressed to avoid treading on her toes. She seemed oblivious to his difficulties, all the more as time went on, and seemingly carried away by the occasion, she called frequently for more drinks between dances. When she finally removed her shoes to assist her efforts on the dance floor, Morgan began to feel a sense of foreboding.

About an hour later his worst fears were confirmed. Mrs Morgan was drunk – more than drunk, positively abandoned. Her dancing technique was becoming more and more flamboyant, putting great strain on the stitching of her skirt, so much so that Morgan steeled himself to see it disintegrate at any moment. He had long ceased to be her sole partner, as she fluttered around the room, glass in hand, inviting various equally bibulous male guests to join her on the dance floor. Even Father Alphonsus did not escape her attention, but his prowess on the floor proved to be unequal to the task of following her frantic gyrations in the confines of her skirt. It was when she fell over in the course of one of these that Morgan decided that enough was enough. Pulling her firmly to her feet he indicated that it was time to go.

126

'But I don't want to go,' she slurred, 'I'm having such a good time.'

Her protests fell in deaf ears. Morgan was adamant, masterly he would have liked to think, and they left the room with Mrs Morgan singing along to one of the interminable country and western ditties, her shoes in her hand, her coat slung carelessly over her shoulder, and Morgan carrying her hat and handbag.

In the hotel lobby Morgan rearranged her dress as best he could. She now bore little resemblance to the picture of elegance which she had set out as that morning.

'Where's the car?' she burbled.

'Forget the car,' said Morgan. 'Thanks to you I'm not fit to drive. We'll have to walk and I'll collect it later.'

Wise as that decision undoubtedly was, it contained the seeds of fresh problems. As they encountered fresh air at the hotel door, he felt his own legs wobble ominously, and he allowed Mrs Morgan to stagger on ahead as he strove to control his wayward progress along the road home. This proved to be a mistake; her performance was not yet over. Turning the corner to the road where they lived he was shocked to find her teetering down the middle white line with a red and white road cone perched on her head.

'I can walk straight,' she shouted back to him, 'now you have a go.'

Morgan strained to summon his fast-fading sense of balance as he lurched unsteadily after her. By the time he reached her his impetus was well out of control and, bundling her to the pavement they hurtled across it and fell heavily into a privet hedge, where they came to rest in total disarray.

'What the 'ell's going on 'ere?' came a voice from the other side of the hedge.

Morgan sighed with relief. Help was at hand. It was Arthur

13

Politicking

It took a long time – months rather than weeks – for Mrs Morgan to recover from the twin humiliation of her performance at the wedding and the indignity of having to be rescued by Arthur. During the autumn and winter of 1974/75 she was subdued and introverted. Christmas was a quiet affair, not to be compared with the previous year when Penny had left her indelible mark on the proceedings. Morgan, a creature of quiet habit, found the more sedate pace of life not unsatisfying but he remained prey to a nagging anxiety about Mrs Morgan's uncharacteristic withdrawal from her usual round of activities. Eventually, early in the New Year, he tackled the problem.

'How about coming to The Maritime tonight?' he enquired tentatively one Saturday morning as he pushed her trolley around the supermarket.

'For everyone to have a laugh at my expense?' replied Mrs Morgan grimly, glancing anxiously around as if the whole store was hanging on her every word.

'Don't be silly,' said Morgan, 'that's all forgotten now.'

He knew from his own forays to the village that, whatever inward impressions she retained about the enormity of her autumn antics, they had long since faded from local gossip. Life in Gatehaven had moved on. Even Arthur, on Morgan's solo visits to the club, had scarcely mentioned the episode. Morgan speculated that by some of the bizarre standards of Gatehaven conduct it was probably nowhere near as remarkable as Mrs Morgan imagined. Throughout that Saturday with gentle persuasion he coaxed her into putting things into perspective. By the evening she had succumbed and they set off for The Maritime

As Morgan had predicted – promised even – things were much as usual – with one exception. Jason appeared to have assumed a greater eminence in the establishment, moving proprietorially around the cocktail bar, dressed in what was almost a dinner suit, saving a polka-dot bow tie, and greeting customers like a landlord to the manner born. Dolores, as always, commanded the bar in exotic fashion but of Sonia – strangely – there was no sign. Morgan wondered briefly what was going on but his main preoccupation was with Mrs Morgan. In this respect the evening was a success. In the weeks that followed, emboldened by her uneventful reappearance at The Maritime, she slipped back into her old social round. No doubt it was something of a shock to her ego, albeit a welcome one, that she was not the talk of the village. But shocks were not to be confined to Mrs Morgan. The next recipient of one was to be Morgan himself and she was to deliver it.

'I've been thinking,' she said to him one evening. Now this was a phrase of hers which always set alarm bells ringing in his mind and he sprang to attention. 'You know,' she went on, 'that we shall be a smaller family this year.'

He knew exactly what she meant. They were coming to the end of a domestic era. Their son would be departing for university in the autumn and their elder daughter had announced her intention of leaving school to enrol as a trainee nurse at the same time.

'Well,' continued Mrs Morgan, 'with just the three of us left at home I shan't be nearly as busy and I have decided that I need some new interest in my life.'

Is that all, thought Morgan as visions of the Women's Institute and evening classes flashed through his mind. What came next, however, could not have been further from his thoughts.

'I have decided,' she said, 'to enter politics.'

Morgan sat bolt upright in his chair. 'Politics,' he said, 'whatever do you mean?'

'I should have thought it was perfectly plain,' she said, 'but I'll spell it out for you if you wish.'

'I think you'd better,' said Morgan, still shocked.

'Well,' she explained, 'you remember the Gatehaven Preservation Society?' How could he forget! He had gone to considerable lengths over the years to avoid contact with it. Was it now to return to haunt him? It was. Mrs Morgan continued, 'They are looking for a bigger say in what goes on around here and they will be contesting seats on the Parish Council in May. I have been approached' – he could have sworn her chest was swelling – 'to stand.'

'Now wait a minute,' countered Morgan, 'isn't the Parish Council something to do with the church?'

Mrs Morgan cluck-clucked in exasperation. 'Of course it isn't,' she said, 'it's the local authority for the village.'

Morgan knew that but recourse to disparagement seemed to be his best hope at this stage.

'Oh, that one,' he went on, 'but they only look after allotments and the like. The County and the District do all the important things.'

She was not deterred. 'Ah yes,' she said, 'but they have

to consult the Parish. It's the law.'

Morgan, in his work, knew something of this kind of consultation and it was not encouraging, but he hadn't the heart to continue trying to deflate her. A different tack was required.

'But it's all party-politics these days,' he said, 'you'll have to join one of the parties to get elected.'

This might just work, he thought. Mrs Morgan was generally disdainful of politicians. It didn't work. She had obviously been well primed by someone.

'Not necessarily,' she responded, 'the Society are going to start a new one. It's to be called the Citizens Party.'

Morgan wracked his brains for a response to this new revelation. There was none. Finally he said lamely, 'But we are all citizens, dear.'

'Exactly,' said Mrs Morgan triumphantly, 'that's why we shall win.'

Morgan capitulated, praying fervently that something would cause this new venture to be still-born.

On this occasion Divine Providence failed to come to his assistance and the practical manifestation of Mrs Morgan's new life direction was not long in coming.

A few days later she announced, 'My agent's coming round tonight for a tactical planning meeting.'

Morgan's first reaction was to see this as a good reason to absent himself from the house – perhaps to the club with Arthur – but it was not to be.

'I'd like you to meet her,' she went on, 'she thinks you may be of help to us.'

He groaned inwardly; this was the last thing he wanted. Suddenly, enlightenment came.

'Ah, but you know I can't get involved, dear,' he said. 'I'm a public servant; I have to be politically neutral.'

'Blanche,' said Mrs Morgan imperiously, 'has already

given that some thought. She says neutral doesn't mean neutered.'

Morgan felt more concerned than neutered. Who on earth was Blanche for a start? And quite what was it they were expecting him to do? Explanations were called for.

'Who,' he said, 'might Blanche be?'

'My agent – Blanche Bickerstaff. You'll like her,' replied Mrs Morgan in the tone she used when she brooked no option.

He tried again. 'But what is it exactly that she's expecting me to do?' he enquired.

'Just be patient,' snapped Mrs Morgan, oddly impatient herself, 'she'll explain everything tonight.'

That evening the doorbell sounded – what was to Morgan – its dread summons. Mrs Morgan went through a final paroxysm of prinking in the living-room as he went to answer it. He recalled another such occasion some years before when Marigold Speke-Johnson had burst into his life in similar fashion to cause him domestic unease ever since. In troubled mind he opened the door. The lady who confronted him was nothing like Marigold Speke-Johnson – at least physically. She was about twice as big, sporting the most generous bust that Morgan had ever seen, to which she was hugging an assortment of files and papers which threatened to disintegrate at any moment into an untidy heap on the floor. Not surprisingly, it did, as she attempted to release from between her teeth a plastic supermarket carrier-bag stuffed with rolls of sickly yellow fluorescent paper, but lacking the spare hand necessary for this manœuvre. Morgan found himself on his knees beside her, gathering up the debris.

'Let me help,' he said involuntarily.

'You're so kind,' she gushed.

With the debris gathered and conveyed to the living-room floor, introductions were effected. Morgan mentally categorized Blanche as a lady of what he thought of as the 'hunting, shooting, fishing' classes, often to be spotted at vicarage garden parties, and prone to espouse vigorously all manner of causes without too much thought to their worthiness. If Marigold was purgatory, he mused, this could be hell. He was not about to be proved wrong. She launched straight into the business at hand.

'The election's in May,' she said, 'that gives us about three months to project our image. We are going to need some lateral thinking.'

Morgan looked blank. What the hell did she mean, he thought, but his reply gave nothing away.

'Of course,' he said jauntily, 'that's exactly the right way to go.'

He was not, of course, privy at this stage to where they were going, or why, or how. Blanche was quick to enlighten him.

'Our candidate,' she said – God, she means Mrs Morgan, thought Morgan as realization deepened – 'our candidate is well known and respected among – how shall I put it – the more perceptive voters' – meaning the Preservation Society mob, thought Morgan – 'but she has got to establish a wider awareness of herself in the village. That is the task we have to address, and this is how we shall go about it.'

Morgan was left reeling at what followed. Firstly, there was to be a leaflet drop – the leaflet was duly produced from the pile of debris showing a beaming Mrs Morgan alongside a stirring call to save Gatehaven from the predatory advance of the city across the Green Belt. Then would come a 'knocking on doors' operation in which Mrs Morgan would follow up the leaflet drop with personal persuasion on the doorstep. At the same time the village would be saturated with the sickly yellow fluorescent posters. Blanche unfurled one of these from the plastic bag. It was her *piece de resistance*. In bold black lettering it said 'VOTE LIFESTYLE – VOTE CITIZEN – VOTE MORGAN'. All this was to culminate in the week before the election in a public meeting to be addressed by Mrs Morgan.

Question after question raced through Morgan's mind.

'Well,' said Blanche, 'what do you think?'

What Morgan thought was unspeakable and he found himself forced to confine his comments to damage limitation.

'I'm not too happy about the poster,' he said, 'people will think I'm the candidate.'

'Nonsense,' said Blanche airily, 'they'll know it's Mrs Morgan by then. In any case, it's a common enough name. Nobody will think it's you.'

Desperation was setting in with Morgan. 'Where do I come in then?' he ventured hesitantly, hoping that he didn't, but fearing the worst.

'That's more like it,' said Blanche. Morgan almost expected an approving pat on the head. 'Now there's the leaflet drop,' she went on, 'we need all the help we can get for that. And there's the putting up the posters and . . . .'

Morgan mustered the temerity to interrupt. 'Just a minute,' he said, 'I can't be seen doing all that – a man in my position.'

It was not a posture he liked to adopt; he felt uncomfortably pompous.

Blanche was not accustomed to interruptions. Her response was supremely dismissive.

'Don't be a silly man,' she said, 'you can do it after dark when no-one's about. Now, let's get on.'

134

Can there be more, thought Morgan. There was.

'Now we come to the question of meeting expenses,' she went on. 'The Society can't fund the entire campaign so we need to enrol new members.'

It was Mrs Morgan's turn to interrupt. 'I'll just go and make a nice cup of tea,' she said.

Coward, thought Morgan, and without further ado, he was enrolled as a member of the Preservation Society, his entrance fee disappearing into Blanche's handbag as he looked on ruefully. Mrs Morgan returned with the tea. Let that be all for one night, prayed Morgan – but Blanche was not finished yet.

'Now you're one of us,' she said, 'there's one more thing you can do.'

'Yes?' asked Morgan wearily.

'It's the venue for the public meeting,' she went on, 'the social club is the only place large enough.'

'Yes?' repeated Morgan, more fearful now than weary.

'Well – I can't think why – but I understand from Mrs Morgan that you're a member,' she said, 'fortuitously, as it happens.'

Morgan looked daggers at his wife. Traitor, he thought.

'But I have nothing whatsoever to do with the bookings,' he protested.

'Ah,' responded Blanche knowingly, 'but that friend of yours – that Potts person – does. Surely you can persuade him to get us a booking.'

Did Mrs Morgan's treachery know no bounds, thought Morgan. That its limits had not been reached became evident to Morgan as Mrs Morgan intervened to complete the ambush.

'I've already explained to Blanche that you can do it, dear,' she said sweetly.

The twin assault was too much for Morgan and he muttered a grudging assent. Blanche left shortly afterwards, her mission accomplished.

'What does she do for a living when she's not "rent-a-causing"?' queried the exhausted Morgan when she was safely out of earshot.

'Nothing now,' replied Mrs Morgan, 'she's retired, but she used to be a headmistress.'

'That figures at least,' commented Morgan.

The following evening, after repeated reminders from Mrs Morgan, he made his way unhappily to the club. Arthur was already in the men's bar, supping cider with a group of 'villagers'. As he always did, he detached himself from them and joined Morgan, who had not yet graduated to supping with the inner circle and sharing their confidences.

'Nice to see you,' said Arthur, 'fancy a drop o' scrumpy?'

While Arthur went to obtain the drinks, Morgan collected his thoughts and planned his strategy. He opted for the casual enquiry.

'Arthur,' he said, 'I've often wondered – how do people go about booking the club for a function?'

'Depends who they are,' replied Arthur, 'an' what they want it for. Committee are very particular about bookings.'

Morgan knew what he meant. He remembered the stories about the ill-fated operatic society venture. He decided to take some protective action to distance himself from what he had to do.

'Well,' he said as casually as he could, 'it's not actually for me – it's for the wife.'

Arthur eyed him curiously. 'What difference does that make?' he asked. 'You'm better come clean with me.'

Morgan came clean while Arthur listened intently. He

136

had scarcely got to mention Blanche Bickerstaff and the Citizens Party before Arthur was shaking his head vigorously.

'Hold it right there,' he said. 'Club has got to be non-political – it's in the constitution.

'Oh,' said Morgan as he strove to digest this unforseen twist. It was undoubtedly a way out of his predicament but it still carried the seeds of conflict, not only with Mrs Morgan, but also with the redoubtable Blanche. Not a comfortable prospect, he thought. He decided on one last attempt, if only to be able to say that he had done all he could to help the cause.

'Well,' he ventured hopefully, 'they're not really political, are they? More like a community group I would say.'

Surprisingly, this last desperate ploy seemed to strike a chord with Arthur.

'Let me think,' he said.

Arthur thought. It seemed like an age to Morgan before he spoke.

'You'm been set up by womenfolk,' he said, scratching his head. There was another pregnant pause as he filled his pipe and lit it, and then, 'but you'm been kind to me and I'll be kind to you.' Morgan waited agog with expectation. Arthur continued, looking around the room conspiratorially. 'I can't promise anything,' he said in a near-whisper, 'but maybe – just maybe – committee would allow a meeting of Preservation Society at which Mrs Morgan happened to be a speaker.'

Morgan could see Arthur's drift but he remained cautious and feigned confusion.

'I don't quite follow, Arthur,' he said. 'Can you explain a bit more?'

Arthur explained at some length. It seemed that he would be prepared to argue to the committee that the

Society was well-intentioned and that its aims did not differ materially from those of the 'villagers' – although, he commented snidely in passing, the latter employed more subtle methods to achieve their ends. Mrs Morgan – who, after all, was a club member – could be invited to explain the aims of the Society to her fellow members but the election would not be mentioned. In that way she would get to the wider audience of 'villagers' that she sought and the committee could deny any fore-knowledge of her political motive.

Morgan marvelled. 'You crafty old dog, Arthur,' he said. 'It's you that should have been the politician.'

Arthur grinned. 'I used to be once,' he said, 'afore all you damned "newcomers" started snaffling the Council seats. But don't count your chickens. I wouldn't do it for anyone else, and it's no cinch that the committee will go along wi'it. I'll let you know next week.'

Morgan returned home to report to Mrs Morgan on the outcome of his mission. On the way he pondered his tactics – after all it was not outright success that he would be able to convey. Inspiration came to him along the road. There would need to be some distortion of the truth if he was to maintain his standing with Mrs Morgan and Blanche. So Arthur's ingenious idea became his, negotiated cleverly in the face of a blank refusal to allow anything at all. Mrs Morgan fell for it; indeed she was impressed. But there was still the task of convincing Blanche.

That task was undertaken later that evening on the telephone. As Morgan anticipated, this was to turn out to be a little more difficult, but Mrs Morgan bore the brunt of it. Her paeans of praise for his ingenuity were of course not a little discomfiting to him, but they were the main plank of her argument with Blanche and he had no option but to endure them. Eventually Blanche

138

conceded, grudgingly, that what had been achieved was better than nothing and Mrs Morgan put down the telephone, her face wreathed in smiles.

'I really can't get over how clever you are, dear,' she said. 'You'll be such an asset to the Party.'

Morgan felt a note of caution was appropriate. 'Not so much of the Party,' he said, 'it's supposed to be a non-political public meeting – remember.'

'Well, you know what it is, and I know what it is, and . . .' began Mrs Morgan before Morgan interrupted.

'And before long everyone will know what it is,' he said sharply, 'just don't go on about it.'

She looked at him curiously; he was not often sharp with her. What she didn't know, of course, was that his motivation was different from hers. He was not over-concerned about the meeting now that he had done his bit to help bring it about, but he had to ensure that the subterfuge remained attributable to him rather than Arthur. The less it was talked about the greater his chances of safeguarding that.

'In any case,' he went on, 'it's not certain yet; the committee still have to agree.'

The committee, swayed by Arthur's standing and cunning advocacy, did agree. Arthur conveyed the news to Morgan the following week, standing on the doorstep where Morgan strove to keep him, lest Mrs Morgan became involved in the conversation and inadvertently blew his cover story.

'Thank you, Arthur,' he said, glancing anxiously over his shoulder. 'Mrs Morgan will be delighted.'

Luck was with him. She had been momentarily distracted by the discovery of wet paw marks on the furniture and her entire attention was directed to disciplining Emma the cat. He went back to the living-room, Arthur safely departed.

'That's it,' he said, 'the meeting's agreed.'

The chastened cat shot out of the living-room as Mrs Morgan's concentration on the disciplinary process instantly lapsed. She clapped her hands in an uncharacteristic display of excitement.

'That's wonderful news,' she cried, 'now we can really get on with the campaign.'

Morgan had a sinking feeling that the trauma of the past few days would be nothing compared with what was about to start. He was right.

14

Campaigning

Over the next few weeks Mrs Morgan was closeted frequently with Blanche at meetings from which Morgan was excluded. For this he was grateful; if he had to play a part in the campaign, he would rather it be as a foot-soldier than a general. It also gave him an opportunity to reflect about the direction in which his wife was headed, dragging him reluctantly along. It was in the course of this reflection that he made a disturbing discovery.

Not to appear ignorant in front of Blanche and the now politically-awakened Mrs Morgan, he had taken the trouble to inform himself about the local political scenario. Naturally, in Gatehaven, it was not at all what one might have expected. The town was divided for electoral purposes into three wards – Central, Coastal and Country. Each of them returned three councillors to the Parish Council and one to the District Council; they were combined to elect one representative for the whole town to the more remote County Council. That much he gleaned from the helpful lady who appeared once a week with the mobile library. The rest of his information came from more informal sources – the barber's shop, the club, and, not least, Arthur.

Although County and District elections were fought on conventional party platforms, they attracted little public interest in Gatehaven. Not so the Parish Council, however. This appeared to have evolved, not on party political lines, but as a forum where 'villagers' and 'newcomers' met to draw the dividing lines between their respective spheres of influence. Actual elections to this body were a rarity. Membership was decided by means of a sort of informal accord between the two factions. Through sheer weight of numbers the 'newcomers' were in a majority of five to four, less than they were entitled to perhaps on the numbers basis, but still a source of discontent with the 'villagers'. The 'newcomers' held all three seats in the Country ward – not surprisingly since it was now largely covered with their 'identikit' houses – and one seat in each of the Central and Coastal wards, which they had only partially succeeded in colonizing. The 'villagers' consequently were confined to two seats in each of the latter two wards. The appearance of Mrs Morgan as an additional candidate for a seat in the Central ward was about to upset this cosy equilibrium and precipitate what might seem to be a totally unnecessary election.

Morgan's first intimation that all was not as it should be came, when – by stealthy eavesdropping and oblique enquiries – he managed to ascertain that the 'villagers' were to field not two candidates, as the accord demanded, but three in the Central ward. This breach of the accord was to be concealed until the very last moment – when nominations were to be published – in order to deny the unsuspecting 'newcomer' candidate the time to embark on an effective counter-campaign. He would know, of course, that there would have to be a poll as soon as Mrs Morgan declared herself but that could be regarded as more an irritant than a full-blown challenge to the established order.

Morgan, whose political intuition had been honed in a

higher league – he was, after all, a senior public servant who worked daily around the fringe of politics – began to smell a rat. He decided to test his suspicion on Arthur.

'You know, Arthur,' he said as disarmingly as he could, 'letting the wife have the club for her meeting came as a bit of a surprise to me.'

Arthur grunted. He always did that when he was searching for the right answer. Morgan recognized the sign. When the answer came it was predictably enigmatic.

'Believe me, lad,' said Arthur, 'they'm doing her no favours.'

That was all, but it was enough for Morgan to complete the picture that was forming in his mind. By capturing all three seats in the Central ward the 'villagers' would regain their long-lost control of the Council at least for a while. What better way to ensure the victory than to encourage Mrs Morgan to stand and hopefully split the 'newcomer' vote! Seen in this light the club committee's decision over her public meeting made absolute but deeply disturbing sense to Morgan. The meeting, he concluded, was likely to be a fiasco, either packed with hostile 'villagers' who had no intention of voting for her, or sparsely attended by the conventional two men and a dog. Either way, he pondered, she would be humiliated – a 'patsy' playing in a game she didn't understand. His thoughts raced on. Worse still, he would be blamed since he had – falsely – claimed the credit for arranging it. It was at this point that Morgan's attitude to her campaign underwent a profound change. It had to if he was to help her make a creditable showing, salve her pride, and, not least, salvage some vestige of his own integrity. The unwilling foot-soldier was about to become a reluctant general.

In the privacy of his thoughts he reviewed the situation. Blanche's policy of wooing the 'villagers', he concluded, was completely mis-directed. Not only would they have no intention of electing Mrs Morgan, but they would also be looking to defeat the 'newcomer' candidate. Her only chance would be to capture the bulk of the 'newcomer' votes and perhaps – but only perhaps – a few 'villager' ones from those whose aspirations may have drifted towards a different perception of their future life-style for one reason or another. No doubt there were some but he was hard put to it to think of any. If Blanche was not willing to change the direction of the campaign, then he would have to do it. He did not relish the thought but needs must. And so, one evening he found himself saying to Mrs Morgan 'I think, dear, that it's time to put a bit of a zip into this campaign of yours, don't you?'

She was clearly taken aback by this unexpected show of interest.

'But I thought you didn't want anything to do with it,' she said. 'I've been trying to persuade Blanche to leave you out of it.'

Morgan took the plunge. 'Things have changed,' he said, and he went on doggedly to explain to her what he had learnt from his covert information-gathering in the village. She listened intently until he administered his *coup de grâce*.

'So I'm afraid that Blanche has got it all wrong,' he said, throwing caution to the wind.

This, of course, provoked a response. 'But she's my agent. She knows about these things,' she cried – a trifle uncertainly Morgan thought.

'So do I,' responded Morgan, encouraged by the slight vacillation in her answer, 'and I'm telling you that if you follow her advice you'll lose and lose badly.'

His perception of her initial response was correct. She

changed tack.

'But how are we to tell her?' she asked. 'You know what she's like.'

He knew very well what she was like and his mental preparation had allowed for it.

'We don't have to tell her,' he said, tapping the side of his nose in a conspiratorial gesture, 'there is another way.'

'Well, I don't know,' said Mrs Morgan despairingly, 'it's all beyond me.'

'Listen,' said Morgan, warming now to his task, 'the door step is the key to this. She wants you to concentrate on 'villager' houses; I suggest you target the 'newcomer' houses as well.'

'But that's every house in the ward to cover,' she protested. 'I'll never get round them all. Besides she'll find out – it's bound to get back to her.'

He played his trump card, dealing with her first objection triumphantly.

'Not you – us!' he said ungrammatically but effectively. 'I'll help you to do the extra calls. We'll wait until she's gone home.'

Mrs Morgan tried to interrupt but he was now in full spate.

'And what if she does find out?' he went on. 'It can't be wrong to do a bit of extra canvassing.'

There was no doubt that Mrs Morgan was impressed with his performance but she mustered one last protest.

'It's so deceitful,' she moaned, 'it's downright dirty.'

'Of course it is,' said Morgan – there was no holding him now – 'it's a dirty game, they're all playing dirty and you'll have to do the same if you're to win.'

She wiped an involuntary tear from her eye. 'I wish I'd

145

never started,' she lamented. Morgan waited expectantly. 'But,' she sighed, 'I can't possibly back out now.'

Morgan's momentary hope receded. Of course she can't, he thought, the loss of face would be a much greater cross for her to bear.

In April the campaign began in earnest. Blanche would arrive each evening, as twilight approached, with her boxes of leaflets and posters, accompanied by a gaggle of Preservation Society members. They were dressed, but for the absence of boot-blacking on their faces, like a group of commandos about to set off for a mission behind enemy lines. Morgan suspected that even they entertained some inhibitions about being recognized as they went about their task. Proceedings would commence with a kind of briefing parade on the Morgans' front lawn. Here Blanche would allocate streets and locations before rostering her troops into groups of two or three and dispersing them with bundles of campaign leaflets into the gathering gloom. Morgan, who was of course participating as a foot-soldier at this stage – his hour had not yet come – became adept at moving cleverly around the lawn to avoid being rostered with the Speke-Johnsons, who were prominent participants on most evenings. That he considered would have been too much to bear. Something like piling Ossa on Pelion, he mused, fondly recalling his success with one of the more obscure clues in a recent *Times* crossword; the leaflet drop itself was ordeal enough – braving dogs and humans alike and trying desperately to look as if he was out for a stroll when anyone approached who might conceivably recognize him. It did occur to him, of course, that subterfuge of that kind would be useless when the time came for him to join Mrs Morgan on the unofficial canvass that he himself had proposed.

146

But for the time being he excised thoughts of that ordeal from his mind, lest courage should fail and all his good intentions wither in the face of abject cowardice.

In this frame of mind the end of the leaflet and poster phase came too soon for Morgan, but come it did as Blanche arrived one evening to brief Mrs Morgan on her doorstep tactics.

At the end she said, 'I shall of course accompany you at a distance but you'll look more confident if you're on the doorstep alone.'

Mrs Morgan looked anything but confident as her eyes wandered towards Morgan's reflecting all the terror of an animal caught in a trap. He decided to intervene.

'I think I'd better come too,' he said, 'just in case there's any trouble.'

It was hardly the right thing to say.

'Trouble?' cried Mrs Morgan, more terror-struck now than before.

'You?' said Blanche as if to question what use his presence would possibly be, if trouble there was.

He struggled for words. 'Well – er, not trouble exactly,' he stammered, 'er – more sort of helping out if discussions got heated.'

'And how, pray, would you do that?' demanded Blanche.

Morgan plumbed the depths of his imagination.

'Well,' he said eventually, as the women waited anxiously for enlightenment, 'I could say that someone had called to see her at home and I had come to fetch her.'

'Humph,' said Blanche dismissively.

Mrs Morgan was less ready to condemn him. She realized that he was trying to reassure her, and, in any case there was the secret second canvass to be considered. It might help him, she thought, to get the feel of things before they attempted that.

'I don't think it will do any harm, Blanche,' she said.

'That's that then,' said Morgan. 'Which night do we start?'

'What do you mean?' replied Blanche, 'tonight of course. There's no time like the present.' She heaved herself to her feet and produced two large yellow rosettes from her omni-present supermarket carrier. 'Sorry I haven't got one for you,' she said to Morgan. 'I never dreamed that you would want to come along.'

He was relieved at that but it was short-lived.

As they left the house, Mrs Morgan whispered frantically to him, 'You'll need one for afterwards – you'll have to get hold of Blanche's.'

Blanche – clipboard in hand – led them briskly towards a row of terraced cottages meandering up from the High Street.

'These are the people you've got to win over,' she said, 'off you go.'

Morgan managed a sly wink at Mrs Morgan as she set off towards the first cottage. There was a nerve-rending pause as she searched for a non-existent door bell; the silence was broken sharply as she finally lost patience and hammered on the door with her fist. A dog howled. Beyond that, nothing. Blanche scuttled down the road.

'Try the next one,' she hissed.

Mrs Morgan dutifully moved on and was soon in an animated, if brief, conversation through a minute crack of an opened door with the occupant of the next cottage. Before long she came disconsolately back down the road.

'They thought I was a Jehovah's Witness,' she said wearily.

'Never mind,' said Blanche impatiently, 'keep going.'

Mrs Morgan set off again, this time it seemed with more success. There were lengthy periods of conversation followed by cheery goodbyes as she moved on to the next cottage. It was then Morgan noticed that Blanche was becoming agitated, looking frequently at her watch and tapping her foot on the pavement almost as if she was frustrated by the time the now-crusading Mrs Morgan was taking on each call.

'Are you in a hurry?' he ventured as they crept slowly along in Mrs Morgan's wake.

It seemed that she was. Morgan listened patiently to a recital of her programme for the remainder of the evening, all planned with near-military precision to the minute – walk the dog, take a shower, listen to a concert on the radio, make her cocoa, drink it, and so to bed, and all by ten o'clock precisely. Meanwhile Mrs Morgan was making good progress along the terrace but not, it appeared, good enough for Blanche.

'This is all taking much longer than scheduled,' she tutted.

Morgan seized the opportunity.

'Look,' he said, 'I think she's got the hang of it now. You go off and see to the dog and all that. We'll allow a bit more time tomorrow night.'

Blanche looked uncertain. 'Are you sure?' she began, but Morgan pressed home the advantage.

'Of course I'm sure,' he said, 'give me your rosette – that will make me an official minder.'

Blanche acquiesced. As she disappeared into the night Morgan ran jubilantly down the street, waving the rosette to attract Mrs Morgan's attention.

'That's enough for tonight,' he shouted, 'she's gone – and what's more I've got her rosette.'

In truth, of course, he could have done without the rosette, but he knew what was expected of him.

'What a cleversticks you are,' said Mrs Morgan, as she came back down the terrace towards him.

They made their way back along the High Street towards the finger of 'newcomer' territory which extended into the Central ward; it was here that their unofficial covert canvass was to begin. Mrs Morgan recounted her experiences as they went. Most of the residents of the terrace didn't know that there was an election on and had been grateful for her for drawing their attention to it – that figures, thought Morgan, there's been no need of one for years. Several others had promised her their votes immediately without waiting to listen to her carefully prepared *spiel* – of course, thought Morgan, the well-tried method of getting rid of an unwelcome canvasser. There was also a 'nice man' – as Mrs Morgan put it – who recognized her and wondered what she did to get such lovely roses in her front garden. Of Blanche's much vaunted leaflets there was no mention; they had either been consigned, unread, to the wastebin with all the other junk mail or – a much more intriguing thought to Morgan – the leaflet droppers had not been as assiduous in their efforts as Blanche expected them to be. No matter, he mused, they didn't rate highly in his own plans for getting Mrs Morgan a creditable vote.

'All in all a successful night's canvassing,' he said with a hint of sarcasm.

Mrs Morgan looked at him knowingly. 'I think so,' she replied, nodding her head.

They turned the corner into 'newcomer' territory. Sea View was the name of the road although the sea had long disappeared from vision behind the ranks of houses opposite. It was here that misfortune overtook them.

150

Struggling along the road, tugged by a villainous-looking bull mastiff was Blanche. Morgan thought furiously.

'Quickly,' he cried, 'she mustn't see us here. Back around the corner and into the public conveniences.'

He pushed Mrs Morgan unceremoniously into the 'Ladies.' 'Stay there until I give the all-clear,' he whispered as he propelled himself towards the 'Gents' next door.

Standing in the shadows near the entrance he watched Blanche's progress as she turned the corner from Sea View. She can't stay around long, he thought, her schedule won't allow it. As she drew level with his vantage point he shrunk back into the dimly-lit interior. To his astonishment she spoke.

'Coo-ee,' she said, 'we're here – Bonzo and me.'

Morgan froze. Was she addressing him? She wasn't. Suddenly there was a sound of movement from one of the cubicles accompanied by the pulling of the flush. As the cubicle door opened he flung himself towards the urinal and assumed the self-conscious posture which men do in that location – all hunched shoulders and bowed head. From the corner of his eye he saw a small figure emerge from the cubicle and make for the door in short bouncing strides common to people of short stature. The man looked vaguely familiar. Tip-toeing to the door, Morgan heard him speak.

'Time for our turn along the prom with Bonzo, darling,' he said.

Bonzo, apparently, didn't think so and began tugging away in the opposite direction, but eventually the combined efforts of Blanche and her companion prevailed and all three disappeared towards the sea-front. Morgan clasped his chest in a gesture of relief only to experience a sense of something missing. His rosette had gone. He looked wildly around to find, to his horror,

151

that it was resting, half-submerged in the trough of the urinal. At that moment the automatic flush operated and completed its immersion.

The voice of Mrs Morgan broke in on his dismay.

'Are you there, dear?' she was whispering at the door.

Morgan had no option but to abandon his rosette to its obnoxious fate.

'Coming, my dear,' he said.

'Did you see that?' cried Mrs Morgan as he emerged. 'She's up to something with Oliver Speke-Johnson.'

Morgan recalled the familiar look of the man as he had left. Of course, he thought, it was him.

'Would you believe it?' he said, 'after all that sauce she fed me about her schedule for the night. I bet she's left her radio and lights on to fool everyone as well.'

'Well, I think it's disgusting,' pronounced Mrs Morgan.

'Surprising anyway,' commented Morgan, 'she's twice as big as him.'

'And a lot older,' added Mrs Morgan.

True, thought Morgan, but only a woman would think of that. His mind was still trying to cope with the vision of such an unlikely pair in passionate embrace.

Back to Sea View they went to begin at last the unofficial canvass.

'You take the odd numbers and I'll take the evens,' said Mrs Morgan authoritatively, almost as if she were assuming the mantle of Blanche.

'They don't have numbers on the houses here – only names,' replied Morgan.

'You know what I mean,' said Mrs Morgan shortly, 'you do one side and I'll do the other. Have you got your rosette?'

'Somewhere,' said Morgan slapping his pockets

vigorously. He was not yet ready to approach the hurdle of explaining the fate of the rosette.

He approached the first house. It was called Maltings for no reason which readily sprang to mind. Edging his way past the two cars ostentatiously parked in the drive – his and hers no doubt, he thought – and negotiating the garden gnomes he reached the door and rang the bell. It was, of course, a set of chimes.

15

Dissension

The chimes of Maltings were to ring in symbolically a new phase in Mrs Morgan's tortuous progress towards the election. Morgan thought so since he was about to enter the fray, but he could not have foreseen that what was to come would be infinitely more stressful than anything that had occurred hitherto and would lead to dissension within and without the Citizen Party coterie. He was already somewhat dismayed, of course, on the evidence of that first evening, by Mrs Morgan's unorthodox – even casual – attitude to doorstep canvassing but he was hopeful that this would change once he had tried his own technique and could demonstrate to her some promises of votes garnered if it was done his way. Regrettably in this he was to fail dismally.

The door to Maltings opened to reveal a bulky, bespectacled man enveloped in a heavy woollen cardigan with an ornate pipe clamped firmly in the centre of his teeth. Morgan mentally categorized him as 'bluff' as he introduced himself as a neighbour; this of course was merely to gain a foothold – his political pitch would follow. It never did.

'Come in,' said the bluff man guiding the un-suspecting Morgan by the arm, 'come and meet the wife.'

Before he could collect his thoughts, he was ensconced – trapped he would soon come to think – in an armchair in the living-room with the bluff man standing over him, arms folded, in an inquisitorial stance. But an inquisition it was not to be – more of a lecture about the life and times of the bluff man and his wife, delivered with machine-gun rapidity in a staccato series of unconnected phrases.

'Neighbour aye,' it began, 'well that's good news, in't it, Sybil?'

The wife appeared from the kitchen. She was a perfect match – buxom and dumpy at the same time, slightly coarse in features and wearing a plastic pinafore decorated with a 1930s print of an advertisement for HP Sauce. The bluff man continued apace.

'Only moved in from up north last week – a reet gradely place this Gatehaven but no-one's spoken to us yet – in't that right, Sybil? Anyroad we're pleased to see you – oh, by the way I'm Cyril Ponsonby and this is Sybil – Cyril and Sybil – got a bit of a ring to it, you see.'

He paused for breath but Morgan was denied an opportunity to reply as Sybil filled the speech vacuum.

'You're dead reet there, luv,' she said.

Cyril returned to the attack. 'First things first,' he went on, 'give the man a drink, Sybil – there's a nice malt in't cupboard – now what about a smoke – don't do it meself – Morgan looked curiously at the ornate pipe – 'doctor's orders you see – just suck this thing for company.'

He wrenched the pipe from his mouth, thumped his chest and retched his way through a simulated paroxysm of coughing to emphasize his point.

These initial exchanges – hardly exchanges since Morgan was mostly mute – were to set the pattern for the next half-hour or so. Morgan could not be exact about the passage of time as Cyril had imposed his bulk in front of the mantelpiece clock and he was too polite to consult his watch under their twin surveillance. He reeled under the torrent of folksy anecdotes about their life in the north and how they finally ended up in Gatehaven. His mind was active of course. He concluded that he had stumbled upon a new breed of 'newcomer' that he liked even less than the old one, and whose future impact upon the delicate balance of Gatehaven society was almost too awful to contemplate. His thoughts were interrupted by a glimpse, through the half-drawn curtains, of a forlorn Mrs Morgan looking anxiously one way and the other for him in the street outside. There was nothing for it now; he had to effect an exit. Any mention of the real purpose of his visit would be fraught with danger, likely to bring forth another time-consuming series of anecdotes. He took the plunge.

'I'm sorry,' he said, bravely interrupting Sybil in the middle of a tale about an extraordinary clever dog that they had once owned in Barnsley. 'I'll have to go. My wife will be wondering where I've got to.'

That, he surmised ruefully, was probably an understatement.

'What a shame,' said Sybil, 'you've hardly told us anything about yourself.'

Chance, thought Morgan as he made his escape, would have been a fine thing.

Mrs Morgan greeted him in high dudgeon. 'Where on earth have you been?' she thundered. 'I've done all my side long ago.'

Morgan explained his predicament as best he could, but there was no way he could clothe his performance with sufficient honour to satisfy Mrs Morgan. Not only did she give him the evil eye but the silent treatment to boot. That night they each clung tenaciously to their own sides of the bed with a large expanse of cold unoccupied sheet between them. Dawn brought no relief and hostilities were still in progress when Blanche arrived in the evening to usher them on their second venture into doorstep canvassing. Or so they thought. She went immediately onto the offensive.

'It has come to my attention,' she said icily, 'that you have been canvassing without my permission in Sea View.' The Morgans were taken aback. Before they could reply she stormed on. 'That kind of thing must cease immediately. It is not our intention to unseat Miles Mallalieu.' Morgan had never heard of Miles Mallalieu but with a name like that he could only be the 'newcomer' candidate. As he searched for a reply, Blanche turned her guns on him. 'I suppose it was all your idea,' she rasped, 'please remember in future that I am the agent here.'

It was at this point that Mrs Morgan sprang into action.

'And you remember that I am the candidate,' she riposted vigorously. 'I decide where we need to canvass so I'll thank you not to make unwarranted attacks on my husband.'

Mrs Morgan always said 'my husband' in a proprietorial tone. In this situation, of course, it had the effect of drawing Blanche's fire back to her, for which Morgan was grateful. He also sensed that her spirited defence of him marked the end of dissension between them. It was inevitably to be replaced by dissension with Blanche. Her dander was well and truly up.

'I think you both need a lesson on the rules of the game,' she said. 'I plan the campaign and I direct it. You do as you are told.'

This was too much for the already smouldering Mrs

157

Morgan.

'And does that include sneaking off half-way through canvassing each night to meet your . . . – she searched for the right word – . . . your paramour,' she hissed venomously.

Blanche was deflated – at least temporarily.

'I think I'd better go,' she said quietly. It would, however, have been too much to expect for her to depart without one last show of defiance. 'But mark my words,' she said, 'if you get yourself elected at the expense of Miles I shall have to think about withdrawing the whip.'

Mrs Morgan looked nonplussed. She probably thinks it's something to do with poor old Speke-Johnson, thought Morgan, but he knew what Blanche meant.

'Please yourself,' he said, happy now to join in the rout of Blanche, 'but with only one councillor that'll do the Party a fat lot of good.'

With Blanche gone things warmed between them. After disposing of Mrs Morgan's dark misconceptions about the whip, Morgan at last had a chance properly to explain his misfortunes at the Ponsonby household and to question Mrs Morgan about her previous night's canvassing. This brought him little comfort but he was anxious not to jeopardize the still precarious restoration of good relations so he listened patiently. She had apparently had an interesting conversation with a woman who wanted her to join her jam-making circle and another with a man who had aroused her interest in wine making, not to mention various other encounters of a similar nature.

'They were all very nice to me,' she commented.

He wondered how all this social tittle-tattle could possibly help to get her elected but he permitted himself just one single shaft of mild sarcasm.

'I don't suppose you kissed any babies,' he said.

She was equal to that. 'Don't be silly, dear,' she said with a twinkle in her eye, 'they were all in bed at that time – but I did pat a few dogs.'

For the next few weeks they planned and executed their doorstep canvassing together. The thrust of their short effort was in 'newcomer' territory, in defiance of Blanche, who was conspicuous by her absence. The poor unsuspecting Marigold Speke-Johnson told Mrs Morgan over the garden fence that she was rumoured to be unwell, but Morgan doubted that. He had spotted some evidence of her likely activity in the appearance around the village of posters announcing the public meeting. The thought of this, of course, did nothing to assuage his ever-present sense of unease about the direction of the campaign. Mrs Morgan had continued her canvassing in the folksy mode which she thought right, but about which he continued to harbour the gravest doubts. In his own efforts on the doorstep he had tried to address the policies which he believed she was advocating, although, to tell the truth, these had become increasingly obscure to him as a result of her attitude and the dissensions surrounding the campaign. For the most part he was received politely, but with what he perceived as an ominous lack of firm commitment. A few days before the public meeting Blanche re-emerged.

It was obvious to Morgan as he opened the door to her that she was a somewhat chastened version of the old battle-axe although her very appearance suggested that she was intent upon resuming some control over events. Her opening remarks confirmed this.

'I'm sorry to bother you,' she said – not a sentiment which came easily to her, thought Morgan – 'but it's about the public meeting.'

Read her like a book, he thought.

'Come in,' he said as doubts began to flood his mind about the wisdom of embarking on that event at all.

In the house, Blanche stood awkwardly, disdaining the offer of a seat, and making no attempt to remove her coat. She's not staying long then, thought Morgan thankfully. Mrs Morgan remained seated, composed and apparently in command of the situation.

'Well, what is it now?' she asked Blanche coolly.

'I've written you a speech for the meeting,' said Blanche, pulling some sheets of paper from her handbag.

'Keep it,' said Mrs Morgan shortly, 'I've already written my own.'

That surprised even Morgan. His occasional anxious reminders to her to prepare for the meeting had invariably been met with a coy smile and an 'all in good time' kind of response. He waited for an explosion from Blanche but there was only a long pause. This was definitely not the Blanche of old.

'In that case,' she replied eventually, 'I'd better have a copy to vet.'

'You can vet it as much as you like,' said Mrs Morgan, 'but I can't guarantee that your suggestions will be accepted.' She went to the bureau and handed Blanche a sheaf of papers. 'There you go,' she went on, ostentatiously consulting her watch, 'you'd better get on with it.'

Blanche turned to leave and then paused. 'Of course you realize that I shall be controlling the meeting from the chair,' she said smugly.

'If you must,' said Mrs Morgan disdainfully, and then pointedly to Morgan, 'what time does our television programme start, dear?'

This time Blanche took the hint and left, speech-less.

The day of the public meeting arrived all too soon for Morgan. With his heart full of misgivings, he escorted Mrs Morgan to the club, arriving about fifteen minutes early. The lounge bar, where the meeting was to be held, was empty except for Blanche and some of her lieutenants from the Preservation Society, conspicuous in their appalling ill-fitting tee-shirts. Morgan was surmising that his 'two men and a dog' theory was correct when he noticed that Blanche was in animated conversation with a man who was even more conspicuous for not wearing a tee-shirt. Tall, grey-haired, moustached and monocled, he was wearing a double-breasted grey suit and a glaringly regimental tie; his brown shoes were polished to a deep shine. Morgan put him down for a retired military man who was lacking his bowler hat and rolled umbrella only because he was indoors and it was not Armistice Day.

Seeing the Morgans, Blanche broke off her conversation abruptly. She rushed across the room, commandeered Mrs Morgan and took her to her place on the stage. Morgan was consigned to a place where the audience would have been, had there been one. He yawned and waited for the action to begin. When it did he was astounded. With barely five minutes to go to the advertised starting time there was a sudden influx of people, comfortably filling the available seats. Many waved to Mrs Morgan as they took their seats; Morgan observed that they were all 'newcomers' – not a 'villager' among them. Seeing them wave, some going to the stage to speak to her as she sat there, smiling smugly, the near unbelievable struck him. These were the fruits of her unorthodox doorstep canvassing. Bless my soul, he said to himself.

Right on time Blanche opened the meeting.

'Good evening ladies and gentlemen,' she boomed

into what in her case was a totally superfluous microphone. That was as far as she got – caught with her mouth open as the room reverberated to an equally stentorian but non-assisted interruption from the floor.

'Excuse me, Madam Chair,' said a voice. Morgan looked around anxiously as a buzz spread through the room. It was the military man, on his feet, moustache bristling. 'Excuse me,' he went on, 'but I wish to protest about the nature of this meeting.'

Blanche replied almost as if on cue.

'And, pray, who might you be and what is the basis of your protest?' she asked.

Morgan experienced a tingle of suspicion. It was all too pat – almost as if it had been rehearsed. Was this to be Blanche's revenge, he thought? The military man took full advantage of the opening so promptly afforded him by Blanche.

'My name is Miles Mallalieu,' he said. 'Colonel Mallalieu as a matter of fact' – naturally, thought Morgan – 'and I am a candidate in next week's election as I believe is this good lady on the platform.' He pointed accusingly at Mrs Morgan. 'It is my contention that she is using these premises for a political meeting contrary to the constitution of the club.'

Morgan waited anxiously but he need not have worried. A wave of protest erupted from the audience. It was garbled and close to cacophony but there was no mistaking the sentiment. They had come to hear Mrs Morgan expound the aims and ambitions of the Preservation Society and Mallalieu should sit down, shut up, and let her get on with it. Blanche's response to this strengthened Morgan's suspicions that something treacherous had been afoot. She was clearly taken aback by the reaction of the audience, but she stuck gamely to what he now saw as her script.

'I must say that in putting it the way he has,' she said, 'Colonel Mallalieu may have a point.'

You silly bitch, thought Morgan, he hasn't said a word yet to substantiate it. The audience seemed to share his view. Uproar now reigned with many of them on their feet and railing at the intrepid but unfortunate colonel and the ever more discomfited Blanche. It was at this point that Mrs Morgan intervened.

'May I say something?' she asked, grabbing the microphone from Blanche.

Try and stop her, thought Morgan.

'Yes,' roared the audience.

Mrs Morgan cleared her throat and waited for the noise to subside. When she spoke it was in moderate tones contrasting totally with the booming of Blanche and the colonel.

'It is perfectly true,' she said, 'that I am a candidate in next week's election. I have never sought to hide that and I would be surprised if there were any people here who did not know it before they came here tonight.'

Shouts of 'True! True!' came from scattered points around the room. Good stuff, thought Morgan. Mrs Morgan continued, 'As for the military gentleman in the audience, I have never met him before and neither, I suspect, have many of you,' she looked pointedly at Blanche, 'though perhaps not all of you.'

She's caught on, thought Morgan gleefully.

'If,' she went on, 'he has been harbouring some objection to tonight's meeting – which is quite clearly advertized as a meeting organized by the Preservation Society – if he has been harbouring such an objection, I would have thought it would have been more sensible to bring it to the attention of the Society prior to the meeting.'

163

A chorus of 'Hear! Hear!' rocked the room. Morgan was now lost in admiration for her performance, but she was by no means finished yet.

'But I realize,' she continued, 'as a politician myself' – cheeky, thought Morgan – 'that such a civilized course of action would not have brought him the electoral publicity that I believe he is courting here tonight.'

This time the applause was deafening – and long. Eventually Mrs Morgan raised her arms in a triumphant gesture to quell the noise.

'So,' she said, 'I am left in no doubt that, should I continue with the advertised programme for this meeting, he is the kind of man who would very likely seek to exploit the situation with the returning officer for the election in an attempt to jeopardize my candidature.'

This time the shouts were of 'Shame! Shame!' She raised her arms again – almost pontifically this time – to calm the situation.

'I do not think,' she continued, 'that such an outcome would be either in my best interests, or in yours, or – let it be said – in the interests of democracy.'

Outright pandemonium broke out. Mrs Morgan waited patiently for it to subside before continuing.

'I have therefore a compromise to propose. Blanche Bickerstaff is perfectly capable of enlightening you about the aims and objects of the Preservation Society. You are welcome to listen to her or' – she paused theatrically – 'you can have now the cup of coffee and a biscuit which I had arranged for the end of the meeting – I'm sure the good ladies of the club could manage that – and we can all chat informally about anything under the sun without breaching anybody's rules. So may I have a show of hands please? All those for Blanche Bickerstaff please show.'

The ensuing silence and lack of raised hands ended in

an outbreak of titters.

'And for coffee and biscuits?' she asked. A forest of raised hands greeted her. 'That's settled then,' she said, smiling ever so sweetly in the direction of Blanche.

Amid the clatter of people getting up from their seats, Colonel Mallalieu turned abruptly on his heel and strode from the room. Blanche huffily gathered up her papers and rushed after him. Morgan elbowed his way through the crush to where Mrs Morgan was attempting to descend from the stage into a throng of well-wishers. Eventually he reached her.

'My dear,' he gasped, 'that was magnificent – no other word for it.'

'I didn't think it went too badly,' she replied, falsely modest as she squeezed his arm, 'but we'll talk later. I have to circulate.'

Morgan bowed to her newly-found wisdom in the matter.

At last, when all the circulating and gossiping was over, they walked home together arm in arm. Morgan was ecstatic about her handling of the meeting. In his mind he could even acknowledge the possibility that she might actually win the election.

'That was the real killer,' he burbled happily, 'the vote on the coffee and biscuits. You know, I didn't even realize that Blanche had arranged any refreshments.'

Mrs Morgan looked at him archly. 'She didn't,' she said, 'I did.'

'But how?' asked Morgan, puzzled. 'You don't have any influence with the club.'

Her eyes twinkled.

'But Arthur does,' she replied.

'Arthur?' said Morgan. 'But you don't talk to him either.'

She was now almost coquettish.

'You have no idea what I get up to when you're away at work all day,' she said teasingly.

16

Consorting

Election Day found Morgan in a quandary. His newly-found faith in Mrs Morgan's ability to win the election was urging him to stay at home for the final phase, but he was dogged by a long arranged ministerial visit to the city at which he would be expected to act as host. He knew in his heart that a Parish Council election in a neighbouring village would not amount to anything approaching a plausible excuse for absenting himself from the presence of the great man. Mrs Morgan was disappointed but she understood and he went off to work as usual, but for a slight detour to cast his vote.

He was determined to keep the minister strictly to his timetable and to get back to Gatehaven as soon as the official cavalcade had departed, but good fortune did not attend him. This particular minister was one of a kind, not unfamiliar to Morgan, who saw himself as a man of the people and could scarcely resist every opportunity for a walkabout and consequent photo session that presented itself. It was a frustrated and irritable Morgan who eventually reached home well into the evening. Mrs Morgan was waiting for him, smartly dressed and rosetted.

'Thank God you've come,' she said, 'I need the car.'

Morgan was puzzled. The polling station was in easy walking distance and he assumed that was where she would want to be.

Not so; Mrs Morgan continued, 'The tellers want it to drive around in to get out our dormant vote.'

He was even more puzzled. She might as well have been speaking in a foreign language. But she read his thoughts.

'You know,' she said, 'the tellers – the people who hang about outside the polling station and tick off your number when you go to vote.'

He was still none the wiser. He had wondered before about the tellers – as he now realized they were called – and had invariably refused to give his number, suspecting that it was all some dark plot to breach the secrecy of the ballot. Mrs Morgan went on, 'They work out which of the Party's supporters have not voted and send a car to get them out.'

'I see,' said Morgan at last, handing her the car key, 'but what about Blanche? Couldn't they have used her car?'

'Blanche,' replied Mrs Morgan wearily, 'is not being as helpful as she might. I'll tell you about it later.'

He went into the kitchen. Mrs Morgan had fed the children – and the cat – but for once he was expected to look after himself. He sat down to a meal of baked beans on toast – a dish which was just about within the range of his culinary capabilities – and immersed himself in *The Times* crossword. The hours passed, the children went to their rooms, the youngest to bed and the elder two to grapple with their homework. Morgan settled in the living-room to indulge his talent of watching television and playing with the crossword at the same time, a feat in which he took a modicum of immodest pride. Shortly before nine o'clock Mrs Morgan returned, hot and bothered.

'Can't stop,' she gasped, 'I've got to get to the count.'

'Right,' said Morgan, kicking off his slippers, eager to join the action, 'hang on a tick. I'll come with you.'

'Ah,' said Mrs Morgan, a trifle hesitantly. 'Er – I'm afraid you can't. It's one of Blanche's little foibles.' They only allow candidates and accredited agents, and she seems to have overlooked you.'

He made a show of putting his slippers back on.

'Well, that's a fine thing,' he muttered peevishly, 'on purpose, no doubt.'

Mrs Morgan hugged him.

'Don't get upset,' she said, 'I'll get back as soon as it's over. Settle down and pour yourself a nice whisky.'

That's something, I suppose, thought Morgan. She didn't make a habit of encouraging him to have a drink. He hugged her back.

'Careful,' she cried, 'you'll crush my rosette.'

He drew back sharply; the watery fate of the spare one was still his secret. He resumed his solitary vigil in front of the television, comforted now by an approved large whisky. One, of course, led to another – and another – as he struggled to assimilate the plot of some late-night soap opera which his customary early retirement had prevented him seeing before. That effort, compounded by the trials of his day with the minister, eventually took its toll. He barely heard the elder children shout their 'goodnights' as he slid into a fretful torpor. He awoke with a start to find Mrs Morgan hugging him furiously.

'I've won! I've won!' she cried.

He looked around the room, bleary-eyed. The television screen was blank, the characters of the soap opera having departed some hours earlier to the ensuing

169

strains of the national anthem; the clock stood at one o'clock. Mrs Morgan could hardly contain herself. She was now on his lap, hat askew, rosette crushed unheeded against him.

'Wake up,' she cried, 'don't you understand? I've done it.'

Morgan struggled to collect his thoughts.

'My darling,' he said at last, 'that's incredible. I'm very pleased for you.'

She was now kissing him furiously, her colour was high, her eyes sparkling and Morgan could detect the faint sickly smell of sherry on her lips.

'And you've been celebrating a bit, I reckon,' he said.

'Only a few quick ones with the Speke-Johnsons,' she said, 'it's you I really want to celebrate with.'

He groaned inwardly. His unusually large intake of whisky over the course of the evening had left his mouth dry and his head aching, but there was no way he could deny her. He got up – Mrs Morgan slid into the chair like a ship at launch as he did so – and moved unsteadily to the drinks' cabinet. She now lay crumpled in the chair, legs apart, uncharacteristically inelegant and still burbling.

'A G and T for me,' she cried, 'none of your damned dry sherry, if you please.'

Morgan obliged, pouring a very small whisky for himself at the same time. He sat down in the armchair opposite her. Lucidity was beginning to return to him – albeit painfully.

'Tell me all about it then,' he said, dutifully.

Mrs Morgan needed no second bidding. She had won, it seemed, by a small majority over the unfortunate 'villager' candidate with Miles Mallalieu coming in a very poor third. Blanche had departed imediately after the announcement with the disconsolate Miles, somewhat to the consternation of Oliver Speke-Johnson, who seemed to be losing touch with the pace of events. Marigold, still blissfully unaware, apparently, of anything untoward, had invited Mrs Morgan and a few loyal helpers back for a celebratory drink or two. Morgan could feel his eyes growing heavy as she rattled on and he was relieved when she seemed to be winding up her account of the night's events.

'Well,' she concluded, 'I suppose I can call myself a proper politician now.'

Morgan stroked his chin thoughtfully. He always did that when he was about to utter something which he considered to be profound.

'My belief is,' he said, 'that you won because you were not a proper politician.'

By this time Mrs Morgan was incapable of divining anything quite so subtle. She got up from her chair, slapping at the creases in her suit.

'You're being silly now,' she said, 'time for bed I think.'

A few days later, an important-looking buff envelope arrived addressed to 'Councillor Morgan'. The whole family waited agog around the breakfast table while she opened it.

'It's my summons to the first meeting of the new Council next Tuesday evening,' she announced, a touch pompously. 'And I have to be there half-an-hour early to be sworn in.'

'That sounds jolly important,' said Morgan. 'Where does all this take place? I've never noticed a Council Chamber in Gatehaven.'

Mrs Morgan consulted her summons.

'That's not surprising,' she said, 'it seems they haven't got one. The meeting is to be held in the function room

171

of The Deerstalker.'

'You're kidding,' said Morgan. 'You mean that pub next to the Parish Church?'

'Apparently so,' she replied, her earlier aura of self-importance now somewhat deflated. As the children began to giggle, Morgan strove to keep a straight face.

'And can ordinary people like me attend this event?' he enquired, tongue in cheek. She stuffed the summons briskly back into its envelope.

'There is, it seems, some limited accommodation for the general public,' she said, frostily.

And so the following Tuesday evening, Morgan accompanied her to The Deerstalker. There was a separate entrance to the function room. Standing at the entrance was a middle-aged lady, severely dressed in funereal black, grey hair secured in a tight bun on the top of her head, who peered at them over the rims of her *pince-nez* spectacles. Morgan recognized her as Miss Noakes, a spinster lady who kept the sweet shop in the High Street. Ignoring Morgan, she addressed Mrs Morgan.

'Good evening Councillor Morgan,' she said. 'I'm Adelaide Noakes, Clerk to the Council – part-time of course. If you come this way we can get on with the swearing-in.'

'Thank you,' replied Mrs Morgan. 'Can my husband come along?'

Adelaide coughed in a gesture of apology.

'Not to the swearing-in, I'm afraid,' she said, 'but he can attend the public session of the meeting if he wishes. Admission is five minutes before the start.'

'I see,' said Mrs Morgan. 'Well, I'll see you later, my dear.'

She disappeared with Adelaide into the function room, leaving Morgan standing in the street outside. He had a slight inkling that the public were not exactly encouraged to attend the deliberations of the Council.

He looked at his watch; there was fully half an hour to go before the start of the meeting, time to sample the delights of The Deerstalker. After all, he mused, not every Council has a pub for a waiting-room. He pushed open the door to the bar. It was not dissimilar to the public bar of The Maritime, but shorn of the reach-me-down fixtures and fittings from the cocktail bar which adorned that establishment, it presented more of a picture of a simple village pub. The bar was deserted except for a couple of 'villagers' and a large dog which was lying in front of an open fireplace containing nothing but uncleared wood ashes. The dog didn't seem to mind the absence of a fire and Morgan surmised that that was his usual spot irrespective of the time of year. Behind the bar was a large ruddy-faced man in a striped apron more suited to a butcher.

'Good evening, sir,' he said, politely enough, to Morgan as he served him with a half-pint of beer.

Morgan passed the half-hour sitting in the corner sipping his beer. He enjoyed doing that and observing the local scene and he made a mental note to return to The Deerstalker on another occasion when it was better patronized. The opportunity to do that was to come sooner than he thought but his mind was now on the Council Meeting. He decided to visit the toilet before he left – he had no idea how long the meeting would last – but it was also part of his assessment of The Deerstalker. The state of the toilets was important to his ranking of pubs and this one turned out to be extremely basic but spotlessly clean, earning a Morgan ranking of second division.

Returning to the function room, he found Adelaide still hovering.

'This way,' she said, ever so slightly officiously, as she led him to some rough benches at the side of the room. 'This is the public gallery. You must remain seated while the meeting is in progress and you are not allowed to say anything in any circumstances.'

Morgan, feeling a little abashed, nodded his understanding, and she disappeared through a door on the opposite side of the room.

Seated alone for the next few minutes, Morgan took in the scene. At one end of the room was a trestle table, covered in a green baize cloth. Behind it were two chairs; one was of the ordinary folding variety but the other was large, high backed and ornately carved. On the table in front of it was a heavy metal inkstand and a gavel. This modest attempt to create an impression of municipal splendour was, however, sadly diluted by the presence on the wall behind of a well-used dartboard. On either side of the room, at right angles to the top table, were two more trestle tables, but these were bare of any covering and equipped only with folding chairs, writing pads and pencils. Completing the square and facing the top table was a solitary small card table also with folding chair and pad and pencil. Suddenly the door on the far side of the room swung open and Adelaide, clutching an official-looking sheaf of papers, led in the councillors. Morgan felt a twinge of excitement; at last the action was about to begin.

With almost military precision, they took their places – four 'villagers' to the left of the top table and four 'newcomers' to the right. Mrs Morgan entered last and was ushered by Adelaide to the solitary card table, before she herself took her place at the top table next to the ornate chair, which remained unoccupied. Morgan wondered why but not for long. Adelaide picked up the gavel and brought it down on its block with a loud

174

crack.

'Good evening lady and gentlemen,' she said – Mrs Morgan was the sole lady – 'our first business is the election of a chairman.'

An awkward silence followed. Again Morgan wondered what was wrong, but that would only become apparent to him as the astonishing events of the next few minutes unfolded. A voice from the 'villager' bench broke the silence.

'I propose young Tom,' it said.

Morgan looked around for a youngster in the assembly but there was none. Adelaide provided enlightenment.

'I take it that you mean Councillor Venables,' she said, stabbing her finger at an elderly man who was sitting self-effacingly with head bowed at the end of the 'villager' bench. Morgan wondered if there was an 'old Tom' and how aged he might be. Adelaide continued.

'Seconded?' she enquired.

'Aye,' responded another voice from the 'villager' bench.

'In that case,' she went on, 'are there any other nominations?'

'Yes,' piped up one of the 'newcomers'. 'I would like to propose Martin Villiers.'

'Second,' said another before Adelaide could put the question.

'I see,' said Adelaide, scratching her head. 'We will have to put it to the vote then. All in favour of Councillor Venables please show.'

Four 'villager' hands shot up.

'Against.'

Four 'newcomer' hands were raised. Mrs Morgan stared straight ahead and made no movement.

'That is not carried,' said Adelaide, sternly. 'Now all those in favour of Councillor Villiers.'

The reverse happened. Mrs Morgan made no move. It was stalemate again. Now all eyes turned towards Mrs Morgan. Adelaide addressed her almost patronizingly.

'Do I take it,' she asked, 'that it was your intention to abstain on both those votes?'

Mrs Morgan gave her the evil eye.

'You may take it as so,' she said coolly. 'Since I have been acquainted with these gentlemen for barely half an hour I have no idea of their respective merits and I have no intention of turning the election for this important post into a farce.'

But that's just what she's doing, thought Morgan. A proper politician would have voted for one of the factions and their policies regardless of who the candidate was. Adelaide clearly agreed with this sentiment as she threw down her pen in frustration and looked in vain for help from the floor. But both she and Morgan should have had more faith in Mrs Morgan. Amid the frantic muttering which was now convulsing both benches, she spoke again, this time with clearly discernable authority.

'I think it would be a good idea if we adjourned to the ante-room for a private discussion about this difficulty,' she said.

Silence again. Mrs Morgan persisted.

'Has anyone got a better suggestion?' she went on.

This time there was a reaction.

'Move the adjournment,' said one of the 'newcomers'.

'Second,' said a 'villager'.

'All in favour,' said Adelaide.

All hands, including this time Mrs Morgan's were raised. Still muttering among themselves the councillors were led by Adelaide through the door from which they had emerged but a short time before, Mrs Morgan bringing up the rear. The general public, consisting, of course, solely of Morgan, were left to await the outcome of the private discussions.

About twenty minutes later they re-emerged. This time, second in line after Adelaide, was Mrs Morgan. She made straight for the top table only to be thwarted by Adelaide's swift intervention.

'Not yet,' she hissed as she guided her firmly back to the solitary card table. Seated at the top table, Adelaide began again.

'Nominations for chairman?' she asked. This time there was no hesitation.

'Councillor Morgan,' said a voice from the 'newcomer' bench.

'Second,' said a 'villager'.

'All in favour?' queried Adelaide. All hands were raised. 'That's carried then. Would you be so kind as to join me here, Councillor Morgan?' she asked, patting the back of the ornate chair.

Mrs Morgan, with a sidelong glance at the by now dumbstruck Morgan, made her way to the top table. Adelaide whispered in her ear and put some papers in front of her, as the assembly applauded.

It seemed like an age to Morgan before Mrs Morgan spoke, but when she did she showed total composure as if the mantle of the chairmanship was already resting easily on her shoulders.

'The next business,' she said, 'is the question of allotment rents.'

This brought a frantic interruption from Adelaide.

'With respect, Madam Chair,' she said, 'there is first the matter of nominating the chairman's consort.' Mrs Morgan's composure gave way to bewilderment. 'It's a totally unofficial appointment, of course,' she went on, 'but it's been a long tradition here.' Mrs Morgan remained silent until eventually Adelaide came to her

177

assistance. 'No doubt you would wish to nominate Mr Morgan.'

Morgan stared at her in utter disbelief. It was all too much. Her being on the Council had been hard enough for him to swallow, but now Chairman with him following along behind as a consort? She avoided his gaze and moved her head almost imperceptibly in a kind of half-nod. That was enough for Adelaide.

'Then it's congratulations to Mr Morgan,' she said as another round of applause broke out. Morgan struggled to conquer his dismay. Believing that some response was expected of him he rose self-consciously to his feet only to suffer sharp rebuke from Adelaide.

'No speaking, please, Mr Morgan. That's only for elected members and me.'

Not only am I consort, thought Morgan, as he slumped back in his seat, but it's a non-speaking part as well.

Meanwhile Mrs Morgan was trying to return to the safe haven of allotment rents but Adelaide was not finished yet.

'That, I think, concludes the public session, Madam Chair. Perhaps someone would like to propose the appropriate resolution to exclude the press and public.'

A strange perfunctory ritual followed.

'Move,' said one.

'Second,' said another.

'All in favour,' said Adelaide, and hands shot up as if they were on a puppeteer's string, except for Mrs Morgan who seemed almost as bewildered as her spouse. Belatedly she raised her hand as all eyes turned once more to Morgan.

He looked around in vain for the press and public until Adelaide said, 'You're keeping the Council waiting,

Mr Morgan.'

God, they mean me, he thought, consort or not, and he got up and walked slowly to the door, dazed and with his mind in turmoil. Mrs Morgan followed his progress, and as he turned at the door, she gestured furiously at the wall behind which lay the bar of The Deerstalker. He got the message. He was to wait for her there.

17

Organizing

Returning to The Deerstalker, Morgan found it very noisy and full. Most of the clientèle seemed to be 'villagers' accompanied by dogs of varying shapes and sizes. Elbowing his way to the bar, he had to be careful not to tread on a carelessly outlaid paw and provoke a canine attack on his ankles. That obstacle overcome, he found himself wedged in a corner at the angle of the bar and the wall, a location bereft of comfort but possessing the advantage of a view of the door through which Mrs Morgan would eventually appear. He waited there with his arms pinioned by adjacent bodies for the barman in the striped apron to catch his eye. When he did, he recognized Morgan from his earlier visit.

'Back again, sir,' he said, 'another half-pint?'

'No,' said Morgan, a mite testily, 'a large whisky is what I need.'

He extricated his pinioned arm from between the backs of two 'villagers', paid for the drink, and settled down to wait. Indulging in his pastime of observing the scene was not easy in the hubbub of conversation, liberally punctuated with 'Ooh ahs' and similar rustic expressions and the heaving of human and canine bodies whenever someone came or went or changed position for one reason or another. He passed an uncomfortable hour, only made bearable by several more whiskies, before Mrs Morgan arrived.

Her entrance was nothing less than spectacular. He glimpsed her head preceded by Adelaide's coming through the door, but then lost sight of them momentarily as they disappeared into the crowd. Then suddenly the crowd parted – something like the waters of the Red Sea it seemed to Morgan – and a corridor appeared through which Adelaide led Mrs Morgan to the bar to a spontaneous burst of applause. As Morgan got a clearer sight of her, he could see that she was now wearing an impressive chain of office. The barman greeted her effusively.

'Congratulations, Mr Chairman,' he said.

Adelaide corrected him.

'Madam Chair, if you don't mind,' she said.

'Sorry – er Madam,' he said sheepishly, 'we'm not 'ad a lady chairman 'ere afore.'

'That's quite all right,' said Mrs Morgan graciously, self-consciously hitching up the chain. It had clearly been designed for broader shoulders than hers.

'Now,' went on the barman, 'a drink, Madam – and Miss Noakes – on the 'ouse.'

At this point Mrs Morgan spotted Morgan in his corner.

'Ah,' she said, 'there's my husband.'

'Bless my soul,' exclaimed the barman, 'I never dreamed. Over here, sir, and join us for a drink.'

Bodies parted again for Morgan to make his way to the cleared space in the centre of the bar where Mrs Morgan, now provided with a high stool, sat as if she were holding court.

'Now – er –,' began the barman.

'Mr Consort,' interrupted Adelaide.

'Now – er – Mr Consort,' he went on, 'the same

181

again?'

'Just a half-pint of beer,' said Morgan. He was grateful for the comparative comfort which his new status seemed to have secured but anxious not to invite criticism from Mrs Morgan over his consumption of whisky.

It was some time before the procession of citizens anxious to shake Mrs Morgan's – and some, to his embarrassment, Morgan's – hand petered out and he was able to have a word with her.

'Well,' he said, 'that's an experience I shan't forget in a hurry. Fancy you becoming Chairman – and by accident as well.'

Mrs Morgan gave him a withering look.

'That, my dear,' she replied, was no accident. It's called the "numbers" game – isn't it, Adelaide?'

A knowing sort of smile briefly illuminated Adelaide's normally stern countenance.

'Oh,' said Morgan lamely, as the extent of her deviousness at last sunk in. 'Well, what about this consort lark?' he went on. 'Did you plan that, too?'

'No,' she replied with the merest hint of an apologetic tone. 'That did take me by surprise. But not to worry – Adelaide's got everything organized. Give him his badge, Adelaide.'

Adelaide took from her handbag an ornate brooch with a motif corresponding to the medallion on the end of Mrs Morgan's chain and pinned it firmly on his lapel. Morgan was shocked.

'But I can't wear that,' he said, 'it's a lady's brooch.'

'I'm afraid it's the only insignia they've got for a consort,' said Mrs Morgan, 'and they can't afford a new one just for one year. You don't have to wear it now, only when you accompany me on official functions.'

Morgan's heart sank but there was no respite.

'And speaking of official functions,' Mrs Morgan went on, 'Adelaide will be letting you have a separate diary of your engagements shortly.'

As things turned out, the first inkling of his own new celebrity came not in a missive from Adelaide, but from an entirely different source just a few weeks later. It was hardly flattering – just a short note on the back of a sheet of school exercise paper delivered by his youngest child from the headteacher at the Convent School, Sister Katherine. The content was curious. She would like to see him about an important matter at his convenience but she would be available from seven o'clock onwards in the convent that evening. He marvelled at the contradiction but finally concluded that it was more of a summons than an invitation.

Shortly before seven o'clock he made his way to the convent. He rang the bell but there was no immediate reply. Eventually, squinting through the leaded glass panel in the door, he caught a distorted glimpse of a flying veil and habit rocketing down the staircase. He stepped back from the door, anxious not to look as if he was peeping. It was the young nun who had very nearly disgraced herself on the trip to Knock. He wondered if she had been given a long sentence of door-opening and telephone-answering as a result of that episode.

'Sorry,' she panted, 'I was at the top of the house.'

'That's quite all right, Sister,' said Morgan, 'I've come to see Sister Katherine. She is expecting me.'

'Will you come into the parlour now?' said the young nun.

Still bruised by his induction to the post of consort, Morgan found the choice of words strangely ominous. Seated in the parlour in a deep old-fashioned armchair under the unwavering and reproving gaze of a picture of the Holy Father on the mantelpiece, a stern discouragement to unseemly thoughts, he waited patiently for Sister Katherine to appear. But then the young nun returned.

'I'm sorry, Mr Morgan,' she said, 'she won't keep you long. She's having her hair done.'

Morgan was startled. He had hardly thought of nuns as having hair, or very little of it anyway, let alone having it 'done'. Come to think of it though, he mused, he had noticed in the last few years of foreshortened veils the odd wisp or two escaping from the headdresses of some of the younger ones. The young nun broke in on his thoughts.

'Would you like a cup of tea while you're waiting?' she asked.

'That would be nice,' he replied, 'but please don't go to any trouble.'

'It's no trouble,' she said. 'I'll be back in a jiff,' and she scurried off in a whirl of veil and habit to return a little later with a pot of tea and a plate of biscuits. 'That should keep you going for a while,' she said.

Morgan wondered how long that while was going to be. He had met Sister Katherine once before when he had enrolled his youngest child at the school, and his knowledge of her was limited to that fleeting first impression. But she had struck him then as a no-nonsense kind of woman with rather an impish sense of humour. What she would have made of the trip to Knock had she gone on it was a thought that Morgan found intriguing but under the stern gaze of the Pontiff from the mantelpiece, he resisted it. When she swept into the room, however, his thoughts ran riot. She was devoid of her veil with greying hair crimped into a tight series of waves, something like the highly coiffured look which Mrs Morgan sported after her weekly visit to the hairdresser. He had never seen a nun without a veil before and he felt slightly uncomfortable, wondering, despite the summons, whether he ought to apologize for being there at all at what he saw as an inopportune moment. Not so Sister Katherine, however, who was completely unperturbed.

'Is that a proper cup of tea she's given you there?' she asked.

'Why, yes,' replied Morgan, 'it's very nice.'

'But is there nothing in it?' she queried.

'Just the one sugar,' said Morgan, 'that's all I need.'

'What I mean is,' said Sister Katherine, with a touch of exasperation, 'wouldn't you like something a bit stronger in it?'

Morgan struggled for an answer but she pre-empted him.

'Just hang on a minute while I go to my room,' she said.

He sat there in astonishment waiting for her to return. His thoughts went back to his first encounter with Father Alphonsus. Looking at the Pontiff, he prayed fervently that this was not going to be a repeat performance.

When Sister Katherine returned, she was carrying a plastic supermarket carrier.

'I have to keep it hidden,' she said, 'some of the older ones like to pretend there's no liquor in the house.' She took out a bottle of whisky and unscrewed the cap. 'But I do like to give a man a drink,' she went on, 'especially when he's come on an errand of mercy.' Morgan's ears pricked up but the nature of his errand was not to be revealed quite yet. 'First things first,' she said handing him the bottle, 'pour a drop in your tea.' He decanted a modest measure into his teacup. 'Not like that,' she said, grabbing the bottle and slopping a more generous measure into the cup, 'have a proper drop. Now taste it and see if it's all right.'

Morgan took a decorous sip. It tasted horrible and he struggled not to grimace.

'It's very nice, thank you,' he said, politely.

'Right,' said Sister Katherine briskly, 'now to business. I'll come straight to the point. I want you to chair the organizing committee for the School Fete in July.' His acceptance seemed to be taken for granted as she went on before he could answer. 'I did think of asking Mrs Morgan, of course, but she's probably much too busy with her civic duties and I'm sure with your experience you could do it just as well.' Morgan didn't take kindly to the idea of being a substitute but the option of refusal was receding by the second. 'In any case,' she continued, 'you would be able to prevail upon her to perform the opening ceremony, I'm sure.'

Ah, that's why she wants me, thought Morgan. He felt trapped and slightly hurt. Sister Katherine continued relentlessly.

'The first meeting of the committee is here in the convent next Wednesday evening at seven. I take it that will be all right for you.' Heaven help me if it was not, thought Morgan, as he nodded tentatively. 'Good,' she said, 'well, until next Wednesday then.'

Morgan recognized the sign of dismissal and levered himself up from the depths of the armchair. She peered past him at the half-full cup he had left on the arm of the chair.

'Don't forget to finish your tea,' she said.

He screwed up his taste buds and downed the liquid in one stomach-churning swig.

Naturally it would have been too much to expect for Morgan's path to the first meeting of the committee to be devoid of pitfalls. The first was to present itself the following day when Adelaide's diary arrived.

'Oh, look, isn't that nice?' said Mrs Morgan. 'Next Wednesday evening we're to pay an official visit to the Old People's Home at Bay Prospect.'

Morgan would hardly have greeted that event with enthusiasm in any circumstances but the clash with the first meeting of the fete committee compounded his problem.

'Have you forgotten, dear?' he ventured timorously, 'that is the evening when I have to chair the fete committee.'

'Well, postpone it,' replied Mrs Morgan pre-emptorily, 'you're the chairman.'

He was now torn between offending the redoubtable Sister Katherine or Mrs Morgan. He leaned hesitantly to the latter option.

'I can't do that,' he said, 'Sister Katherine has made all the arrangements.'

'Sister Katherine, so what?' retorted Mrs Morgan.

It was beginning to look as if her elevation to the chairmanship of the Council had gone to her head.

'Well,' continued Morgan bravely, 'she's not exactly the sort of person you can mess about like that.'

'And I am, I suppose?' snorted Mrs Morgan.

'You know I don't mean it like that,' said Morgan as contritely as he could in the circumstances, 'but it's you that the old people will want to see. I'm just a bit of an "also ran" when you're around.'

He had hoped that a modicum of flattery would have worked but she continued to huff and puff. His brain was frantically trying to assess the balance of advantage. Eventually he concluded that avoiding the visit to the Old People's Home – particularly if he had to wear his silly brooch – plus retaining the favour of Sister Katherine narrowly outweighed the agony of a short period of the 'frozen' treatment from Mrs Morgan. He decided to stand firm and resign himself to that. Mrs Morgan, of course, was far from pleased.

The second pitfall started innocuously enough on the evening before his meeting with a telephone call from Sister Katherine. Mrs Morgan answered it.

'Oh, Sister,' she gushed, 'how nice to hear from you and how kind of you to ask my husband to chair your committee. Yes, of course, he's here. I'll call him for you right away.' She covered the mouthpiece. 'It's that damned nun for you,' she said abruptly changing tone.

Sister Katherine's message to Morgan left him with a faint sense of foreboding. She wanted him to come to the convent half an hour before the meeting to discuss certain difficulties which had arisen.

'What difficulties?' enquired Morgan apprehensively.

'Nothing that you and I can't overcome together,' was the enigmatic reply. 'See you tomorrow then. God bless!'

And so it was that Morgan found himself once more in the parlour of the convent waiting for Sister Katherine. It was not long before she swept in, this time somewhat more conventionally attired in a sort of half-habit with a miniscule veil.

'I'm so glad you could come early,' she said, 'we have something to sort out before the others get here.' Morgan waited expectantly. 'It's like this,' she went on, 'we have some new parishioners – a man and wife – who are showing great interest in the fete. In fact, they have made all sorts of donations which I can't really turn down.'

'Well, that's good news then,' commented Morgan, not discerning anything sinister in that.

'Not entirely,' she responded, 'there's a snag. They want to chair the committee.'

Morgan fell silent. He was by no means unhappy

about someone else chairing the committee but he had a nagging doubt over the likely reaction of Mrs Morgan in her new *persona*. Sister Katherine took his silence for disappointment. 'Don't feel too badly about it,' she said, 'I have a plan.'

'A plan?' asked Morgan, still grappling with his thoughts.

'Yes,' she said, 'we can let one of the Ponsonbys chair the . . . .'

Morgan interrupted. Alarm bells were ringing in his brain.

'One of the who?' he gasped.

'Ponsonby – that's their name,' said Sister Katherine, unaware of his dilemma.

He felt that his humiliation was complete. To be relieved of the chairmanship was one thing but to serve under Cyril or Sybil Ponsonby was quite another. He flirted with the idea of extricating himself from the committee entirely, but Sister Katherine was moving on, clearly not contemplating any such outcome.

'My plan is to let one or other of them take the chair but for you and me to continue to work together behind the scenes on the real organizing. That way we can present them with a series of *faits accomplis* and run things our own way.'

Morgan was far from convinced. Given his experience of the Ponsonbys on the election canvass, the thought of anyone succeeding in presenting them with a *fait accompli* seemed quite unreal, even if it was someone as overpowering as Sister Katherine. True to form, however, she was not to be diverted.

'Well, that's settled then,' she said, 'they'll be here in a minute.'

The committee assembled. Apart from the Ponsonbys, Sister Katherine and himself, there were two earnest young mothers from the Parent Teacher Association, whom Morgan guessed would be no match for the Ponsonbys in full flow. He was right. After Cyril and Sybil had greeted him effusively as an old friend – an unpardonable impertinence, he thought – and other introductions were made, Cyril started to take over the meeting.

'Down to brass tacks, lads and lasses,' he said, 'the first thing is to sort out the stall-holders. Now I suggest . . . .'

'The first thing,' interrupted Sister Katherine, with a suggestion of haughtiness, 'is to elect a chairman.'

Sybil intervened as if on cue.

'I propose Cyril,' she said.

An awkward silence followed before Sister Katherine seconded, surreptitiously winking at Morgan.

Cyril resumed his flow.

'As I was saying,' he said – before he was so rudely interrupted, thought Morgan mischievously – 'we have to decide who is going to do what. Now Sybil has kindly consented to put on her fortune-telling act' – naturally, thought Morgan – 'and I' – his chest seemed to swell – 'will do my Father Christmas.'

That was too much for Morgan. 'Father Christmas?' he said incredulously, 'but the fete's in the middle of July.'

'Ah,' said Cyril, tapping the side of his nose as if to emphasize his guile, 'that's the trick of it – advance orders for Father Christmas – it's a novelty, you see. Got it?'

Nobody had actually got it, but in the face of Cyril's enthusiasm for the idea and its sheer effrontery there was no concerted opposition. He took that as assent and carried on.

'Now,' he continued, 'there's the bottle stall, the "As-Nu" and the hoop-la. I have already sounded out a few people to take these on and . . . .'

This did provoke a reaction from Sister Katherine. Morgan had been wondering how long she could take Cyril's steamroller tactics.

'Excuse me, Mr Ponsonby,' she said, 'you may not be aware of this, but traditionally here the bottle stall has always been run by the convent sisters and the "As-Nu" by the Union of Catholic Mothers.' The earnest young mothers muttered their concurrence. 'I see no reason to change that,' she went on.

Morgan revelled in Cyril's sudden consternation.

'But I've already approached folk,' he said testily.

Sister Katherine was not one to let an Achilles heel pass her by.

'Well, you will have to un-approach them, won't you?' she said tartly. 'We can't go around upsetting people who have been supporting us for years.'

Morgan was beginning to enjoy things now. The rest of the meeting was virtually a dialogue between Cyril and Sister Katherine, at times a blatant crossing of swords with no quarter given, but ending in what appeared to be an honourable draw. Morgan could see that it wasn't, of course. He marvelled at the way Sister Katherine had managed things, allowing the Ponsonbys just enough leeway to make them believe they were having their way, but getting her way on the points she considered critical. He and the earnest young mothers played little part in this process but for him just being there was a delight.

As he left at the end of the meeting, Sister Katherine squeezed his arm – almost affectionately – and whispered, 'See how it's done.'

He nodded. She winked knowingly at him, a sly smile flitting over her face.

'I'll telephone you tomorrow,' she said.

18

Feting

The first telephone call Morgan received the following evening was not, however, from Sister Katherine. It was from Cyril. It seemed that in all the jockeying for supremacy during the meeting, he had neglected to allocate tasks to some of the committee members. How would Morgan feel about selling raffle tickets at the fete?

Morgan's feelings about that were, to say the least, mixed. He had been surprised – even pleased – to escape from the meeting without attracting any specific responsibilities but he felt in his heart that he ought to justify his position on the committee by doing something. Nevertheless, the lowly task of selling raffle tickets did not seem to him to sit well with his erstwhile status of chairman-elect. He seemed to be in free fall from near celebrity to hired hand. He wondered if Cyril had some inkling of his plotting with Sister Katherine and was wreaking his revenge. More to the point, what would Mrs Morgan think of it all?

While these thoughts were cascading through his mind, Cyril was chuntering on in an orgy of self-adulation about the success of his organizational efforts so far. Morgan was barely listening, merely trying to say 'yes' or 'no' in the right places as he did sometimes when

Mrs Morgan was in full flow. On this occasion he must have miscalculated his responses. Suddenly he became conscious of Cyril thanking him for his acceptance of the position of raffle ticket seller before he rang off with a hearty 'Toodle-loo'.

When Sister Katherine telephoned a little while later, he was resolved to seek her advice. This proved somewhat difficult at first as she, too, was bent on recounting her own organizational triumphs and particularly her manipulation of the previous evening's meeting. Eventually he seized one of her infrequent pauses for breath to unburden himself, but her reply was enigmatic and afforded him little comfort.

'Leave things just as they are for now,' she said, 'I want him lulled into a false sense of security while we get on with our tasks.'

What these tasks might be was still a mystery to Morgan but he was not about to be enlightened.

'Heavens! Look at the time,' she said, 'I'll ring again tomorrow. I have to rush off to Vespers.'

That came almost as a shock to Morgan. He was beginning to have difficulty in appreciating that she was first and foremost a nun.

In the event it was Mrs Morgan, not Sister Katherine, who afforded him the excuse for relinquishing his raffle ticket duties, although the manner of it would not be much to his liking. She was still openly contemptuous about his apparent fall from grace in the matter of the fete committee chairmanship, contrasting it with her own triumphant progress through the web of local politics to her present eminence. But when he told her sheepishly of his latest humiliation, her contempt was softened by amusement, even perhaps a shade of sympathy.

'Well, that caps everything,' she chortled. Morgan

prepared himself to suffer in silence. 'But you can't possibly do it,' she went on. 'If I am to open the fete you'll be there in your official position as my consort.'

His mind seethed with mixed metaphors; frying pans to fire and devil and deep blue sea jostled for supremacy. To throw off the yoke of raffle ticket selling only to have to appear wearing his brooch and walking two steps behind his wife was by no means the avenue of escape that he would have chosen. He had by now reconciled himself to the programme of visits to old people's homes, libraries, schools and the local hospital – even the official opening of a new public convenience – which Adelaide had scheduled for him over the coming months, but this was different. They were semi-private occasions with a limited and often captive audience, but at the fete there would be scores of his friends and acquaintances – 'villagers' and 'newcomers' – all too ready to titter behind cupped hands at his subordinate role. It was not now the machinations surrounding the fete committee which were uppermost in his mind; it was the impending ordeal of the fete itself.

During the next few weeks, he attended, reluctantly but dutifully, one or two functions in his consort role. Mrs Morgan, mercifully, was now better disposed towards him. His dereliction of duty on the evening of the first meeting of the fete committee seemed to have receded into distant memory. What mild friction there was between them revolved around the frequent telephone calls he received from Sister Katherine to whom Mrs Morgan referred to variously, depending on her mood, as 'the nun' or 'Kate' or his 'girl friend'. For the most part the calls were innocuous enough, usually seeking his *post facto* approval to things she had done to spike the guns of Cyril and Sybil. One evening, however, just over a week before the day of the fete, Morgan answered the telephone to be greeted with a cry of distress.

'We have got a great catastrophe on our hands,' wailed Sister Katherine.

He braced himself for a calamity. There was none – only what seemed to him a minor difficulty over car parking for the fete which seemed to have assumed the proportions of a major disaster in her mind. In previous years, apparently, the local constabulary had always turned a blind eye to parking along the road beside the school during the fete, regardless of the restrictions which normally applied there. This year the county engineer had intervened and imposed an embargo. The news had been conveyed to her that very morning by a somewhat embarrassed local police sergeant. Intervention by external authority was not, of course, the norm. in Gatehaven. Morgan greeted the news with a typically low-key response.

'Well, most people are within walking distance anyway,' he said, a trifle too casually.

Sister Katherine exploded. 'That is not the point,' she responded vigorously, 'we have always enjoyed special parking arrangements and now this person – this foreigner – from County Hall – Tomkins I think they call him – has poked his nose in and ruined everything.'

Morgan couldn't follow the logic of that argument. It failed completely to answer his own comment about walking distance. But his ears pricked up at the mention of a name.

'It is Philip Tomkins you're talking about, isn't it?' he asked, 'the county engineer, personally.'

'That's the varmint,' she said. He could envisage her fuming. 'I've arranged to go and see him on Monday at nine-thirty and I would be obliged if you would come with me.'

Morgan was thinking on his feet now. Here, it seemed, was an opportunity to re-establish his credibility both with her and Mrs Morgan, not to mention giving Cyril and Sybil one in the eye at the same time. Tomkins was well-known to him through his work, and if he could be persuaded to relent, few people were better placed to do that than himself. He decided to keep this card up his sleeve for the time being; the deviousness surrounding the organization of the fete was beginning to prove infectious.

'Good,' he replied, 'I'm at work on Monday but I can meet you at County Hall just before nine-thirty.'

Over the weekend he mulled over the problem. The solution came to him in the course of his Sunday afternoon stroll which took him past the school. Opposite the school gate there was a public open space which he judged could accommodate not a few cars. He also knew that it was owned not by Mrs Morgan's Parish Council but the District Council. This was important. He was anxious to retain the initiative and the credit for solving the problem himself. The task, as he now saw it, would be to persuade Tomkins to prevail upon his colleagues in the District Council to make the space available for a few hours in the overriding interest of road safety. But, he thought, not a word to Mrs Morgan. Irrespective of ownership there would always be a danger that her new-found eminence might compel her to intervene and syphon off any glory from him.

On Monday morning he arrived at County Hall, located oddly enough in the city not far from his office. Sister Katherine was waiting. She was devoid of veil and dressed in a smart suit, looking for all the world like one of those superior secretaries who populated the business quarter's pubs and cafés during the lunch hour. Her sole concession to her religious status was a miniscule cross in the lapel of her suit which Morgan had difficulty in spotting without his spectacles. He was disappointed at her appearance. Tactically he felt it would have been better for her to have been wearing some vestige of a habit. In his opinion nuns – provided they looked like nuns – tended to attract a sympathetic hearing from officialdom. He lacked the courage, however, to comment. They were ushered into Tomkins's office.

'Morgan,' said Tomkins, cordially extending his hand, 'what are you doing here?' Morgan explained his role as an organizer of the school fete. 'Oh,' replied Tomkins, 'and this lady must be another. But I was expecting Sister Katherine.'

'This lady,' said Morgan, coughing over his words and studiously avoiding her gaze, 'is Sister Katherine.'

Tomkins was suitably contrite. 'I'm so sorry,' he said, 'I wasn't thinking.'

To Morgan's horror this proved to be a signal for her to go straight on the offensive.

'Just like you weren't thinking, I suppose, when you decided to mess about with my fete parking,' she said.

Morgan knew that this would be totally the wrong approach but it was too late to stop her now; battle was joined. He sat silent and helpless as argument and counter-argument raged – quiet and politely rational from Tomkins, it was true, but overwhelmingly impassioned, if somewhat short on logic, from Sister Katherine. After a while, however, it occurred to him that these fierce opening exchanges might provide just the right platform for him to enter the fray as the voice of reason when the time was opportune. He allowed the tempest to continue for about ten minutes or so and then interrupted quietly but firmly.

'May I suggest something?' he asked.

197

Tomkins was anxious for some relief from the onslaught.

'Please do, Morgan,' he sighed.

Morgan chose his opening words carefully, meticulously avoiding once more the gaze of his companion.

'I understand perfectly,' he said, 'the desire of the County to keep the cars from the road.'

Tomkins began to fidget uneasily with the papers on his desk, not quite sure of what was coming. Morgan could sense Sister Katherine's steely gaze on him. He prayed that she wouldn't intervene at this crucial juncture, reinforcing his silent supplication to the Almighty with a sharp tap on her ankle under the table, before he went on.

'There is,' he continued, 'a public open space across the road from the school. Perhaps you could persuade the District Council to let us use that for parking for a few hours while the fete is in progress.'

Tomkins grasped the opportunity gratefully.

'I don't see why not,' he said, 'but you could ask them yourself. After all I believe your wife has some influence in the area.'

Panic gripped Morgan for a fleeting moment. Was he to fail at the last hurdle by conceding Mrs Morgan's intervention? He resorted to flattery.

'Ah, but they'll take much more notice of you,' he said hopefully.

His ploy worked. Tomkins leaned back in his chair, arms folded, preening himself.

'Perhaps you're right,' he said, falsely modest, 'but I'll have to make a phone call or two. Can I ring you later?'

In the lift going down from Tomkins's office Sister Katherine was jubilant.

'We've done it,' she said.

Morgan didn't share her view about the plurality of their success but this was no time to be churlish.

'I have to get back to the office now,' he said, 'I'll ring you when Tomkins has confirmed the arrangements.'

'Oh,' she said, disappointment clouding her face, 'I thought we might find a pub and celebrate our victory.

Morgan glanced anxiously at his watch.

'Sister,' he said, 'it's only just past ten o'clock. They won't be open yet.'

Thank God for British licensing hours, he thought.

Tomkins duly confirmed the parking arrangements to Morgan later that day, but as things turned out, total victory was not to be his; or so it seemed. The final meeting of the fete committee on the evening before the event was to take place coincided with one of his consort duties. It would be Sister Katherine's privilege to confront Cyril with the details of the 'rescue package' concerning the car parking problem. Morgan guessed that she would claim – falsely in his view – at least some of the credit, but he didn't mind that too much. His real satisfaction lay in the fact that he had achieved it without the assistance of Mrs Morgan in her official capacity. He reminded Sister Katherine on the telephone before the meeting that stewarding would need to be arranged for the parking area, and also to let Cyril know that, because of official duties, he would be unable to discharge the task of raffle ticket selling.

The Saturday of the fete turned out to be bright and sunny after overnight rain. Adelaide arrived at the Morgan house just before two o'clock in her slightly battered car which did duty for the chairman as official transport as and when required. Morgan was still apprehensive about the ordeal of the fete as he reluctantly pinned his consort brooch to his lapel, but he took some comfort from dwelling on the discomfiture that Cyril and Sybil must surely have endured at the hands of Sister Katherine the previous evening.

Arriving at the school, Adelaide pulled into what was now signposted as the official car parking area. Here was a surprise. Cyril, clad in gumboots, was striving to marshal dozens of cars into some semblance of tidy parking.

'What on earth are you doing here?' asked Morgan innocently. 'I thought you were supposed to be Father Christmas.'

Cyril glowered at him, red in the face.

'Chance'd be a fine thing,' he rasped. 'I wish you and that damned sister had let me know earlier.'

'Ah,' began Morgan, but Cyril's attention was rapidly diverted by the need to pacify drivers and passengers alighting into a sea of mud. The overnight rain and the cars had combined to create a less than attractive *entrée* to the great event. To Morgan's inner delight poor Cyril was attracting the blame.

Meanwhile Mrs Morgan's ears had pricked up at Cyril's remarks.

'What's all this about you and Sister Katherine?' she asked Morgan.

'Nothing for you to worry about, my dear,' he replied, 'I'll tell you all about it later.' He was looking forward to that.

'Well, the mud is,' snorted Mrs Morgan. 'How am I supposed to get from the car to the school?'

Adelaide came swiftly to the rescue.

'No problem, Madam Chair,' she said, and pulling some galoshes from under her seat she was soon squelching her way to the boot of the car. Here she produced a wad of flat pieces of cardboard which she proceeded to lay out like stepping-stones across the sodden turf to the dry safety of the adjacent pavement. Mrs Morgan, holding Morgan's hand, did her best to negotiate these with a dignity becoming to her office, but could not quite avoid giving an impression of a highly nervous horse in a dressage competition.

The fete was already in full swing. Crowds of 'villagers' and 'newcomers' jostled around the school playground, which was gaily bedecked with bunting and balloons, looking for early bargains from the second-hand stalls, at the same time trying to placate offspring impatient to try their luck and their parents' money on the amusement stalls with their tawdry prizes. One corner of the playground was, however, curiously free of this tumult. There – in a prominent position naturally – were two tents, one placarded with Father Christmas cut-outs and the other with a notice reading 'Madame Zorro – Fortune Teller'. Both were closed. Morgan could understand why this was so for the Father Christmas stall – after all the stallholder was busy marshalling cars – but what, he wondered, could have happened to Sybil and her fortune telling act? A sharp tap on his shoulder answered his unspoken question.

'Can I interest you in buying a raffle ticket, sir?' said Sybil icily.

After a while, not without some difficulty, Morgan managed to manœuvre a rather dishevelled Mrs Morgan to a dais, complete with microphone, in the centre of the playground where Sister Katherine was standing. Mrs Morgan was far from pleased with things so far.

'I thought I was supposed to open the fete,' she said, haughtily.

'So you will, so you will, my dear,' replied Sister Katherine sweetly, 'we are just waiting for the chairman of the fete committee to come and introduce you. He has,' she went on, winking at Morgan, 'been detained for a little while on his other duties.'

At that point Cyril arrived, breathless and mud-spattered.

'I think all the cars are in now,' he gasped. 'I'll get on and introduce you, Mr Mayor.'

'Madam Chair,' said the ever watchful Adelaide, reprovingly.

Cyril clambered onto the dais, leaving great lumps of mud from his gumboots in his wake. Mrs Morgan ostentatiously picked her way after him through the mud, her nose wrinkled in what was to Morgan a familiar sign of displeasure. He sought to remain in the comparative obscurity of the crowd which was gathering expectantly around the dais, but Mrs Morgan beckoned him impatiently to follow her, while Adelaide reinforced the gesture by pushing him firmly in the back. He sighed in an involuntary acknowledgement of the inevitable. His most embarrassing moment had arrived.

On the dais, Morgan stood beside Mrs Morgan with Cyril at the microphone. He tried to look anywhere but at the crowd as Cyril launched into an ever-effusive introduction extolling the virtues of Mrs Morgan and how she had interrupted her busy schedule just to be with them at the fete. This was totally untrue, of course, and had it been anyone else but Cyril speaking, Morgan would have put it down to sarcasm, but he concluded that subtlety of that order was hardly likely to be present in Cyril's armoury. Eventually the microphone was passed to Mrs Morgan and she started to speak. It was then that yet another minor calamity occurred.

In the middle of welcoming everyone and urging them to spend their money in support of the school, her voice disappeared abruptly from the p.a. system. Morgan look around anxiously for the microphone cable. It ran back across the playground and along a grassy bank beyond to the nearest school building and electric point. On the way it passed close to the entrance to the beer tent situated on the grassy bank. Here, it was obvious to Morgan, was the source of the trouble. Just outside the beer tent, spreadeagled on his stomach, lay Father Alphonsus vainly trying to retrieve his straw hat with the coloured band as it threatened to blow away down the bank. Sister Katherine, her gaze following Morgan's, was not slow to enunciate the problem.

'The silly old buffer,' she said, 'he's come out of the beer tent and tripped over the cable. It'll be disconnected, you mark my words.'

Morgan returned his attention to Mrs Morgan who was ploughing on with her speech, unaware that no-one could hear. Morgan thought that she was doing a passable impression of a silent film star. So, apparently, did her audience from the giggles which were now becoming audible around the playground. He knew that he had to act. Gently propelling Mrs Morgan to one side, Morgan bravely took centre stage.

He cupped his hands to his mouth and bellowed as best he could, 'Ladies and gentlemen – sorry for the technical hitch. On behalf of the chairman of the Council, I declare this fete well and truly open!'

A huge cheer erupted followed by sustained applause and shouts of 'Good old Morgan' and 'Well done, Mr Consort'. Morgan didn't know whether to feel pleased or embarrassed. The latter feeling prevailed, however, as he scanned the crowd to see Arthur and a group of regulars from the men's bar of the social club furiously waving their fete programmes and leading the shouting. The first few wavering notes of 'For He's A Jolly Good Fellow' was all too much for him to bear. He turned abruptly and led the bewildered Mrs Morgan from the dais.

Sister Katherine struck out boldly in the direction of

the beer tent.

'We all need a drink after that,' she said.

Father Alphonsus, meanwhile, had quickly picked himself up and melted into the anonymity of the crowd, no doubt fearful of the gathering rage of Sister Katherine. In his haste he had left his straw hat on the ground directly in the path of her advance to the beer tent. With a well-directed kick she sent it spinning into a nearby bush.

'That'll teach him,' she snorted.

Seated in the relative calm of the beer tent, drinks were dispensed and small talk took over. Further disruption, however, was not long in coming. A persistent rat-tat-tat on the canvas roof of the tent signalled the arrival of a heavy rainstorm.

'Oh dear,' commented Mrs Morgan, 'what a pity!'

Sister Katherine was unperturbed.

'It's all right now,' she said, 'we make all the money in the first half hour. They're all greedy for the bargains you see.'

The social side of the event, it seemed, was not of paramount importance to her.

Morgan pulled back the flap of the tent and surveyed the scene. Across the road the fete's patrons were scrambling into their cars and departing the scene in a cacophony of screeching brakes and tyres. The rainswept playground was deserted but for a few stallholders vainly trying to protect what was left of their wares from the elements. His gaze panned around towards the school buildings to reveal and extraordinary sight. Father Christmas and Madame Zorro had just emerged from the school only to be brought up short on the path by the force of the storm. They stood there forlornly, dripping with rain, as they took in the near-empty playground now sadly devoid of customers for their planned spectacular.

Sister Katherine stood on her toes to look over his shoulder at the hapless pair.

'Now isn't that a perfect end to the day,' she said waspishly.

Morgan was beginning to wonder how they would get Mrs Morgan to the car unscathed by the rain. Had she brought her umbrella, he thought. Strangely for her she hadn't but the ever-efficient Adelaide was prepared for any eventuality it seemed. From her hold-all she produced two small collapsible brollies. Morgan assumed one was for him, but alas, no! Amid quick goodbyes, Mrs Morgan and Adelaide scurried off in the direction of the car while he battled through the rain in his accustomed place, two steps behind and umbrella-less. In the car he wiped the rain from his face and head as he tried to put the best complexion on things.

'Well, that wasn't too bad, was it?' he ventured a trifle unconvincingly.

Mrs Morgan's reply was ominously measured.

'I'll say one thing,' she said, 'it was not the best organized function I've attended as chairman.'

Morgan opted wisely for silence.

19

Controversy

Mrs Morgan's year of office as chairman of the Council proceeded majestically into the early months of 1976. Morgan played his part as consort resolutely, resigned to the temporary loss of informal social contact through pub and club which he savoured most about life in Gatehaven. She, and by association he, were too eminent for that. It was almost unthinkable for her to appear in public unless she was resplendent in her chain and accompanied by her faithful acolyte, Adelaide. As a concession to necessity, Morgan was allowed to shed his municipal dignity once a week to do the household shopping. It was unfortunate that her near royal progress had to slide into controversy as she neared the end of her term. Ironically it was the long-suffering Morgan who was to be the unwitting perpetrator of this disaster.

For some time his Department of Government had been concerned about the spread of unofficial gypsy encampments about the region and the apparent lethargy of the County Council in tackling the problem. Following a rash of trespassing, public protest, legal actions and evictions in the summer and autumn of 1975, Morgan came under strict orders from London to turn the screw on the County Council. Dire threats to the Clerk of the Council of Ministerial reaction of the nastiest kind provoked a response which was to intrude not only on his work but on his personal life as well. He was never to discover if this was intended, but dark suspicion dogged his thoughts for years afterwards.

On his return from work one evening in January, he was greeted by an excited Mrs Morgan.

'Have you heard the news?' she asked, as he took off his coat and shoes and ritually donned his cardigan and slippers – on the front doormat, of course.

From any other questioner it was the kind of silly question which might have produced a tart reply. He had heard lots of news that day – the Cold War, the rate of inflation, the comings and goings of the Royal Family and much more – but given no clue as to what particular piece of news she was referring to, he could only answer in the negative. In any case he knew his place. When Mrs Morgan had something to impart it was never a good policy to pre-empt her pleasure by disclosing prior knowledge. She beamed at him.

'The County Council are going to set up a gypsy camp here and the Parish Council may be asked to manage it,' she said, only just failing to add a self-congratulatory 'so there'.

His heart sank.

'Is that supposed to be good news?' he replied.

'Of course it is,' she went on excitedly. 'Can't you just see it? The painted caravans, the horses, the gypsy markets and all that. It's just what we need to give Gatehaven a bit of colour.'

Things were worse than he had thought.

'But, my dear,' he said, 'they won't be that kind of gypsies.'

Mrs Morgan bridled. 'Whatever do you mean?' she asked. 'Gypsies are gypsies. I remember from when I was a girl. Romanians I think they were called.'

'I think you mean Romanies,' he said wearily, 'but these will not be like that. They'll be tinkers – travellers I think they call them nowadays – and they'll come in old bangers and engage in car-breaking and scrap metal dealing and the like. They won't be popular with the locals.'

Mrs Morgan was never one to allow herself to be confused by logic. She thought deeply for a moment and when she spoke it was in her regal mode.

'But they're still people who have nowhere to live,' she said, 'and we as a community – of which I am the leader – have a civic duty to help them.'

Oh God, thought Morgan. I'm on an all ways loser here, as he hurriedly reviewed his options. He could, of course, have bolstered his standing with her by revealing his own part in the affair. But all his instincts told him that the arrival of the travellers would provoke all sorts of local mayhem and that Mrs Morgan's support for them would bring her – and him – into conflict with 'villagers' and 'newcomers' alike. He resolved to say nothing about his own involvement and to try persuasion. His long experience of Mrs Morgan should have told him that this would be counter-productive. The more he argued the more set her attitude became. Not only did she continue to dispute his view of what a gypsy encampment would be like – still invoking half-remembered images of her childhood – but her 'even if' fall-back position became ever more self-righteous. From this high moral ground she questioned poor Morgan's decency, even his Christianity. In the end he gave up and waited with trepidation for the next stage in the affair.

It was not long in coming. Early in February, Mrs Morgan returned from a meeting of the Council in tears.

'They're all against me,' she cried, 'eight to one

against. I've never been so humiliated in all my life.'

It was a phrase she often used when she failed to get her own way; normally Morgan would have ignored it, but on this occasion he sensed that it was close to the truth.

'Come and sit down,' he said gently. 'I'll make you a nice cup of tea.'

The trappings of normality, reasoned Morgan, might defuse her anger. They didn't.

'I shall fight,' she went on. 'I shall call a public meeting. The people will be on my side, you'll see.'

Privately Morgan doubted that, but he stuck to his 'calming' approach.

'Tell me what happened,' he said, 'you'll feel better if you talk about it.'

It seemed that the official communication from the County Council had provoked uproar at the meeting; no doubt much of this had been simmering since the media leak of the proposal a few weeks earlier. Not only did the Parish Council decline to manage the proposed gypsy site, but they also resolved to use all possible means to galvanize public opposition to its location in Gatehaven. Mrs Morgan's lone opposition from the chair had been greeted with universal derision in a rare display of unity between the 'villager' and 'newcomer' factions on the Council. Eventually she stormed out amid choice epithets from the 'villagers' and sneers from the 'newcomers'.

'Well,' said Morgan, still looking for reason to prevail but failing fast, 'that's democracy you know. You have to go along with the majority.'

Not, it seemed, in Mrs Morgan's interpretation of political philosophy.

'Democracy,' she thundered in reply, 'tolerates opposition. We shall see what the people think.'

209

Morgan called a truce. His appeal to logic and reason was not going to get him anywhere. He could not, for the life of him, see how she was going to ascertain what the people thought, and he was sceptical about whether it would be what she wanted to hear in any case. He had not taken her threat to call a public meeting seriously, but a few weeks later posters started to appear around the village announcing just such an event. The fact that many of them were defaced or torn down as soon as they appeared only served to confirm his fears. But his mood sank to even lower depths of apprehension when Mrs Morgan let it be known to him that his presence at the meeting would be mandatory.

The evening of the meeting was one of those which sapped the will of endeavour – dark, dank, cold and depressing. Adelaide, whose own loyalty must have been strained, drove them to the function room of The Deerstalker where the meeting was to be held. The room was in darkness and when Adelaide switched on the lights, the scene which confronted them compounded Morgan's dismay. It had not been cleaned from whatever had taken place there the night before – overflowing ashtrays, bottles and beer-cans littered the tables and the floor was festooned with discarded serviettes and spent balloons. Mrs Morgan bristled with anger.

'I'll soon see about this,' she said, making for the door which led to the bar of The Deerstalker.

Adelaide was swift to restrain her.

'There's no time for that now,' she said, 'let's get to work.'

Brooms and dustpans were produced from the ante-room and some semblance of order and cleanliness was restored. With Mrs Morgan looking anxiously at her watch, a few rows of seats were assembled in front of the dais. She then took her accustomed place in the high-backed chair, furiously brushing dust – real and imagined – from her suit, with Adelaide, notepad and pencil at the ready, beside her. Morgan sat sheepishly in the front row, arms folded tightly in front of bowed shoulders, as if ready to defend himself against whatever might befall them.

Nothing befell them. The appointed time for the start of the meeting came and went as they sat there in dismal isolation. Morgan counted the cracks in the yellowing ceiling. Mrs Morgan tapped irritably on the table with her pencil, and Adelaide sat with her head bowed as if in prayer. It was the antithesis of Mrs Morgan's triumphal entry to the local political scene in the same room less than twelve months earlier. Morgan suspected that an astonishing alliance of 'villagers' and 'newcomers' was busy wreaking a terrible revenge on her for the manner in which she had out-witted them all at that time. Political depths were certainly being plumbed, but not, it seemed, Mrs Morgan's resources.

'That's it then,' she said at last. 'I shall have to take my campaign to the streets.'

Over the next few weeks, visions of anarchy and civil disobedience troubled Morgan's mind, but as with most periods of impending storm there was a preceding lull. True, County Council workmen could be seen levelling and tidying the designated site alongside the derelict harbour, often to the accompaniment of raucous abuse apparently orchestrated by the 'villager' councillors. Their 'newcomer' colleagues were said – according to village gossip – to be employing more sophisticated tactics. Morgan learnt that they were making representations to any form of authority they could identify, regardless, it seemed to him, of locus or standing in the matter. The threatened joint effort to galvanize public support failed to materialize because, so Morgan

211

gleaned, Mrs Morgan's abrupt departure from the last Council meeting had at least had the effect of returning both factions to their usual entrenched positions where agreement on tactics proved impossible to achieve. As for Mrs Morgan, she stayed uncharacteristically introspective and rarely mentioned the matter. Her own threatened campaign on the streets never materialized either, probably, surmised Morgan, because she could see that it would not be necessary. As time went on, there was a sense of inevitability about the ultimate arrival of the gypsy families, and in the face of this protest began to look distinctly futile. Morgan himself took some comfort from the way things were going and began to anticipate that the arrival itself might turn out to be something of an anti-climax. This perception, however, did not turn out to be entirely correct.

Foreboding, bordering on panic, resurfaced in Morgan's mind when Mrs Morgan announced to him one breakfast-time that the first gypsy families would be arriving the following day, and that she would be there to welcome them 'officially'. Her stress on the word 'officially' led him to assume – correctly – that he would be expected to accompany her. His resistance to this was predictably token.

'But, darling,' he said, 'I have important appointments at work.'

'I see,' she replied.

That was all, but there was an inflection in her voice which spoke louder than words and which demanded a review of his options. The balance of advantage hardly favoured him, of course. His natural desire to distance himself from whatever unsavoury scenes of hostility might be provoked by the official welcome stood little chance against the consequences of his absence from it – the wrath of Mrs Morgan for one, then the awful thought that she might be in physical danger if matters got out of hand, and, perhaps decisively, his inner secret knowledge that it was he, albeit innocently, who had brought it all to pass. He always did what he considered to be the decent thing and his reluctant consent to accompany her was merely a matter of time. She knew that, of course.

Next morning they awoke to torrential rain. Strangely, there was no Adelaide to transport them in style – albeit meagre style – to the site.

'She's supposed to be sick,' commented Mrs Morgan by way of explanation, but somehow managing to convey scepticism and condemnation at the same time.

'I'll have to drive then,' said Morgan, 'we can't walk in this weather.'

Privately he was grateful for the intervention of the elements, reasoning that they would be safer in the car than on foot. Replete in chain and badge they drove the short distance to the harbour-side and parked near the entrance to the site.

A small crowd had gathered nearby, huddled under umbrellas, some waving placards. Morgan, peering through the rain-washed windscreen, his vision fragmented by the sweep of the wipers, strained vainly to identify the demonstrators. Mrs Morgan sat upright in her regal position staring straight ahead. Suddenly shouts from the crowd broke the dismal silence. Morgan craned his neck in the direction of the road behind them leading to the site. He could just make out a lone car and caravan trailer making its way slowly towards them. Mrs Morgan made as if to open the car door, but Morgan put a restraining hand on her arm; the crowd was growing more restive and chants of 'Gypsies out' were now audible. The car came to a halt and a man emerged. His

213

well-pressed grey slacks, carelessly knotted cravat and suede shoes were not what Morgan expected a gypsy to be wearing. At this juncture a familiar figure detached itself from the crowd. Blanche Bickerstaff, swathed in oilskins and galoshes, advanced towards the car, raised her arms in a gesture reminiscent of crucifixion, and prostrated herself in front of the car. The crowd cheered; the car driver scratched his head.

Morgan was still admiring the dramatic effect of Blanche's entry to the scene when Mrs Morgan decided that her hour had come. Pausing only to activate her umbrella, she leapt from the car and strode towards the action, with Morgan scampering after her. The driver looked even more startled as she bore down on him, as if to join the prostrate Blanche in the mud at his feet. Her intention, of course, was quite different. Handing her umbrella to Morgan she assumed her speech-making pose.

'Good morning to you,' she said, raising her delivery to stentorian pitch to overcome the chorus of 'Boo's which had greeted her appearance. 'I am here to welcome you on behalf of the citizens of Gatehaven. I am sorry about this – er – person in the road, but my husband will arrange to have her removed forthwith.' Turning to Morgan she hissed, 'Find the local Bobby.'

This posed a minor dilemma for Morgan. He had no idea where the local police could be found which would not involve abandoning Mrs Morgan to the mercy of the crowd – and indeed the elements, since the oratorial pose in which her body was now set did not allow for her carrying her own umbrella. He was rescued by a prompt response from the bewildered car driver which dramatically changed the course of events.

'This is all very kind of you,' he said to Mrs Morgan, 'but I don't understand what all the fuss is about. I'm actually looking for the Westcliff Holiday Park to deliver my new caravan to its site, but I seem to have lost my way.'

All those in earshot were momentarily dumbstruck. Blanche was the first to recover. Levering herself onto her elbows, a sorry sight with mud spattering her clothing and face, she gasped, 'You're not a gypsy then?'

'Whatever gave you that idea? Is it some kind of joke?' the man replied, now beginning to show a hint of irritation.

Morgan intervened politely.

'I'm sorry, sir,' he said, 'it's a long story and you've been delayed enough already. I'm afraid you've taken the wrong exit from the motorway. You need to go back and take the next one going west. The Holiday Park is sign-posted from there.'

'Thank you,' said the man. 'I hope you manage to sort out whatever is going on here.'

He returned to his car. Blanche trooped wearily back to her fellow demonstrators. Mrs Morgan remained standing at the scene of confrontation as if to defy the crowd. Morgan looked around apprehensively.

'I think we'd better get back in the car,' he said.

'Shush,' said Mrs Morgan, peering into the rain. 'I think I can hear another car coming.'

Morgan wiped his eyes and squinted down the road, fearful of the prospect of a repeat performance. But suddenly the approaching car sprouted a blue flashing light. The Gatehaven police force had arrived.

The Gatehaven police force consisted of a sergeant and four constables. Sergeant Plomley was one of the old school, large and red-faced, who always appeared to have been stuffed into his uniform, and who would have looked more at home on one of those bicycles with the extra-high crossbar; a decade or so earlier he would

215

probably have been riding one. The constables, by contrast, were young and fresh-faced, of the *genre* who always made middle-aged people feel older than they actually were. In the absence of bicycles they now relied on a solitary patrol car, a medium-sized saloon of not quite the latest vintage. All five officers were packed into it as it arrived at the gypsy site that day; evidently some measure of civil disturbance was expected.

Sergeant Plomley levered himself, huffing and puffing, from the car and approached Mrs Morgan as he struggled to replace his helmet and salute.

'Sorry, Madam Chairman,' he gasped, 'should have been here earlier, but County Hall detained me on the phone. It seems that them there gypsies won't be coming.'

'Not coming!' exclaimed Mrs Morgan. 'Whatever do you mean?'

'Well,' said the sergeant, growing even redder in the face, 'they've been down hereabouts – all secret like – to 'ave a look-see and it seems they don't much like the place. County Hall say they will have to find them another site.'

'I really don't understand this,' persisted Mrs Morgan, 'the County were supposed to have consulted before designating the site.'

'Oh, they did that all right, ma'am,' said the sergeant – Morgan could have sworn a flicker of derision crossed his face – 'with everyone but the gypsies, it seems.'

Morgan look around the miserable rain-swept scene. It was now a sea of mud. To one side stood the protesters, rain-soaked and forlorn, no doubt beginning to wonder why they were there and what they should do next. To the other, Mrs Morgan and the sergeant, equally unsure as to what happens now. Mrs Morgan broke the deadlock.

'I think I'd better disperse the crowd,' she said.

216

'No, ma'am, that's for me to do,' said the sergeant gallantly, 'you get off now in case there's any aggro.'

Morgan guided her back to the car.

'Well, that was a strange outcome,' she commented as they pulled away.

'Not really,' said Morgan, 'it might have been more sensible to have consulted the people most concerned before all you politicians struck your attitudes.'

It was a brave statement for him to make. Normally a criticism so direct would have brought a spirited reaction from her, but this time she remained silent, and – he sensed – not a little dejected. At that moment, as they left the desolation of the harbour-side, Morgan guessed that the heady days of her political triumphs were drawing to a close. Indeed they might already have ended. A period of transition was about to begin.

20

Transition

Mrs Morgan's term of office as chairman was due to expire in May 1976. Like its start, the ending was not to be without a touch of the bizarre. The question of who was to succeed her and enjoy the benefit of the chairman's casting vote was greatly exercising the minds of the 'villager' and 'newcomer' factions on the Council. She, of course, could have resolved that question at a stroke by making her own choice and casting her vote accordingly. But the affair of the gypsy encampment had soured her attitude towards both groups. Her inclination was to be perverse and abstain, creating a deadlock in which neither group could muster a majority to secure the election of their own candidate. Morgan detected a certain amount of glee in her attitude when she told him of her intention, which left him uneasy of mind. He didn't really approve of this deliberate frustration of the machinery of government, even at Parish level, but he was reluctant to become involved in yet more controversy and, none too bravely, he kept his own counsel.

Not so Mrs Morgan, who derived great pleasure from conveying her plan to the poor beleaguered Adelaide on the day before the Council meeting. It was this that led to Adelaide telephoning Morgan that day at the office to plead, tearfully, for his intervention. After much soul-searching, his innate decency triumphed and he promised to speak to Mrs Morgan about it that evening. And so he came to the point of raising the subject as they did the washing-up after supper.

'I've been thinking,' he said.

Mrs Morgan was in a frivolous mood.

'Not too painful was it?' she replied.

'Seriously,' went on Morgan, 'you can't leave them without a chairman.'

'But I'm not,' she replied, 'I'm merely exercising my right to abstain. They can sort out the chairmanship among themselves.'

'You know they won't be able to agree,' persisted Morgan, 'this kind of squabble will bring the whole Council into disrepute.'

'Too bad,' was the uncompromising reply. 'None of them is fit to be chairman anyway.'

An uncomfortable twinge of suspicion entered Morgan's mind.

'You're not thinking about getting yourself elected for a second term, are you?' he asked anxiously.

'God forbid,' she said, 'after that business with the gypsies.'

He was thankful for that. He also saw the merest suspicion of a loophole through which he might break the deadlock.

'You really just want to get your own back for that, I suppose,' he said speculatively.

She looked him straight in the eye, questioning his motives.

'You could put it like that,' she said.

He judged this to be a time to break off the engagement; a more subtle tactic was required and he needed time to think.

An hour or so later, as they sat in the living-room – cocoa, knitting, and crossword time – he resumed his mission.

'I've got an idea,' he said.

Mrs Morgan put down her knitting.

'What is it now?' she asked.

Her tone hardly conveyed patience and at that point he almost gave up, but Adelaide's tearful entreaties continued to haunt him.

'Well?' said Mrs Morgan.

He took the plunge.

'Why don't you seize the opportunity to let off steam, tell them what you think of them and then enjoy the embarrassment of their difficulty about the election of chairman?' he said.

'That's exactly what I intend to do,' she replied, taking up her knitting again as if to close the discussion.

Morgan was not dismayed. That was exactly what he expected her to say. He paused for a moment, revelling in the elegance of his own subtlety, before he continued.

'Ah, but wait a moment,' he said, 'you can get more out of it than that if you play your cards right. You deserve the satisfaction of all that, but you can also rub their noses in the dirt by finally saving the situation.'

Mrs Morgan discarded her knitting again – a sure sign of concentration.

'There is no question,' she said, 'of my serving a second term or of demeaning myself by choosing one of their damned candidates.'

It was Morgan's turn to show – or in his strategy feign – impatience.

'You're not following me, my dear,' he said, 'you can still have all your fun and then present yourself once more as the saviour of the situation.'

'How, precisely?' asked Mrs Morgan haughtily.

Morgan warmed to his task. He was about to deliver his punchline.

'By publicly – very publicly – tossing a coin to decide how you should vote,' he said.

Mrs Morgan sat bolt upright in her chair.

'Toss a coin,' she exploded, 'you don't do municipal business like that.'

Morgan was prepared for this reaction.

'Normally I would agree,' he conceded, 'but this is not a normal situation. What better way to underline your displeasure with all of them and still avoid the accusation that you were disrupting the system?'

He sat back in his chair, arms folded, an an attitude of barely concealed satisfaction. It was not, of course, in the nature of Mrs Morgan to concede immediately that she had been out-thought, especially if Morgan had been doing the thinking.

'Um!' she said. 'I think I'll go to bed now.'

Morgan recognized the sign of a partial capitulation.

He could not be sure, of course, and all next day he wondered whether he had done enough. Mrs Morgan had not mentioned the matter at breakfast, and when he arrived home from work that evening – as bad luck would have it delayed by pressing business at the office – she was already preparing to leave for the Council meeting. By the time Adelaide arrived to drive her there, he was no wiser as to her intentions. As he stood at the door to see her off, he tried to avoid Adelaide's eyes, pleading for some assurance from him. Then, quite by chance, an opportunity presented itself for him to give what little comfort he could. Mrs Morgan stopped abruptly at the car door.

'I've forgotten my agenda papers,' she said, as she bustled back into the house.

Morgan turned to Adelaide.

'I've planted the seed,' he said, 'pray God it will germinate.'

What poor Adelaide was to make of that enigma might have made for an interesting exchange but Mrs Morgan's imminent return prevented any elucidation, although to Morgan it was to bring some further satisfaction.

'Good luck, my dear,' he said to her.

She winked at him.

'Luck may have quite a lot to do with it this evening, I fancy,' she said.

Morgan breathed a sigh of relief. As the car moved away he gave a triumphant 'thumbs-up' sign. Mrs Morgan responded with a wave. Adelaide continued to look bewildered.

The smile on Mrs Morgan's face when she returned from the meeting told Morgan all he wanted to know. It had all gone as he had said it would, except, of course, that the plan seemed to have become theirs rather than his through some overnight transformation, but it was not a time to quibble. He enjoyed her obvious satisfaction as much as she did as he listened to her account of events. To complete her satisfaction the turn of the coin had put a 'villager' into the chair, much to the chagrin of Blanche Bickerstaff and Miles Mallalieu who had been sitting in what passed for the public gallery. 'I think they were holding hands, too,' digressed Mrs Morgan.

Morgan hauled her swiftly back on course.

'What are your plans now, then?' he asked.

She was conscious that she had another two years to serve as a councillor, still holding the balance of power, but not with quite the same dominance on those occasions when absence or abstention could bring into play the casting vote of the new chairman. There was no hint that her interest in Council affairs might wane now that she no longer would enjoy the pre-eminence of the chairmanship, but Morgan had a feeling that it might. Over the course of the long hot summer of 1976 he was proved right. She began to miss the odd Council meeting or civic occasion and look to him more and more to squire her to the club for bingo with Bridie – absenting himself in the men's bar, of course, for the duration of the actual proceedings – and to The Maritime for occasional social dalliance with the wider community. Naturally, he welcomed this transition in their domestic activity – it was much more to his liking – but there were other changes occurring in Gatehaven which he would come to regret.

These began to manifest themselves towards the end of the year as the hot spell broke up and the darker nights were drawing in, heralding a season of parties and merry-making. More than a year before Morgan had half-noticed that things were changing at The Maritime when he had tempted Mrs Morgan back there in the process of rehabilitating her from the fiasco of the wedding of Jason and Dolores. At that time Jason's apparent rise to greater eminence had puzzled him momentarily, but the ensuing trauma of Mrs Morgan's year of office, when casual visits to pub and club were denied him, had driven any impression of things untoward from his mind. One Friday evening as they strolled through the twilight towards The Maritime it was to return with stunning clarity.

The first indication that things were not what they used to be came when they were still a good quarter-mile from their destination. It was a distant but insistent throb of what sounded like a steam-hammer.

'What the devil is that noise?' asked Mrs Morgan, stopping with her hand cupped to her ear.

223

Morgan listened intently until he could just make out the faint twang of a guitar between the insistent thumping.

'Ah, I've got it,' he said, 'it's music.'

'Is it?' replied Mrs Morgan, her nose wrinkling in distaste. 'You may call it that but I don't.'

'Well, anyway,' said Morgan, not yet suspecting the worst, 'it's probably some youngsters having a fling in one of the houses. Let's get on.'

He was, of course, quite wrong. As they drew nearer to The Maritime, the thumping beat with its occasionally audible guitar accompaniment grew louder and louder, until as they entered the cocktail bar it overwhelmed their hearing.

But hearing was not the only sense to be assailed at this point; their sight too was to take a battering. The bar bore little resemblance to its old ambience. One half of it at least had been cleared of chairs and tables to accommodate some kind of monster music machine. Not only did this discharge the thumping beat at an unimaginable decibel level but it also treated the room to a kind of *Son et Lumière* display of flashing multi-coloured beams of light which transformed the appearance of those present to make them look like 'dayglo' caricatures of real people. In front of this monster a low wooden stage had been laid on the carpet, which shuddered to the gyrations of a few dozen young people of both sexes, although Morgan found it hard to distinguish which was which. Jeans, tee-shirts and flowing locks seemed to conspire to create some kind of 'unisex' look which defied instant discrimination. At the end of the bar furthest from the source of the noise and light a group of older people were gathered in what looked like a defensive huddle.

He guided Mrs Morgan to this end of the room and

224

secured her firmly to a vacant bar stool. Dolores was serving but her Hispanic look had been replaced by the anonymity of the all-pervading jeans and tee-shirt.

'What can I get you, Mr Morgan?' she asked politely but unsmilingly.

'A couple of ear trumpets would be useful,' replied Morgan huffily. 'What the hell is going on here?'

Still no vestige of a smile crossed her face.

'Friday and Saturday are now disco nights,' she said.

From the way she spoke and the blank expression on her face, she seemed to Morgan like a robot, programmed to give a standard reply.

'I see,' he said, not really seeing the point, or indeed hearing too well either, 'in that case I'll have a pint of bitter and a gin and tonic.'

'Eh?' said Dolores, cupping her hand to her ear.

Morgan shouted his order again, trying to muster a smile to lighten the proceedings. Dolores, however, remained solemn and unsmiling – sullen even. Later in the evening he would discover why.

Sipping his pint, he surveyed his fellow refugees from the music machine. There was something odd about them, he thought. Suddenly it came to him. They were 'villagers' to a man – literally to a man, since wives accompanying their menfolk to bars was scarcely part of the 'villager' tradition. One or two of them nodded to him, simultaneously grimacing and inclining their heads towards the cacophony at the far end of the room. He wondered where the 'newcomers' were; after all the cocktail bar used to be their undisputed territory. By now his eyesight was adjusting to the flashing beams and he began to make out the faces of individuals on the dance floor. To his surprise two of them were Sonia and Jason, alternately gyrating around each other in what seemed to be some primitive mating rhythm, and then clasping each other in close embrace. Sonia's part in this process seemed to Morgan to possess all the grace of a Sumo wrestler, but he gave her full marks for effort. Her ample proportions were also packed into a standard set of jeans and tee-shirt, but they seemed to be fighting a constant battle to escape. It was only when she stopped to mop her brow that the wobble of her bosom – for all the world like two puppies trapped in a sack – subsided sufficiently for him to read the inscription on her tee-shirt. 'Maritime Movement' it proclaimed. That figures, thought Morgan.

During this brief pondering he had scarcely looked at Mrs Morgan, but it would have been too much to expect for her to remain out of the action for very long. When her intervention came it was characteristically decisive.

'I've had enough of this,' she said, 'drink up and let's go.'

Morgan downed his pint obediently. It was no hardship, he too had had enough. As they left the bar he noticed the 'Specials' menu on the blackboard. Today's delicacies were hamburgers or hotdogs. What else, he thought. In the hall an idea occurred to him.

'Let's try the public bar,' he said. Mrs Morgan hesitated. 'Come on,' went on Morgan, 'it's too early to go home yet.'

She shrugged her shoulders in grudging assent. Sally, the check-out girl greeted them.

'Welcome,' she said, 'long time no see – come in and shut the door or we'll not hear ourselves speak, even in here.'

Morgan looked around in amazement; the public bar, once the exclusive domain of 'villagers', was entirely populated by 'newcomers'. As he ordered the drinks he leaned over the bar and addressed Sally in a

226

conspiratorial whisper.

'Can you tell me what is going on here?' he asked.

She was equally conspiratorial.

'Shush,' she said, looking nervously along the bar, 'it's that Jason's idea since he took over as manager.'

'Manager?' choked Morgan, temporarily abandoning his *sotto voce.*

'Shush,' repeated Sally, as if she was suffering under a reign of terror, 'keep your voice down. Sonia made him manager when she took up with him.'

'Took up with him?' questioned Morgan.

'You know what I mean,' whispered Sally, blushing slightly, 'he's her fancy man.'

'But Dolores is still there,' persisted Morgan. Then it came to him. 'It must be a *ménage a trois*', he said.

Sally's brow wrinkled.

'I dunno what that means,' she said, 'but they're all living together like a threesome.'

Exactly, thought Morgan, as Sally bustled off along the bar to attend to her other customers. Now he understood why Dolores was so sullen; everything was falling into place in his mind. The 'newcomers', appalled by the new image of the cocktail bar, must have migrated to the public bar and by sheer weight of numbers had driven out the 'villagers'. Most of the latter, no doubt, had retreated to more convivial territory in the social club or The Deerstalker, except for a poor stubborn rump who preferred to make their point by resisting the awful clamour of the music machine. Mrs Morgan interrupted his mental analysis of the situation. She had overheard his conversation with Sally and formed her own conclusion.

'I'm glad we popped in here,' she said, 'it's all very interesting.'

Morgan was not so sure that 'interesting' was how he

would have described things. What happened next, however, would disturb him even more.

A little later on they were approached by one of the 'newcomers', a small blonde woman whom he vaguely remembered as Fiona something-or-other. That he remembered her first name was something of a miracle. But she was attractive in a pert kind of way, just missing being pretty, and the male in him had taken note of that.

'How are you both?' she gushed, although she seemed to be addressing Mrs Morgan rather than him.

As often happens with women in such circumstances, a conversation ensued which he found so trivial as to be banal and boredom quickly set in. He resolved to enter the exchange if only to bring it to an end.

'Er, how is . . . ?' he ventured, vainly trying to recall the name of her husband.

'Nigel,' said Mrs Morgan, sensing his difficulty.

'Ah, yes,' said Morgan gratefully, 'Nigel – how is he?'

Fiona's response was strangely cool and measured. Morgan wondered what he had said wrong.

'I'm not with him now,' she said.

The significance of the reply was lost on him.

'Oh, off for a night out with the boys, is he?' he responded, falsely jovial.

The awkward silence which followed was finally broken in desperation by Mrs Morgan, whose reading of the situation was ahead of Morgan's.

'I think Fiona means, dear,' she said, choosing her words ever so carefully, 'that she and Nigel are no longer what you might call a couple.'

He blushed furiously. Fiona, somewhat put out by his crassness, made her excuses and departed to the other end of the bar to rejoin her escort. Naturally this was not

Nigel. Morgan was now catching on fast. He peered after Fiona.

'The fellow she's with,' he spluttered, 'he's what's-'is-name – married to the woman who ran the As-Nu stall at the fete.'

Mrs Mogan nodded sagely.

'I know,' she said, 'and they're not the only ones who seem to have changed partners. A lot of things appear to have happened while you and I have been off serving the public.'

Morgan fell silent. He found the evening's revelations deeply disturbing as if the settled order of life, which he treasured, was breaking up before his eyes – first The Maritime itself, then the curious situation surrounding Sonia, Jason and Dolores, and now a bewildering change of partners among people, who, if not close friends, had been frequent social companions. On the way home, Mrs Morgan intruded once more on his introspection.

'Penny for them,' she said.

'I don't like it much,' he moaned, 'all these changes. It's not like Gatehaven.'

'You don't notice much, do you?' replied Mrs Morgan, 'It's exactly like Gatehaven. I find it fascinating.'

She was obviously titillated by it all. That worried him even more.

21

Partying

The winter months that followed that visit to The Maritime saw some dissension in the Morgan household. Mrs Morgan liked to go out on Friday nights, and she saw nothing amiss in spending an hour or two in the public bar observing the marital permutations of its patrons. But Morgan, at his most sanctimonious, stubbornly refused to go. He argued that it was a lowering of their standards to mix with such people. After all, he would say to her, it was not just one or two but a whole community that seemed to be engaged in an orgy of extra-marital dalliance. Moreover, he would go on, a mite pompously even for him, someone had to set some sort of example. She thought he was a prude; naturally, she said so – frequently.

Worn down by the taunt, and if truth were known, not a little bored by a diet of indoor pursuits at the weekends, he eventually conceded a compromise. They would go on Thursdays. Morgan was playing a clever ploy here. He didn't want to go to The Maritime at all and his ultimate objective was to persuade Mrs Morgan to patronize The Deerstalker. He reasoned that Thursday night at The Maritime would be nowhere near sufficiently lively to suit her. His observation of the 'newcomer' way of life had taught him that expensive houses, two cars and foreign holidays – all essential qualifications to membership of the more *avant garde* fringe of the 'newcomer' set – posed such a drain on resources, that drinking sessions at The Maritime and any consequential pleasures were almost certainly restricted to weekends.

He was right. The Thursday evening expeditions were a disaster. The cocktail bar was silent and deserted but for a few recalcitrant 'villagers' still stubbornly staking their claim to the territory in the brooding presence of the mute music machine and the sullen Dolores. One or two of the 'newcomers' were to be found in the public bar, but they were not of the *genre* which had provided so much vicarious pleasure for Mrs Morgan. Jason was also present – noticeably drinking rather than managing – and, so Morgan thought, following the trend by displaying a remarkably keen interest in Sally the barmaid whenever Sonia was not looking. Sonia bustled about as usual, trying to inspire some semblance of joviality among the meagre custom and occasionally complaining to the Morgans about the paucity of patronage. Morgan was tempted to offer her an explanation for that but discretion kept him silent.

It was not as if it was only the ambience of the place that had suffered. There was also a noticeable decline in standards. Any suggestion of a food menu had vanished and sustenance of that kind was now confined to a few sandwiches and sausage rolls encased in a fly-blown plastic cover behind the bar. Morgan could have sworn that the same morsels remained there untouched – at least by human hand – for several weeks. Ashtrays too always seemed full, not only with cigarette ends but screwed up crisp packets and other less easily identifiable detritus, and Mrs Morgan's habitual gesture on arrival – running her finger across the seat of her chair before she sat down – would more often than not reveal a generous coating of dust. There was, thought Morgan, an all-pervading air of decay about the place.

After some months of perseverance, matters came to a head. Mrs Morgan had steadfastly pretended to enjoy Thursday evenings while Morgan patiently waited for the mask to slip. Eventually it did.

'I'm getting a bit bored with Thursday up there,' she said casually – a little too casually, thought Morgan.

His reply was suitably restrained.

'No – it's not what it used to be,' he said.

'Well?' said Mrs Morgan.

'Well what?' responded Morgan, toying with her as his plan unfolded.

'What do you suggest we do?' she persisted.

He stroked his chin to emphasize his deep consideration of the matter.

'Perhaps the club, then,' he said tentatively, hoping to eliminate the options one by one.

'No! No! No!' she riposted vigorously, 'that's all right for bingo – it's not the same kind of evening out.'

The time had come for him to play his trump. 'Well,' he said, reverting to the chin-stroking to emphasize his point, 'that more or less leaves only The Deerstalker.'

'The Deerstalker?' she gasped with a surprising degree of incredulity.

The incredulity was lost on Morgan as he ploughed on into a eulogy about the delights of The Deerstalker. He should have known better. The inevitable interruption was not long in coming.

'Just hold on a minute,' she said, 'you well know that it's the haunt of the Council mob and their cronies. Did you really think I would want to spend Friday evenings with that lot?'

Poor Morgan! How suddenly his carefully crafted plan had collapsed. He found himself suddenly speechless, a condition which Mrs Morgan was characteristically swift to exploit.

'That settles it,' she said, 'we shall have to go back to Fridays at The Maritime.'

He was in no state to protest. In a way the desolation of Thursday evenings was as much anathema to him as the Friday evening hob-nobbing with what he regarded as sin. He didn't much like staying in at weekends either, and his abortive plan to promote The Deerstalker had only succeeded in eliminating the club as a viable alternative. He resigned himself to the depravity – as he saw it – of The Maritime on the following Friday – at least until the intervening Sunday when relief came from a most unexpected source.

Sitting in his pew at the end of Mass, Morgan was scratching around for some small change. Father Alphonsus had just announced a second collection which was to be taken during the final hymn. It struck no blinding chord of sympathy with Morgan but as usual he was prepared to make a gesture. But Father Alphonsus's next announcement was an altogether different matter. He was, he announced somewhat extravagantly, about to revive one of the great Catholic traditions of Gatehaven, which had fallen into disuse – to wit the weekly parish party on Friday nights. A murmur which Morgan sensed to be approval swept the congregation, and – was it his imagination – the final hymn was sung with rather more gusto than usual. A buzz of excited conversation permeated the singing of the last verse and the normal rush for the door which usually accompanied that stage of the proceedings seemed to decline to a mere trickle as people lingered to discuss the good news.

Morgan wondered what Mrs Morgan's reaction would be. They were half-way home before he summoned up the courage to broach the subject.

'Sounds like a good idea – the parish party,' he ventured speculatively.

She eyed him quizzically.

'You didn't have anything to do with that little development, I s'pose,' she said.

'I swear . . . .' began Morgan, before she interrupted.

'God forgive me for evil thoughts,' she said, 'coming out of Mass too. I suppose we'll have to go and support the parish.'

Morgan felt sufficiently encouraged to speak the unspeakable.

'But we won't be able to go to The Maritime,' he said.

'I know,' she replied, with just the suspicion of a sigh, 'The Maritime will have to wait awhile.'

A long while, I hope, thought Morgan.

And so the next Friday evening they made their way to the parish hall. This was not an inviting venue. Its grey stone structure dated from the last century when it had served as a church until burgeoning congregations had forced and financed the building of a new one. Its leaded windows resisted the intrusion of much natural light, giving it a sepulchral interior, except when some garish strip lights, mounted precariously in the rafters, were turned on for social occasions. This illumination tended to emphasize the run-down state of the interior with its peeling distempered decor, disfigured by condensation or damp – probably both. Nevertheless, on this occasion, valiant efforts had been made to relieve the gloom of the place. A circulating globe, reminiscent of dance halls of an earlier generation, had been rigged between the strip lights in an attempt to deflect their garishness. Balloons and streamers festooned the walls and ceiling, mostly strategically placed to cover the worst of the decorative blemishes, and at one end a trestle table, its rough surface disguised by sheets of what looked like wrapping paper left over from Christmas, groaned under the weight of an array of assorted bottles.

Father Alphonsus stood at the door wearing his blazer and panama hat – a sure sign whatever the season that hilarity was on his mind.

'Fifty pence a head,' he bellowed, pushing a church offertory basket at each arriving partygoer, 'and the first drink's free.'

The place was already quite full when the Morgans arrived. Having paid their entrance fee, they jostled their way towards the makeshift bar in search of the promised free drink. Behind the bar stood the ubiquitous Sally in her Maritime uniform – recruited, no doubt, to add a touch of class to the proceedings – presiding over the assorted bottles. These ranged from genuine wine bottles to more humble flasks which had once contained lemonade or orange squash, but in each case the original label was now obscured by a plain white one. These read 'Elderberry' or 'Potato' or some such name followed by a date.

'Free firsts, Mr Morgan,' said Sally. 'Which one would you like?'

'It's just wine then,' said Morgan, in the forlorn hope that it wasn't.

'Not just wine,' said Sally, shaking her head in mock reproof, 'all genuine vintage from the Gatehaven Winemaking Circle and guaranteed to blow your head off.'

'Oh,' said Morgan, 'in that case I'll have two glasses of that one there,' pointing to a pale liquid which to his unpractised eye looked rather more innocuous than some of the more full-blooded red varieties on display.

'An excellent choice, if I may say so,' said Sally, pouring two glasses full to the brim.

'I say,' said Morgan, 'that's a very generous measure.'

Sally winked at him.

'You get a bit extra with Sally,' she said.

Morgan didn't know what to make of that.

Turning from the bar, he sipped his wine. It was sweet and cloying to the palate, and its passage from mouth to stomach left him with a slightly uncomfortable sensation. He resolved not to drink too much of it. Mrs Morgan pronounced it delightful. By this time Father Alphonsus was standing in the middle of the room, rocking back on his heels, fingers clasping his lapels; an important announcement was clearly imminent. At a wave of his hand the crowd shuffled back to form a circle around the dance floor. With an exaggerated gesture he produced a packet of what looked like crystals from his pocket and proceeded to sprinkle them over the floor in a manner worthy of a liturgical rite. That done, he resumed his place in the centre of the floor.

'Are you all ready for the dancing?' he asked, and scorning a reply, pointing dramatically to the corner beside the bar, 'right – take it away, George!'

Morgan peered through the crowd to the corner beside the bar. There stood an old-fashioned turntable of the kind which stacked the records on top of one another and dropped each one in sequence as the playing arm rose simultaneously at the end of each disc. It was connected to two non-matching amplifiers by a bewildering array of wires. The contraption was guarded by George, a 'villager' whom Morgan recognized, looking self-conscious in his best suit and tie. At Father Alphonsus's command, George depressed a switch but apart from a loud click nothing happened. He tried again with the same result. Amid murmurings and titters, Father Alphonsus tapped the floor impatiently as his face grew redder and redder. Suddenly he launched himself in the direction of the apparatus and rapped it sharply on the side with his fist. This time there was a whole series of clicks as the playing arm jerked into position. A small cheer erupted as the strains of a rather old Glenn Miller recording crackled into life. Father Alphonsus strode from the corner, his face wreathed in a self-satisfied smile. Now came the usual shuffling to see which intrepid couple would lead the dancing. Everyone looked round expectantly. Morgan felt a sharp push in his back.

'C'mon,' said Mrs Morgan, 'it's a quickstep. You can do that.'

He moved forward hesitantly only to find his way barred by Bridie, the priest's housekeeper.

'Just a minute everyone,' she shouted, trying to make her reedy voice heard above the music. George obligingly turned the volume down. 'That's better,' she went on, 'now we used to have a custom at these parties.' A chorus of 'ah's rose from the 'villagers' while the 'newcomers' looked on bemused. Bridie paused for breath and continued, 'The first dance should be started by the parish priest and the superior of the convent.'

He won't relish that, thought Morgan, remembering Father Alphonsus's attitude towards nuns. All eyes turned to the end of the room where Sister Katherine emerged from the ranks. She was wearing what seemed to be her party dress – a sort of buttons and bows creation which would not have been out of place in an early Shirley Temple movie. She stood self-consciously in the middle of the floor, waiting. Of Father Alphonsus there was no sign.

Cries of 'Where's Father?' and 'Dunno' and 'He was

here just now' mingled as confusion grew. Then Bridie reasserted her authority.

'Hold it everyone,' she cried as she marched purposefully towards the door marked 'Gents' and flung it wide open. Father Alphonsus emerged sheepishly without a word.

'Off you go, Father,' said Bridie as she propelled him firmly in the direction of Sister Katherine.

The ensuing performance was something of a disaster. Whatever terpsichorean skills either might have possessed in days gone by vanished in a stiff-armed stand off, as they sought to match the demands of the rhythm with the minimum amount of physical contact. When, in the course of a somewhat ambitious manoeuvre – given the awkwardness of their stance – Father Alphonsus's panama hat fell off, he seized gratefully on the oppportunity to break off the engagement, slapping his chest and feigning shortage of breath. Sister Katherine, no doubt equally relieved, melted gratefully back into the crowd as other couples took to the floor.

The party continued in jovial fashion. As Morgan had noticed on previous occasions, tribal divisions between 'villagers' and 'newcomers' seemed to fade at parish functions as if subsumed in a stronger allegiance to a common faith. Father Alphonsus, once recovered from the embarrassment of the inaugural dance, skilfully encouraged the mingling, announcing a 'Paul Jones' whenever it seemed to flag. Between dances there was liberal consumption of the home-made wine. The matrons of the parish emerged from the kitchen to parade proudly around the room with trays laden with mountains of sausage rolls, quiches and sandwiches. All in all, thought Morgan, it was an agreeable experience – simple, almost rustic, pleasure all the more enjoyable for its lack of sophistication.

It was about ten o'clock that the mood changed in a way that was to ruin Morgan's cosy perception of the occasion. People started to drift away in twos and threes – the clergy, the nuns and mainly the 'villagers' until at half-past-ten all that remained was a rump of a few dozen 'newcomers'. Morgan noticed that George had been replaced as the provider of music by one of the 'newcomers'. Now the records being played were slow and romantic and the frenetic nature of the dancing had changed to close contact swaying on the spot with minimal feet movement. Morgan felt slightly ill-at-ease.

'C'mon,' he said to Mrs Morgan, 'it's time to go.'

Her response surprised him. Drawing him on to the dance floor in a sinuous embrace, she whispered in his ear, 'Not yet, dear. I like dancing with you like this.'

He racked his brains to recall any previous expression of a similar predilection on her part, but none sprang easily to mind. He didn't much like it; it seemed too much like making love in public. Or perhaps he was a prude after all. There was certainly pleasure and advantage in feeling close to Mrs Morgan. It helped to counteract those little disagreements – about Friday nights at The Maritime for instance – which seemed to have such a disproportionately spoiling effect on their twenty-odd years of mutual love and affection. Nevertheless, the behaviour of the fellow dancers continued to disturb him.

Suddenly his unease was compounded. One of the 'newcomers' made an announcement which at first he found puzzling.

'Right,' he said, 'all form a circle and gentlemen's car keys into the ring.'

The circle formed amid much giggling from the women and chortling from the men. Morgan drew back

239

from it, still unsure about what was happening. Mrs Morgan tugged on his arm.

'It's a kind of party game,' she said, 'let's join in.'

Then he realized what was happening. His mind raced back to his early days in Gatehaven and the wife-swapping rumours which had sealed the fate of the fledgling operatic society. He was horrified. By now the keys were in the ring and the women were tumbling in after them.

Mrs Morgan hissed in his ear. 'Your keys, your keys,' she said, 'we'll miss the game.'

More by luck than design he had an answer.

'I haven't got my car keys,' he said, 'we walked up – remember?' Mrs Morgan pouted. 'In any case,' went on Morgan firmly, 'it's not what you think. We're leaving,' and grabbing her by the arm he ushered her unceremoniously to the door. Outside the hall, Mrs Morgan exploded.

'What did you do that for?' she shrieked. 'I'm sure we could have joined in somehow.'

'Shush,' whispered Morgan, looking anxiously down the darkened street. 'You don't understand. They're wife-swapping.'

'Wife-swapping!' exclaimed Mrs Morgan. 'Your morality has gone to your head. It's a parish party, for God's sake.'

He took her firmly by the arm and guided her in the direction of home. Somehow he felt a need to put some distance between them and the goings-on in the hall. Patiently he explained his suspicions to her. They struck a chord.

'I wondered what some of them were doing there,' she said.

'Some of who?' asked Morgan.

'Some of the crowd we saw in The Maritime the other

240

Friday,' she replied, 'and they're not even parishioners either.'

'I see,' said Morgan, 'that figures then.'

He had intended that to be the end of the matter but Mrs Morgan was not one to shirk a crusade when she saw one.

'What do you intend to do about it?' she asked.

'Me?' said Morgan. 'Avoid the place like the plague, I reckon.'

Naturally that was not good enough for Mrs Morgan. Her abrupt change of attitude on the short journey from the hall to home had to be justified.

'It's got to be stopped,' she said. 'You'd better get up to the presbytery and see Father Alphonsus in the morning.'

Morgan groaned.

'Do I have to?' he asked. 'It's none of our business. Besides you were prepared to tolerate it at The Maritime.'

'That,' said Mrs Morgan, 'was different.' Morgan couldn't see how. She enlightened him. 'It's almost on holy ground,' she said. 'Someone's got to do something about it.'

Why me, thought Morgan wearily, as they reached the house.

22

Crusading

The next morning, being Saturday, Morgan would normally have slept a little later than usual. But he awoke early with a nagging feeling that something was amiss, although, as often happens, in his drowsiness he could not quite pinpoint what it was. Mrs Morgan, with a dig in his ribs, was swift to put him out of – or rather into – his misery.

'Up you get,' she said, 'you have things to do.'

'It's too early,' muttered Morgan irritably.

'Not if you want to catch Father Alphonsus before he's out and about,' she replied, throwing off the bed-clothes.

Then it all came back to him – the disturbing culmination of the parish party and Mrs Morgan's avowal to sort it all out, with him in the van of things, of course. Over breakfast he attempted a damage limitation exercise.

'Don't you think you should come with me?' he ventured speculatively.

Mrs Morgan was clearly going for a B echelon position on this one, as he feared.

'No,' she replied emphatically, 'this has got to be man-to-man stuff with no holds barred.' Morgan groaned. 'Naturally you have my full support,' she added, but he found that cold comfort.

He decided to protest.

'But you're the one who wants to do something about it,' he said. 'I just want to forget all about it.'

She rose from her seat and stood in the middle of the kitchen, hands on hips; Morgan felt trapped.

'You do agree it should be stopped?' she asked.

'Well – er – yes,' responded Morgan.

What else could he say?

'But you would prefer someone else to do it?' she went on. He had an uneasy feeling that the trap was about to close. He searched for an answer but by now she was turning the screw. 'Like me, for instance?' she continued.

He was floundering now in the face of her belligerence, and she knew it. It came as no surprise to him to find himself an hour later – alone – ringing the bell marked 'Visitors' at the presbytery door. Bridie opened the door.

'Ah,' she said, 'you will have come about the parish party.'

Was she clairvoyant, wondered Morgan?

'Well, yes,' he replied. 'How did you guess?'

'I didn't guess,' she said tartly. 'Old George has already reported. Father's in the kitchen. Go on through.'

Father Alphonsus was seated at the kitchen table, bleary-eyed and looking distinctly unclerical in his string vest, rolling one of his obnoxious cigarettes.

'Come in, my son,' he said, 'fancy a cuppa?' He reached to the unit behind him and filled two enamel mugs. 'Help yourself to milk and sugar,' he said, gesturing towards a half-used bottle of milk and a sugar bowl at the end of the table.

Morgan took a demure spoonful of sugar. Father

243

Alphonsus took three. As Morgan sipped his tea he realized why. It was hot and strong and slightly stewed. He quickly took another spoonful to make it more palatable as he sought to conceal any involuntary sigh of distaste. Father Alphonsus continued the rigmarole of rolling his cigarette. Suddenly he looked up and fixed Morgan with a baleful stare over the top of his spectacles.

'It's a bad business, this, my boy,' he said.

Morgan hesitated a moment before he realized that the ball was in his court.

'Yes, Father,' he began. 'Mrs Morgan feels . . .' suddenly he felt disloyal, 'No – Mrs Morgan and I feel that it has to be nipped in the bud.'

Father Alphonsus lit his cigarette and attempted to blow smoke rings towards the ceiling.

'And so it will,' he replied – then a pause for more smoke rings – 'but I need your help.'

Morgan's heart sank. He had hoped that he would have been able to report back to Mrs Morgan that Father Alphonsus was dealing with the situation and that there his own involvement would cease. But there was nowhere to retreat.

'Yes, Father?' he said lamely.

'Good man,' said Father Alphonsus, slapping his chest in a paroxysm of coughing as the effort of blowing smoke rings got the better of him. 'This,' he croaked, 'is what we are going to do.'

What they were going to do was simple enough, but in Morgan's view fraught with dangers. At the following Friday's parish party, Father Alphonsus and a few friends would remain behind after the ten o'clock exodus and by their very presence dare the offenders to attempt anything untoward. Morgan's thoughts raced. What if they carried on regardless? What if there was a scene?

244

Surely there must be some other way of tackling the problem, preferably one that didn't involve him. He strove in vain to think of one. The irreverent notion crossed his mind that the proposed solution would also extend Father Alphonsus's imbibing time, but that was hardly an argument to carry any weight with him. His mind was still in turmoil when Father Alphonsus broke in on his thoughts.

'So you and the missus are game then,' he said.

Morgan's silence and the merest suspicion of a nod were taken as consent.

'Good,' said the priest, 'now I must be off on my rounds.'

Back at home, Morgan explained the plan to Mrs Morgan. It was instantly rejected.

'Not on your life,' she said. 'If you think I am going to sit there with all that going on, you're very much mistaken.'

Morgan's patience snapped – well not quite, but his irritation showed.

'The idea,' he said sharply, 'is to stop it happening.'

'But will it?' she retorted equally sharply, 'and what a kerfuffle there'll be if it doesn't.'

Morgan was now in a deep quandary. In his heart he agreed with her but he knew that to show the slightest sign of this would immediately catapult him into reneging on his undertaking to Father Alphonsus. He could see no alternative but to go through with the plan and hope – even pray – for the best. It was imperative to persuade her. There was nothing for it but to go on the offensive. He sought to expose her weaknesses.

'I don't really understand your attitude,' he said, shaking his head sadly to emphasize the point. 'First you lap it all up when it happens at The Maritime, then you are shocked and want to mount a crusade when it occurs somewhere else – the parish party as it happens – but it's the same sin wherever it occurs. And now you want to wash your hands of it.'

She fell silent, and then suddenly broke off the engagement.

'It's time we did the shopping,' she said.

Morgan scented success. It was by her standards an admission of defeat. Final capitulation came as they pushed their heavily laden trolley towards the supermarket check-out.

'Just this once,' she said, 'but on your head be it.'

Wasn't it ever thus, thought Morgan ruefully. And so the following Friday evening the whole charade recommenced. The inaugural dance proceeded with Father Alphonsus and Sister Katherine locked in animated conversation as they shuffled around the floor without too much regard for rhythm. Morgan guessed – rightly as it turned out – that he was recruiting her to the cause. Adversity makes strange bedfellows, he mused, and then mentally reproached himself. In this case 'bedfellows' was hardly the right analogy.

The 'witching hour' of ten o'clock arrived. Old George abandoned his turntable duties, the 'villager' contingent shrugged on their coats and left and the seductive slow rhythms began. Morgan looked anxiously around to see who were to be their fellow crusaders. Not the clergy, certainly, Father Alphonsus excepted. The other priests had made no appearance at all, and Morgan, remembering his early exchanges with Father Alphonsus all those years ago, wondered if they were all still busy planning to change parishes or professions, but still being outwitted by their devious superior. Not the nuns either, but for Sister Katherine, it seemed. Morgan caught a glimpse of her ushering the young nun of Knock fame towards the door. He and Mrs Morgan remained

246

standing near the bar waiting for something to happen, when a hearty slap on his shoulder and a boisterous ''Ow's thee, lad', announced a familiar presence.

Cyril and Sybil Ponsonby were standing behind him. Morgan had not previously associated the Ponsonbys with the wife-swapping circle and his initial reaction was one of shock. Cyril quickly allayed his anxiety.

'Here to help us sort things out – eh, lad?' he said.

Sybil tittered and blushed.

Morgan felt relieved. Father Alphonsus was now beckoning to them from across the room and they moved hesitantly towards him. In no time at all he had marshalled them into a row of seats against the wall. At a gesture from him Sally appeared from behind the bar with a tray of drinks.

'On the slate,' he said.

'Naturally, Father,' she replied, almost as if the exchange was scripted.

They all sat there, Father Alphonsus, Sister Katherine, the Ponsonbys and the Morgans in a kind of gallery as if waiting for the main event of the evening to begin. Naturally this extraordinary manœuvre did not pass unnoticed by the 'newcomers'. They had started what should have been the 'smoochy' dancing, but with an eye to the gallery, their performance was so decorous and restrained that they might as well have been participating in a veleta. There was a bout of whispering and turning of heads towards the unexpected spectators, who, following the example of Father Alphonsus, sat silent and forbidding. Of course, it couldn't last. Eventually one of their number was deputed to seek clarification. He sidled over-casually up to the gallery.

'Staying later tonight?' he enquired.

Father Alphonsus took a lip-smacking swig from his drink and reached for his cigarette-making equipment –

always a sign, mused Morgan, that he was playing for time to concoct an answer. When it came it was typically uninformative.

'Celebrating,' he said, 'that's it – celebrating.'

'Oh,' said the emissary, 'something nice?'

Heads turned anxiously towards Father Alphonsus, But there was no cause for anxiety. He, at least, had gathered his thoughts and charted his course.

'Nothing nicer,' he replied, 'Sister Katherine's birthday.'

Hypocrite, thought Morgan, as he switched his gaze to her. She was sitting stone-faced, staring straight ahead, decidedly un-birthdayish.

After congratulations were offered to which Sister Katherine offered a muttered 'Thank you' with eyes averted, the emissary made his way back to his companions. They had now abandoned the pretence of dancing and all stood in a huddle awaiting events. But Father Alphonsus was not finished yet. In a loud voice he pressed home his advantage.

'Sally, my girl,' he bellowed for all the room to hear, 'another round of drinks here,' and then equally audibly, 'George – don't worry about locking up. We'll be here for some time yet. I'll see to it.'

It was game, set and match. Very shortly afterwards, amid much muttering, the 'newcomers' left in two and threes. Father Alphonsus sat puffing his cigarette, smiling broadly, and calling out 'God bless, now' to the departing backs. Sister Katherine sat, arms folded, impassive and staring straight ahead. Morgan fidgeted in his seat. He had a strong premonition that all was not as it should be.

Cyril was naturally anxious to get into the action. Prolonged silence was not his normal state, and he appeared to be untroubled by the kind of doubts about what was to happen next which were sorely afflicting Morgan. He clapped his hands in a gesture of finality.

'Tha's sorted that out then, Father,' he said, and then turning to Sister Katherine, 'now then, Sister, what a pleasant surprise. Drinks all round again I reckon.'

No-one responded, not even Sally at the bar, who glanced towards Morgan with the tiniest hint of resignation in her eyes. She knows what's going on, he thought. Sister Katherine broke the awkward silence.

'That, Father,' she said icily, 'was a downright lie about my birthday.'

He stroked his chin contemplatively.

'But plausible, my dear,' he said. 'Nobody would have expected me to be celebrating my birthday on this hooch would they now? And it worked, didn't it? Ends sometimes justify means, you know.'

She was beginning to rise to the taunt.

'And what convoluted treatise on morality did you pluck that pearl from?' she asked, eyes blazing.

Morgan felt obliged to intervene.

'It doesn't really matter, does it?' he said, 'there had to be some false reason for us to be staying once they'd asked us why. I'm sure God will forgive such a small peccadillo in such a good cause.'

Sister Katherine's anger subsided; she was fond of Morgan.

Goodbyes were said. Father Alphonsus strolled down the road with the Morgans. As they reached the presbytery he stabbed his finger at the neon sign of The Maritime a little way down the road.

'That's the source of our problem,' he said, 'used to be a half-decent sort of parish pub till they got other ideas.'

Morgan was puzzled. So far as he knew the 'newcomers' still met in the public bar on weekends to pursue their marital infidelities and he couldn't understand why they had seized upon the parish party for this purpose.

'I know things have changed there, Father,' he said, 'but surely the gang who tried to hi-jack the party could still use the place for their . . . ,' he searched for a decorous word, 'their goings-on.'

'Have you been there lately?' asked Father Alphonsus.

'Well, not this week,' replied Morgan.

'Ah,' replied Father Alphonsus knowingly. 'Things have changed more than you think. You try it next Friday.' He paused. 'On your way to the parish party,' he added.

Morgan was disinclined to follow that advice. Nor was he too enamoured of crusading at the parish party each Friday. The Deerstalker was beginning to look like a very inviting option. Mrs Morgan shared his view about the party but she was intrigued by what they had heard – or not heard – about developments at The Maritime. Morgan stood no chance against her re-aroused curiosity. The following Friday evening found them making their way there.

Nothing appeared to have changed as they approached. The loud monotonous rhythm came into earshot long before they reached the door and the flashing lights could be seen illuminating the windows of the cocktail bar as they entered the hall. They turned into the public bar. To their surprise it was empty except for Sonia, perched precariously on a bar stool, munching from a packet of crisps. Of Sally the barmaid there was no sign. Morgan assumed that she had been given the night off to officiate at the parish party.

'Welcome, folks,' said Sonia, 'what can I get you?'

She attempted to launch herself gracefully from her stool but it was more of a slip and slide really.

As she shuffled around the bar rubbing her hip – a casualty of the sudden dismount it seemed – Morgan enquired, 'Where is everyone tonight?'

'Search me,' she replied, 'gone to Father's alternative attraction, some of them, I s'pose.'

Morgan doubted that in view of the previous week's happenings but it was not something he would find easy to discuss with her. They sat alone sipping their drinks. Sonia opened another packet of crisps and remounted the stool. She seemed strangely disinclined to converse. After about ten minutes of almost complete silence, relieved – if that is the right word – only by crisp munching from Sonia, there was suddenly an explosion of noise and activity. The first sound was the rumble of a heavy vehicle entering the car park at speed and coming to rest with a screeching of brakes. Morgan peered through the window. In the flickering light of the neon sign he could make out about twenty burly young men in dungarees and gumboots leaping excitedly from a mud-spattered lorry. Their laughing and shouting – punctuated with choice language – was clearly audible in the bar. This was a signal for Sonia to spring into action.

Launching herself precariously once more from her stool, she rushed into the hallway, cupping her hands to her mouth and shrieking in the direction of the kitchen, 'Stand by, Jason – it's the residents.'

Hardly had she gone when she was borne back into the bar on a wave of bodies as the 'residents' poured in. Smoothing her overtight skirt back into place and fussing with her hair, she strove to reach the safety of her side of the bar. The Morgans sat slightly cowering in their seats as the 'residents' spread themselves boisterously and noisily around the room. Back behind the bar, Sonia took command of the situation.

'First things first, lads,' she screamed above the hubbub. 'Orders for supper. For your delight tonight we have a choice of bacon or sausage with egg and chips; bread and butter is extra.'

It was at this juncture that Jason suddenly appeared as if on cue. Morgan felt he was about to witness a new nightly ritual. Jason was resplendent in a cook's overall and cap, albeit somewhat marred by a kind of off-white grubbiness, and armed with a pad and pencil.

Sonia shrieked again, 'Food orders to Jason, drinks to me at the bar.'

The ensuing cacophony was near indescribable as orders flew around the room. Morgan marvelled how Sonia and Jason made any sense of it, but soon Jason had departed, clutching his pad, in the direction of the kitchen. What a hellhouse of activity that must be, mused Morgan.

Meanwhile, Sonia, having satisfied all immediate liquid requirements, emerged from behind the bar with a large tray of cutlery, condiments and innumerable bottles of tomato ketchup and brown sauce. These she proceeded to distribute around the tables including the one where the Morgans were sitting.

'All go, ain't it?' she gasped to them in passing, mopping her brow with a kitchen cloth which rivalled in grubbiness the overalls worn by Jason.

Morgan stole a sidelong glance at Mrs Morgan. Her nose was already wrinkling in a familiar gesture of distaste.

Now came a jostling for table places as the 'residents' anticipated their evening repast. One young man in muddy boiler suit and gumboots inserted himself into a totally inadequate space between Mrs Morgan and the wall. Her frantic efforts to slide along the seat only succeeded in propelling Morgan into even closer proximity with another.

'Evening, missus, I'm Terry,' said the young man beside Mrs Morgan, grasping her hand in his wedge of a fist. Her response was a triumph of civility over embarrassment.

'How do you do?' she said, extricating her hand with difficulty. 'You're staying here, then?'

'Ay, missus,' he replied, 'for the next few months any road, while us is working on motorway widening.'

'How interesting,' said Mrs Morgan, her tone casting doubt upon any deeply-held feeling of interest.

In no time at all Sonia and Jason were back in action distributing the food. A plate of bacon, greasy chips and a runny barely-fried egg slid along the table in front of the Morgans in the general direction of Terry. He leaned over her, doused his cigarette in the ashtray – spilling a fine layer of grey ash over the table – and swept the sauces and condiments towards him all in one sudden movement. It was all too much for her.

'Time to go,' she announced, squeezing herself from her cramped space twixt Morgan and Terry, gulping the remains of her gin and tonic, and then feverishly picking at her teeth to extract some shreds of lemon which the gulping had deposited there.

Sonia paused in her distribution of the plates.

'Going so soon?' she asked, almost as if she was daring them to stay.

Morgan could not bring himself to answer and he led Mrs Morgan from the room with a curt nod in her direction. Once outside, Morgan took a deep breath.

'No wonder the wife-swappers don't go there anymore,' he gasped, 'what a carry-on. That's the last time for us, too.'

'You can say that again,' said Mrs Morgan, still furiously picking at her teeth, 'and did you see those eggs

– barely shown the pan I would say.'

The state of the eggs was not uppermost in Morgan's catalogue of complaints but he was well-used to the butterfly nature of her thought processes.

'Well,' he said, 'it's off to the parish party now I s'pose.'

'Must we?' groaned Mrs Morgan. 'I've had just about enough of all of it for one night.'

That was music to his ears but he tempted fate by seeking confirmation.

'But what about Father?' he asked, hesitantly.

'Oh – blow Father,' she replied, stamping her foot.

There was no arguing with that. Besides, she had ruled out any subsequent domestic repercussions by effectively taking the decision.

They trudged wearily home.

23

Intrusion

Over a period of about two years following the *débâcle* at
The Maritime and the strange events surrounding the
parish party, Morgan withdrew into the role of an
observer rather than a player in the game of Gatehaven
comings and goings. It was not entirely his choice. Mrs
Morgan had lost interest in the Parish Council, quietly
relinquishing her seat in the non-election of 1978, when
the traditional carve-up between 'villagers' and
'newcomers' had reasserted itself. Instead, unaccount-
ably to Morgan, she had re-kindled her old enthusiasm
for the Preservation Society and was once more
embroiled in the round of coffee mornings, sherry
parties and pseudo-historical lectures in the company of
Blanche Bickerstaff – apparently now forgiven for the
electoral misdemeanours – the Speke-Johnsons and the
rest. Naturally, Morgan studiously avoided involvement
in this, hence his lapse into more solitary and
contemplative pastimes. Not that this bothered him
overmuch; he liked his own company up to a point and
there was always the odd visit to the club in the company
of Arthur and his 'villager' chums to nip in the bud any
faint inkling of the onset of boredom.

This period of relative calm enabled him to indulge his
penchant for observing life in the community as it

evolved around him, often from a corner seat in The Deerstalker, thus fulfilling an old ambition from the heady days of Mrs Morgan's chairmanship of the Council. Regrettably, he did not like all that he saw. Gratuitious vandalism and crimes against property and person, hitherto seen as a big city disease, seemed to be on the increase, even in Gatehaven. Mrs Morgan – simplistically in Morgan's view – blamed it on what she saw as the insidious influence of The Maritime disco, now rumoured to be a hotbed of under-age drinking. Morgan felt it was more than that. He would ponder on the growth of materialism – greed, in plain speaking – fed by a surfeit of media advertising which seemed to question the adequacy of those who failed to drive fast cars and take foreign holidays and aspire in countless other ways to what the advertising fraternity perceived as the concomitants of the good life. The acquisition of the wherewithal for all this, he would muse, would hardly be confined to gainful employment.

In all this there was one curiously local phenomenon about which he experienced mixed feelings. He could distinguish clear signs now of the beginnings of a breakdown in the hitherto rigid social division between 'villagers' and 'newcomers'. For this he could agree with Mrs Morgan that the decline of The Maritime was an important source. His visits to The Deerstalker on those occasions when Mrs Morgan was out vainly trying to preserve what, in his opinion, no longer existed or did not deserve to exist, brought illustrations of this change. The Deerstalker, unlike The Maritime, was a pub with only one bar, and a small one at that. It had been, in the main, a haunt of 'villagers' seeking an occasional alternative to the social club. But some of the 'newcomers' who had abandoned The Maritime were now also seeking refuge there and enforced proximity to 'villagers' in convivial surroundings, lubricated by alcohol, was creating a kind of shared *bonhomie* which in former years did not exist. Morgan was not surprised to learn from Arthur that this was beginning to spill over into the social club, where 'villager' members, fresh from evenings spent supping at The Deerstalker, were now beginning to press for the admission of one or two of the more bibulous 'newcomers'. In many ways, of course, Morgan could see that this was an admirable trend in the development of the community. But sometimes, secretly and guiltily, he found himself resenting it. To him it was the start of the ending of an era.

His self-indulgent semi-isolation was not, however, to last. In the autumn of 1979 there was an incident which was not only unpleasant in itself but which immediately was to draw him back into community activity. Naturally, it all began with Mrs Morgan. With their youngest child away spending a half-term holiday with Morgan's sister, she was heavily engaged that week in the activities of the Preservation Society. To her immense disappointment, however, Blanche telephoned on the Thursday to tell her that a lecture planned for that evening – about pony trekking in the nearby wetlands – had been cancelled. Apparently the lecturer, over-enthusiastically research-ing his subject, had fallen from his pony and caught a cold from involuntary submersion in a ditch. Over supper she seemed restless and bored.

'I suppose you'll be off to The Deerstalker,' she said wearily to Morgan.

He knew instinctively what was expected of him.

'Why don't you come along for a change?' he replied.

After some demurring, so false that even Morgan was not fooled, she agreed. It was a fine dry evening, still light, when they left the house. When they returned, barely two hours later, being the time of year it was, it was dark, storm clouds were menacing and the first drops of thundery rain were beginning to fall. Morgan experienced a sense of something ominous in the dark deserted house framed in lowering skies.

Emma the cat greeted them in the drive. In that instant Morgan's vague forebodings became stark anxiety. The cat had been in the house when they left. There was no cat-flap. How had she got out? Morgan looked anxiously at Mrs Morgan but she showed no awareness of anything amiss as she fumbled in her handbag for her front-door key. He laid his hand gently on her arm.

'Just a minute, dear,' he said, 'I'll go first.'

That prompted her curiosity.

'Is anything wrong?' she asked.

'I'm not sure,' said Morgan grimly, fearing that there was.

He unlocked the door and switched on the light, at the same time shielding her from a view of the interior. It was a shambles. The hall cabinet had been overturned and its contents were strewn over the floor. He turned to her and took her in his arms.

'I'm afraid, my dear,' he said, 'we've been burgled.'

They entered cautiously, hand in hand, stepping over the debris on the floor of the hall. Reaching the living-room they found a wasteland, every window wide open, curtains blowing in, and glass littering the settee and floor below the frame where entry had been forced. Gaps along one wall, heightened by the hitherto unnoticeable change of hue in the wallpaper, announced the disappearance of television set and music centre. Books, ornaments and papers were scattered around the floor in obscene confusion. Morgan felt a sense of utter desolation such as he had never known before.

Mrs Morgan was shaking with emotion, bordering on

hysteria. She clung to Morgan, sobbing uncontrollably. Gently he disengaged himself.

'I'll have to call the police,' he said.

As he went wearily to the telephone, Mrs Morgan, as if by instinct, started to gather up bits and pieces from the floor. Morgan reacted quickly.

'Don't touch anything,' he said sharply, 'the police will want to inspect it first.'

Her initial sense of shock appeared to be receding. Her reply was aggressive.

'And what am I supposed to do?' she asked, 'just stand here in this mess for God knows how long until they come?'

Morgan was caught in two minds, with one hand on the telephone and the other outstretched towards her as she stood forlorn but defiant in the centre of the room.

'Just for once,' he sighed, 'let's do things my way, shall we!'

She burst into tears again.

He was now in charge. He dialled the emergency code and explained their predicament. Putting down the telephone, he went to the kitchen. It was untouched. He bounded up the stairs to find the bedrooms in the same condition. Thank God for that, he said to himself as he returned to the living-room and beckoned to Mrs Morgan.

'It seems to be only in here,' he said, 'come into the kitchen and put the kettle on – the police will be here soon.'

Sergeant Plomley and one of his absurdly young-looking constables were the first to arrive. He was puffing with exertion, red in the face, and looking more than ever as if he was about to burst the silver buttons down the front of his tunic.

'Well, sir,' he said, looking around the living-room, 'what have we here?'

What a bloody superfluous question, thought Morgan, now beginning to experience a sense of outrage at the invasion of his privacy. He could scarcely control the sarcasm in his reply.

'I would say, Sergeant,' he said, 'that it has all the hallmarks of a burglary, wouldn't you?'

If Sergeant Plomley noticed the sarcasm he didn't show it. Turning to the young constable, he said, 'Check the rest of the house and garden,' then turning to Morgan, 'it's a job for CID this one – I'll go out to the car and radio.'

Morgan followed him to the hall, not quite sure what was expected of him now. It all seemed to be passing from his control. He wandered, almost dazed, back to the kitchen. Mrs Morgan had made the tea and was sitting at the table weeping.

'I'll never get over this,' she said. 'I feel as if I've been raped.'

He put his arms around her but he too was shaking and she squeezed his hand gently to still his rage. It was all in vain.

'I'll kill them,' he hissed through clenched teeth.

Outrage had now given way to a naked desire for revenge. It was not at all like Morgan.

'Calm down, dear,' whispered Mrs Morgan. 'You'll do yourself no good by getting into a state.

Control of the situation was reverting to her. In the Morgan household of course that was where it would normally reside.

The young constable was the first to return.

'The rest of the place looks OK,' he said, 'but I'll need you to verify that in due course.'

Before Morgan could answer, Sergeant Plomley

260

bustled back into the kitchen.

'CID'll be here in a jiff,' he said, taking his pencil and notebook from his pocket. 'Now, constable, what have you found?'

'All untouched by the look of it,' replied the constable.

Sergeant Plomley scratched his head.

'Very strange,' he said, 'but I'll need you, Mr Morgan, sir . . . .'

'Yes, I know,' interrupted Morgan irritably, 'to verify it in due course.'

'May I suggest, Sarge . . .,' began the young constable, stopping in mid-sentence as Sergeant Plomley continued to scribble furiously in his notebook. After a while he looked up.

'Well, lad?' he asked.

The young constable, it seemed, harboured ambitions to become a detective.

'In my opinion there are two theories here,' he began.

'Is that so?' asked Sergeant Plomley, plainly exhibiting the exasperation of experience.

The constable pressed on, undeterred.

'Either they got what they wanted,' he said, 'electrical goods all easily disposable in pubs in the city, or,' he paused for effect, 'more likely Mr Morgan disturbed them when he returned.'

'Mm,' said Sergeant Plomley, pen in mouth, 'mebbe, mebbe.'

He sounded far from convinced.

It sounded plausible to Morgan. He reacted sharply.

'What you mean,' he said, anger rising once more, 'is that if we'd got home a few minutes sooner . . . .'

Mrs Morgan's intervention did nothing to allay his

261

growing rage.

'I told you not to have the last drink,' she said bitterly.

Morgan sensed danger. Was it all now to be laid at his door, he thought.

Fortunately for Morgan, further pursuit of his culpability by the now aggressive Mrs Morgan was prevented by the arrival of CID. This turned out to be a smooth young man in a smart suit with a Clark Gable moustache and sleek brilliantined hair. He exuded none of the cosy familiarity of Sergeant Plomley, as ignoring the Morgans, he immediately began to quiz his colleagues about the case. No doubt correctly, he seemed to be more concerned with the perpetrators of the crime than its victims. Morgan found him cold and detached; he felt an instant dislike for him.

Sergeant Plomley was attempting to brief him from his notebook, but all the time having to vie with interruptions from the young constable trying to promote his theory about the confinement of the mayhem to the living-room. It did nothing for the sergeant's dignity when CID seemed to agree.

'Right,' he said, 'we'll have the fingerprint boys in and the dogs in case they're still in the vicinity.'

With that he disappeared, presumably to make the arrangements – not a word to the sorrowing Morgans. Cold bastard, thought Morgan, not a local – slight London accent, presumably a high-flyer.

Sergeant Plomley, as if to make amends for CID's lack of concern, sat down beside Mrs Morgan and put his arm around her shoulders.

'Cheer up, my dear,' he said, 'it could have been a lot worse, I can tell you. Now what about that cup of tea?'

Shortly afterwards two men in green overalls arrived,

one carrying a black box.

'Evening all,' said one matter-of-factly. 'Where's the damage?'

They sounded to Morgan as if they had come to repair a domestic appliance. Sergeant Plomley was more impressed.

'They'm the fingerprinters,' he whispered almost reverently, then, 'in the living-room, chaps. The constable will bring you a cup of tea.'

They were in the living-room about fifteen minutes before one of them returned.

'That's it, missus,' he said to Mrs Morgan. 'You can clear up now.'

As they left, CID returned. Sergeant Plomley and the constable leapt to their feet as if to receive some great pronouncement. It fell somewhat short of that.

'Nothing for the dogs,' said CID 'trail's gone cold. I reckon that's about it, then. Perhaps you'd call at the station to make a full statement tomorrow.' He paused and then added 'Sir' as if he resented it.

Morgan's dislike of the man grew.

'Is that all you can tell us?' he asked. 'Will you catch them?'

CID paused at the door.

'Maybe,' he said. 'Who knows? But you'll not be likely to get your stuff back. I should get on to the insurance first thing in the morning if I were you.'

He turned abruptly on his heel and left.

Sergeant Plomley fidgeted with his tunic; Morgan sensed he was embarrassed by the manner of his colleague.

'Don't be too upset, ma'am,' he said to Mrs Morgan. 'It's all in a night's work to the likes of him. Now we must be off. See you at the station tomorrow, Mr Morgan.'

Morgan accompanied them to the front door.

'It doesn't look very hopeful,' he ventured.

Sergeant Plomley would not be drawn.

'We'll talk about that tomorrow, sir,' he said. 'You try and get a good night's sleep now.'

Fat chance of that, thought Morgan.

When he returned to the living-room, Mrs Morgan was already on her knees with pan and scoop extracting slivers of glass from the carpet. He knelt down beside her.

'No office for me tomorrow,' he said, 'there's the window to get repaired, insurance to see to, statement to make – God, what a palaver.'

Mrs Morgan was way ahead of him.

'I can arrange about the window and the insurance and I'll get the place straightened up quicker without you under my feet,' she said. 'You go to the office and sort out your work. Then you can come home at lunchtime and go to the police station.'

He was grateful for that. He had several important meetings scheduled for the following morning. Contrary to expectations, they slept well that night – mental and physical exhaustion had taken their toll.

The next day when Morgan returned at lunchtime wonders had been worked. But for the absence of the television set and music centre, the living-room and hall were back to their usual tidy and welcoming state.

'How did you get the window repaired so quickly?' he asked.

'Arthur,' replied Mrs Morgan triumphantly. 'He got one of his cronies from the club to come round right away.' She could not resist a small gibe. 'He has his uses, I s'pose,' she added.

Morgan ignored that minor provocation. He was full of admiration for her achievements.

'You've worked wonders, my darling,' he said, kissing

her.

She was immediately modest.

'Oh, it was nothing,' she said airily, 'the blessed police made as much mess as the burglars – mud on the carpet, tea stains on the table and all that.'

'Well,' said Morgan, surprisingly decently in view of his feelings about CID in particular, 'they have their job to do I suppose. Oh,' he added by way of an afterthought, 'what about the insurance?'

'Claim form's in the post,' she said, bustling past him to the kitchen, 'now come on – lunch'll be ready in half-an-hour. You've just got time to go and make your statement at the police station.'

He felt better as he made his way to the police station but not for long. It was an old Victorian building not far from his house but at the top of a steep hill. He made light of the climb, buoyed by Mrs Morgan's stoic reaction to events, but all his frustration returned when he reached the door. Pinned to it was a sheet of paper, yellowed from daily use, which read 'Closed for Lunch'. Making his way back to the house, he sought to control his returning anger. As he entered he called out to Mrs Morgan.

'You'll never believe this,' he said bitterly. 'If you want to commit a crime in Gatehaven, lunchtime's the time.'

When he explained, she roared with laughter; that was a help. Crisis, he thought, seems to bring out the best in her. After lunch he trudged back up the hill to the station. This time the door was open and he found himself standing at the counter behind which sat a middle-aged lady doing her knitting.

'Ah,' she said, 'you'll have come to see the sergeant about last night.'

She rang a small bell on the counter and Sergeant

Plomley appeared from a door at the rear. He was in shirt sleeves and braces and stuffing the remains of a sandwich into his mouth.

'Come into the office, Mr Morgan, sir,' he said.

The 'office' was a small bare room with bars on the window. Presumably it did duty as a cell on the rare occasions when some local miscreant needed to be detained for any length of time. Furniture was sparse – a trestle table with a typewriter on it and two folding chairs on each side. A naked light bulb hung from the ceiling. Sergeant Plomley reached for his tunic and helmet from a hook behind the door and donned them decorously, slapping dust from his tunic as he did so.

'There,' he said, pulling his tunic tightly over his stomach and easing the strap of his helmet over his chin, 'now we're all official like – let's get on wi' it.'

Morgan sat down at the table as Sergeant Plomley positioned himself behind the typewriter.

'What are the chances of catching them?' he enquired.

'With respect, sir,' replied the sergeant, rather officiously it seemed to Morgan, 'that's my concern. We'm here to record your official statement.'

'Oh,' said Morgan lamely, and waited for the next development.

This took a little time as Sergeant Plomley rummaged through a pile of papers beside the typewriter.

'Must do it on the proper form,' he said, 'ah – that's 'im. Now tell me in your own words everything that happened when you came home last night.'

Morgan began only to be interrupted almost immediately.

'Whoo – not so fast, sir,' said the sergeant, as he pounded the keys furiously with two fingers.

There followed a period of laborious dictation. When

it was over Sergeant Plomley slapped the paper down in front of Morgan.

'There you go, sir,' he said, 'read 'im carefully and sign at the bottom – close as you can under the last line.'

Morgan read through the document not without difficulty. The typewriter ribbon was past its best. He signed it and pushed it back across the table.

'Fine,' he said, 'but there is only one 'l' in television if you don't mind me saying so.'

'Bless my soul,' said the sergeant, ''ow did that 'appen? Glad you spotted it,' He reached for a pen and made the alteration. 'Now you initial that, sir,' he added, 'can't have HQ thinking there's been any tampering, can we?'

Morgan couldn't quite see the significance of that but he guessed that rules were rules and that Sergeant Plomley lived by them. Certainly that seemed to be the case when he tried once more to draw him on the likelihood of apprehending the culprits. All this produced was a series of 'officialese' comments which were so bland and anodyne that they conveyed nothing. That, it seemed, was that. Morgan rose wearily to his feet, bid goodbye to the sergeant and left. The lady behind the counter had resumed her knitting and tranquillity had returned. As he started down the hill he wondered what was the point of it all. Then a strange thing happened. Sergeant Plomley was at the door of the station calling him back. He turned and retraced his steps. Sergeant Plomley grabbed him by the arm and propelled him around the corner of the building, looking anxiously from side to side as if he was about to commit some terrible misdemeanour.

'Off the record, sir,' he said, 'can't speak in front of 'er,' nodding his head towards the station door. 'It'd be all over the village in no time.'

267

Morgan waited expectantly. Sergeant Plomley gulped and mopped his brow with his handkerchief.

'Truth is, sir,' he half-whispered, 'yours is not the only place to have been done in the last few weeks. We think it's a gang from the city but they've been too crafty for us so far. It needs someone to catch 'em red-handed, I reckon.'

Morgan was nonplussed.

'But how can I help?' he asked.

Sergeant Plomley tapped the side of his nose with his forefinger.

'Have a word with some of your neighbours,' he said, 'a word to the wise – nuff said.'

At that moment the grey-haired lady from the counter appeared at the corner beckoning agitatedly to him.

He drew himself up to his full height and said, in a voice designed to be plainly audible to her, 'All I can tell you, sir, is that we shall be pursuing our inquiries. Good afternoon now.'

Morgan was deep in thought as he made his way home.

24

Vigilance

In the weeks following the burglary, Morgan continued to think deeply. As it happened, he found himself with plenty of time to do so. Mrs Morgan had decreed that he should remain at home each evening for fear of a repeat of the ordeal. This, of course, did not prevent her from going off to her Preservation Society functions, but it left him housebound, introspective and, as a consequence, irritable. His train of thought ranged widely. On the one hand he continued to bemoan inwardly the changes in social behaviour occurring around him, of which he now saw his own domestic misfortune as the illustrative centrepiece. Probably the truth was that he was yearning for a permanence that was impossible to guarantee anywhere – let alone Gatehaven; in his heart he knew this but he found it saddening nevertheless. On the other hand, he found himself addressing the enormous practical difficulties of his own nightly confinement. Would he never again occupy his contemplative seat in the corner of The Deerstalker? Would he and Mrs Morgan never be able to go out together again? And what about holidays?

Mrs Morgan, prodded no doubt by his increasing irritability, was not entirely oblivious to the problem. One evening, about a month after the burglary, she broached the subject.

'All this staying in at night seems to be getting you down, dear,' she said.

Seems, thought Morgan, it must be obvious to an idiot. But he was stuck for an answer. The simple solution that she should stay in sometimes without him was a non-runner. She had already made that clear.

'What else can we do?' he asked despairingly.

Evidently she had been thinking.

'We could get a burglar alarm,' she said.

He dismissed that abruptly.

'That's only practicable if all three of us are out,' he said, adding by way of an afterthought, 'and the cat – she could set it off.'

Mrs Morgan persisted.

'But surely that's something,' she said, 'at least the house would be safe when we were all out.'

All of them being out was not uppermost in Morgan's mind. He continued his disparagement.

'You reckon,' he replied, 'you get the house all wired up like Fort Knox and bells go off which no-one takes any notice of – just like the shops in the High Street.'

That, he thought, was a convincing argument, but she brushed it aside imperiously – she often did that to him.

'You're way behind the times,' she said, 'it's a lot more sophisticated than that nowadays. You just think about it.'

He did think about it but the idea continued to leave him unexcited. He began to see it as another intrusion on his privacy. Mrs Morgan, of course, having planted the seed, continued to nurture it. It was just the odd aside now and then, usually preceded by 'Wouldn't it be nice if . . .' but it rankled him. He had to find some other way – but what? He cast his mind back to Sergeant Plomley's

270

somewhat enigmatic off-the-record remarks at the police station. Perhaps he ought to discuss the problem with the neighbours. Some kind of communal vigilance, for instance, might be the answer.

And so, despite some initial sarcasm from Mrs Morgan – she was not accustomed to having her own ideas discarded – he invited Arthur and the Speke-Johnsons to come in one evening for a chat. When he raised the subject at the meeting first reactions were far from encouraging. Although sympathetic about the Morgans' unfortunate experience, they all showed the usual signs of believing it to be something which happened to other people and not to them. Besides which they were not an easy mix of audience – Arthur, the archetypal 'villager', and the Speke-Johnsons, as near to typical 'newcomers' as one would be likely to find. Communication, let alone collaboration, was difficult enough. But Morgan, driven by the need to find some way out of his problem, stuck to his task. It was Mrs Morgan, however, who turned out to be unintentionally helpful. She needed little encouragement to launch into a tale of the events of the night of the burglary which was so horrifically graphic that Morgan found it difficult to reconcile it with his own recollection of the affair. But he didn't demur. It was all grist to the mill.

Arthur was the first to succumb to her heart-rending account. This, of course, surprised her since that was hardly her intention. But he was a kind man who had never forgotten the help of the Morgans in the Penny affair all those years ago.

'I reckon us ought to do summat about it,' he said, sucking reflectively on his pipe.

At that moment the door-bell rang.

'Damn,' said Morgan aloud.

Mrs Morgan tut-tutted.

'Answer it then,' she said.

Little did Morgan suspect as he went to the door that events were about to take an unexpected turn – in fact a whole series of them. It was Blanche Bickerstaff and Miles Mallalieu.

'We've come to your security meeting,' announced Blanche.

He strove hard to hide his surprise and dismay as he ushered them into the living-room. Mrs Morgan had gone to the kitchen to make coffee. He followed her there.

'What the hell are they doing here?' he asked. There was anger in his tone – at least what passed for anger in his necessarily circumspect altercations with Mrs Morgan. 'They're not even neighbours,' he added.

'I invited them,' she replied. 'They don't live too far away,' here a note of triumph intruded, 'and besides Blanche has already got a burglar alarm.'

He was inwardly furious.

'But we are not intending to discuss burglar alarms,' he said tersely.

'We might be later when Blanche has had her say,' she replied in her 'game, set and match' tone.

Morgan resorted to desperation.

'But what about Oliver and all that funny business with Blanche,' he said. 'This could be very embarrassing.'

'Not at all, not at all,' replied Mrs Morgan airily, 'we're civilized folk in the Preservation Society. All that has been forgotten long ago.'

Morgan was beginning to feel that his initiative was slipping away from him. What he had planned as a meeting to seek an alternative to the burglar alarm was about to become a rally in support of it. As it was to turn out, his anxiety was misplaced. Events were about to take another turn which was so unexpected that even the conniving Mrs Morgan could not have anticipated it.

When they returned to the living-room, Miles Mallalieu – typical, thought Morgan – was lounging in Morgan's favourite chair. Blanche, through some miscalculation of space, was on the settee, her considerable bulk squeezed uncomfortably between Arthur and Marigold Speke-Johnson. Oliver was hovering, not quite knowing where to put himself. Blanche, it appeared, had been enveloped in mid-sentence by a thick blue cloud of Arthur's pipe-smoke. She was beating her breast in a fit of coughing and the resultant wobbling of flesh was dispersing the smoke in fascinating patterns around the ceiling. At the same time, the flailing of her left elbow, like the flapping of a chicken's wing, was posing a severe physical threat to the diminutive Marigold as she shrank into her corner of the settee.

'Well?' said Mrs Morgan, looking at Morgan.

That meant she expected him to say something but whether to rearrange the seating or to get on with the business of the meeting he was not sure. He opted for the latter.

'Thank you all for coming . . . ,' he began, but Blanche interrupted.

'Excuse me,' she said, aggressively emphasizing the 'me'. 'I was just in the middle of pointing out one or two things.'

'Oh,' said Morgan with a shrug of his shoulders, 'point away then.'

They waited expectantly while she meticulously straightened her blouse to repair the ravages of the breast-beating.

'There,' she said at last, 'now as the only other person here to have suffered the indignity of being burgled . . . .'

Mrs Morgan, taken aback, reacted quickly.

'But you've got a burglar alarm,' she said, 'I've seen it.'

'Ah,' said Blanche, 'you may have thought that you saw it, but all you saw was a red box on the front of my house. Miles put it up for me, didn't you, Miles?'

Morgan sensed a hint of venom in the question and – unusually – felt slightly sorry for Miles. His sympathy increased as she went on relentlessly. 'And you said it would fool anyone, didn't you Miles?'

But Blanche was not at this stage about to be diverted from her theme just to bait the hapless Miles. That, no doubt, was for later.

'What I really wanted to say was that even if it had all been connected up – which it wasn't – it would still not have deterred an intruder.'

'Just a minute,' said Mrs Morgan, no doubt sensing danger to her own objectives, 'perhaps the burglar found out that it was just a red box.'

'That,' said Blanche, folding her arms dismissively across her chest, 'is where you're wrong. Not even my dearest friends knew. Not even you knew.' – pointing dramatically at Mrs Morgan.

Morgan speculated as to whether Mrs Morgan was surplus to the 'dearest friends' or included among them. No matter – he was enjoying the exchange and Blanche, unexpectedly, seemed to be promoting his cause. Meanwhile she continued, undeterred by Mrs Morgan's niggling interruptions.

'In fact,' she went on, 'only Miles knew and he would have no reason to break into my house.'

Morgan permitted himself a lascivious thought. Not for the purpose of burglary at any rate, he said to himself.

'So,' said Blanche, 'Miles has drawn on his military

experience to devise a plan. Over to you, Miles.'

Morgan felt a strange urge to clap but he controlled it. Miles, who had been cowering in his chair from Blanche's thinly-veiled degradation of his earlier efforts, now came into his own. He rose and marched stiff-legged to the far end of the room.

'Roger,' he said.

It seemed to Morgan that the picture was incomplete without some flip-over charts and a pointer but these were not, of course, normal accoutrements of the household. Instead Miles stood at attention, red-faced, chest swelling and moustache bristling.

'The way to beat these Johnnies,' he barked, 'is to anticipate their next move. Forewarned is fore-armed!'

And so the great plan unfolded. Basically it was to be a duty rota for each household to patrol the others when the occupants were absent. It seemed reasonable enough to Morgan as far as it went, but he could tell from the look on Mrs Morgan's face that she was far from pleased. This was hardly surprising. Her advocacy of the burglar alarm solution had been well and truly shattered by Blanche and the plan made no concession to her fear of remaining at home should Morgan wish to go out. This aspect worried him too. His lone forays to The Deerstalker and the club still appeared to be under threat. But he was, at least, halfway to his objective and perhaps one final effort might secure it completely.

'Very good,' he said when Miles had finished, 'but there's just one snag as far as we are concerned. Since the burglary Mrs Morgan is a bit nervous about staying at home at night when I am out and . . . .'

That was too much humiliation for Mrs Morgan. Her interruption was swift and incisive.

'Whatever gave you that idea?' she asked.

Morgan could hardly believe his ears. He seemed to

275

have accomplished all his aims at a stroke, though not quite in the way he had intended. Good old Blanche, he thought – probably for the first time in their acquaintance. Suddenly, doubt set in. What if she was putting on a show for Blanche only to renege later? But he could hardly raise that issue now – or could he chance his arm and maybe seal it? While he was pondering the rest were waiting. Eventually Miles interrupted his reverie.

'Well, Morgan?' he asked.

Morgan opted for discretion.

'Oh – nothing,' he replied, 'it doesn't matter.'

Arthur, predictably, was willing to give the plan a try, but the Speke-Johnsons remained luke-warm, each, it seemed to Morgan, for different reasons. Oliver, he suspected, remained bruised by his earlier experiences with Blanche and was anxious not to be involved in any fresh association with her. Naturally he couldn't say so and his mild demurrals lacked any real substance to support his position. Marigold was different. She came over as a delicate creature who abhorred anything with overtones of violence so much that she pretended that it didn't exist. Neither was any match for Blanche. Morgan, whose instinctive knee-jerk reaction to any suggestion by that particular lady was one of blind opposition, now found himself in the curious position of espousing her as an ally. He let the rout of the Speke-Johnsons take its inevitable course, but he remained uneasy about Mrs Morgan. She had been silent for far too long, but that couldn't last. Eventually she spoke.

'Well, I'm not sure,' she said. 'It seems too much to me as if we are taking the law into our own hands.'

Morgan sensed danger. At the very least she was laying herself open to another humiliating salvo from Blanche. Worse still, if she overcame that and won the day, his entire plan could be sunk without trace. He had to intervene.

'That may be true, my dear,' he said – outright contradiction, of course, would have been fraught with future domestic perils – 'and I see your point' – piling on the reasonableness of his attitude – 'but I am not sure that the law is able to supply us as individuals with the kind of protection you have in mind.' He quailed inwardly as he saw her eyebrows rise. It was usually the prelude to an outburst. 'Not, of course, that you're not entitled to it,' he added hastily. Had he conceded too much, he asked himself? 'In a perfect world, that is,' he went on in a desperate attempt to limit any damage.

Blanche came to his assistance once again.

'Exactly,' she said, 'I couldn't have put it better myself.'

Morgan felt the beginnings of panic. Had Blanche come to his aid once too often? Continued alignment with her could be his undoing, particularly if she now turned on Mrs Morgan. He had to go on.

'Look,' he said, 'we're all reasonable people' – the words almost stuck in his mouth but ends on this occasion had to justify means – 'let's try it for a few months; if it works – well and good – we'll all know about the level of burglaries roundabout and if we all escape the plan will have worked. If it doesn't, we'll have to think again.' Then he played his ace. 'In that event, my own reaction would be to give serious consideration to a burglar alarm,' he went on.

It didn't sound to him like particularly convincing stuff but it was the best he could manage impromptu. To his surprise it worked. His final half-promise about the burglar alarm seemed to have persuaded Mrs Morgan to meet him halfway. In fairness to her she usually did in the end.

'All right,' she said, 'a three month trial – that'll take us through the winter. But I still don't think it'll work.'

Miles took his cue obediently from Blanche and set about the business of arranging the rosters; naturally he was to take the first week. That being sorted out, they took their leave.

As Morgan ushered them out, Mrs Morgan called out to him, 'Bring my umbrella in from the porch, will you dear.'

He felt reasonably satisfied with his night's work as he waved goodbye to the departing guests – but not for long. When he looked around to retrieve her umbrella it was nowhere to be seen. The significance of this failed to register at first.

'You must have brought it in earlier,' he said innocently, 'it's not here.'

She came to the front door.

'I certainly did not,' she said, stamping her foot ever so slightly, 'someone's stolen it.'

Morgan tried to make light of it.

'Well, it's only an umbrella,' he said, you've got a whole battery of 'em in the hall cupboard.'

That was a mistake.

'My dear,' she replied in her exasperated tone, 'that is not the point. Something has been stolen even with all you . . .' she searched for the right word . . . vigilantes a few yards away. So much for communal watching.'

He felt obliged to protest; it was so unreasonable, even for her.

'Come on,' he said, 'the plan wasn't even in operation' – and then a flash of inspiration – 'even your burglar alarm wouldn't have prevented that.'

'That's as maybe,' was the reply, summarily dismissing reason, 'but I'll be keeping a close eye on this watching business all the same.'

Morgan wondered what she meant by that. He was soon to find out.

25

Watching

Morgan spent the next few days wondering about what Mrs Morgan was up to. Predictably, when she made her move he failed to spot it. Naively, he welcomed it.

It was the evening of the Wednesday after the meeting and he was reconciled to another boring few hours watching TV programmes that he didn't want to see – and worse that he wouldn't have wanted friends and colleagues to know that he had seen. Had he been alone, of course, he might have read a book or listened to the radio, but Mrs Morgan would be at home too, and her simultaneous desires to follow her favourite 'soap operas' and at the same time enjoy his company left him no way out.

He was surprised and delighted when she said after supper, 'I think we'll need the services of the chief vigilante tonight.'

Just like that – completely out of the blue. Before he could overcome his surprise, she went on.

'I think it's time you and I had a night out together.'

Brilliant, thought Morgan. Then a snag invaded his growing euphoria.

'But what about . . . ,' he said in a whisper, pointing to the bedroom where their younger daughter, now a teenager of course, was struggling with her home-work.

'No problem,' said Mrs Morgan. 'I've already had a word with her. She doesn't mind staying in by herself.' The merest suspicion of a supercilious grin was beginning to form on Morgan's face. 'And don't you laugh,' she went on.

'I wouldn't dream of it, dear,' said Morgan hastily.

'In any case,' continued Mrs Morgan tartly, 'your communal watch will be on, won't it?'

He wondered why it was 'his' communal watch.

Hats and coats were donned before Morgan realized that he had not yet informed Miles of their intention.

'Oops – nearly forgot,' he said, 'where are we going? He'll need to know.'

'You may say,' replied Mrs Morgan, 'that we are going to The Deerstalker.'

Good, thought Morgan. Even that slightly curious response failed to arouse any suspicion. He telephoned Miles who responded in 'gung ho' fashion – he would, wouldn't he? thought Morgan. Miles signed off with 'Roger and out' and off they went. Morgan still felt good. Things were looking up – or so he thought.

The first indication that things were not going to turn out quite as he expected came at the front gate. Mrs Morgan, her umbrella daintily picking out the path ahead of her, set off in entirely the wrong direction.

'Hold on,' said Morgan, 'you're going the wrong way.'

'No I'm not,' she said, 'we're taking a little stroll first. It's a fine night.'

Now a fine night it was not. Cold with black threatening clouds scudding across the sky obliterating moon and stars, it was anything but.

'But you said we were going to The Deerstalker,'

protested Morgan.

'No I didn't,' said Mrs Morgan. 'I told you to tell Miles we were going to The Deerstalker. That's different.'

'Different?' spluttered Morgan, 'but you've made me tell him a downright lie.'

'Not if we go there afterwards,' she replied.

'After what?' asked Morgan, now thoroughly bemused.

She stopped and leaned nonchalantly on her umbrella.

'After we have checked on the chief vigilante,' she said, affecting a touch of exasperation, 'if everything's as it should be we'll go to The Deerstalker.'

Now it was clear to him. He knew exactly what she had been planning. She was out to find fault in the communal watching. He sought confirmation.

'You mean you're going to spy on Miles to see if he does his watching?' he questioned.

'Exactly,' she said, 'except that it's we, not me, who will be doing it. Now let's get on. If everything's all right I'll buy you a drink.'

She rarely did that. Morgan was fearful at her confidence.

They moved into 'newcomer' territory – rows and rows of identical houses with mock latticed windows behind which, no doubt, dry sherries were being sipped prior to dinner. Only 'newcomers' had dinner, invariably at eight o'clock. 'Villagers' ate it in the middle of the day. The Morgans, now falling somewhere betwixt the two, ate supper at about six o'clock.

At the end of the road where Miles lived, Mrs Morgan stopped abruptly and pulled Morgan into the shadow of a garden hedge.

'Sh,' she said superfluously – he hadn't said anything – 'that's his house there.'

She pointed across the road with her umbrella.

'What do we do now?' asked Morgan wearily.

'We wait,' she whispered. 'If he's doing what he's supposed to be doing it won't be long.'

Sure enough, a little while later the door to Miles's house opened and he emerged.

As he shut the door behind him they heard him call out, 'Won't be too long, dear. Just off on my little patrol.'

'Who's he talking to?' hissed Morgan.

'Sh,' said Mrs Morgan, finger to his mouth, 'that'll be his wife.'

'I didn't know he had one,' persisted Morgan. 'What about this thing with Blanche?'

'You tell me,' said Mrs Morgan. Then she panicked. 'Oh God – he's coming towards us. Quick – closer to the hedge. Kiss me.'

Morgan pecked her demurely on the cheek.

'Not like that, for God's sake,' she said, drawing him closer to her and further into the hedge. He felt raindrops from the ruffled privet rolling down the back of his neck as he responded as enthusiastically as he could. Miles marched past them, rolled black umbrella over his shoulder. He never seemed to just walk.

'Evening,' he said as he went by.

'Do you think he saw us?' asked Mrs Morgan anxiously as he disappeared down the road.

'Of course he saw us,' said Morgan irritably, 'he spoke, didn't he?'

'Don't get uppity with me,' said Mrs Morgan, 'you know what I mean. Did he recognize us?'

'Hardly,' replied Morgan, 'he would have had a bit more to say if he had. Now that's enough for tonight. He's on patrol and you owe me a drink.'

'Not quite, I fancy,' said Mrs Morgan. 'I want to see

where he goes.'

She set off furtively in the shadow of the hedges in the direction which Miles had taken. Morgan brushed the wet privet leaves from his collar and padded after her. To Morgan's chagrin, it soon became obvious that Miles was not proceeding in the direction of the Morgan residence. He made for a bungalow a few streets away, still well in 'newcomer' territory. Darting from one bit of cover to another some distance behind, they were just in time to see the porch light of the bungalow go on framing Blanche as she gave Miles a rib-shuddering embrace.

'I told you so,' said Mrs Morgan triumphantly.

'Told me what?' asked Morgan – but he already knew the answer.

'That this whole thing is nothing more than a ruse for him to get away from his wife to see Blanche,' she said.

She hadn't actually told him that before, but it seemed irrelevant now. The evidence seemed to be all in her favour. He tried one last ploy.

'Let's wait a while,' he said, 'perhaps he'll come out again in a minute and get on with his patrolling.'

That was the best he could do but he knew it wouldn't work. His cause was lost. They waited in vain for an hour. Mrs Morgan, who had reached her conclusion, and was not anxious to imperil it, pressed him continually to take her home. Eventually the onset of rain decided it and they made their way back to the house. He didn't dare mention The Deerstalker.

Mercifully, Mrs Morgan did not crow over what she undoubtedly regarded as a vindication of her unease about the communal watching scheme. On the contrary, she chose to show the mercy of the victor. The following week she suggested to Morgan that he might care to resume his lone sallies to The Deerstalker – that night in fact. Rashly, Morgan revived memories of the Miles affair.

'Do you want me to tell Arthur?' he said, 'he's on watch this week.'

Her reaction was appropriately contemptuous.

'Humph,' she snorted, 'if he's anything like that Mallalieu creature he'll be a fat lot of use. No – you carry on but be back by nine.'

As Morgan gleefully donned his coat the doorbell rang. He opened it to be confronted by a burly figure in a black Balaclava and anorak, carrying what looked like a shotgun. His panic outpaced his shock.

'No you don't,' he cried, slamming the soor shut.

Mrs Morgan called out from the living-room.

'Steady on,' she said, 'you'll have the glass out of the door, slamming it like that.'

He stood inside the door wondering what to do next when the letterbox rattled.

'It's me, Arthur,' croaked a disembodied voice through the aperture. He breathed a great sigh of relief, opened the door and stepped outside, closing it ever so gently behind him.

'What the hell are you doing, Arthur?' he asked, 'dressed like that – and is that a shotgun you've got there?'

'I be on patrol this week,' said Arthur, 'and I be ready for them. Speke-Johnson and 'is missus are out to a party and I wondered if you wanted a bit o' watching as well.'

'Definitely not,' said Morgan, 'you'd frighten Mrs Morgan to death if she saw you. What's all this with the gun?'

'He'm all right,' said Arthur, 'he'm licensed.'

Licensed for what, thought Morgan.

'But you can't go shooting at people,' he said, 'Not

285

even burglars.'

'Don't you fuss,' replied Arthur. 'I'll just gi' 'em a bit of a fright.'

Morgan was uneasy but weak. His precious drinking time until nine o'clock was ticking away.

'OK,' he said, 'but be careful and for God's sake keep away from Mrs Morgan with it. I'm off to The Deerstalker.'

It was not a wise decision.

Promptly at ten minutes to nine he downed the remains of his last pint, made his farewells and set off home from The Deerstalker. Arthur's activities had dogged his thoughts all the evening. As he drew level with the Speke-Johnsons his worst fears were realized. There was a loud bang. Please God, let it be a car back-firing, he prayed. He looked up and down the road. Not a car in sight. It was then that Arthur appeared, tugging off his Balaclava and waving his shotgun.

'I've winged one of the varmints,' he shouted excitedly.

Morgan froze to the spot.

'Come on,' said Arthur, tugging at his sleeve, 'let's catch the bugger.'

His thoughts were in turmoil as Arthur dragged him down the drive towards the back of the house.

''ere – 'old the torch,' he said as he propelled Morgan towards some thick bushes in the back garden. 'Over 'ere,' he went on, 'there was some rustling in them there bushes. I shouted "'alt or I fire" as us used to in th'army but 'e kept on so I let 'n 'ave it. Only the one barrel, mind you.'

Morgan hastily pushed the barrel of the gun away from him and halted their scrambling progress towards the bushes.

'But, Arthur,' he said, 'you may have killed

someone.'

Arthur was unimpressed.

'Firing low for the legs, ain't I?' he said.

Morgan was equally unimpressed.

'What if he was crawling?' he asked.

For the first time Arthur's tone faltered.

'Blimey – 'adn't thought o' that', he quavered.

Morgan drew a deep breath.

'There's only one way to find out,' he said, 'give me the gun.'

Arthur snapped on the safety catch – God, it's been cocked all the time, thought Morgan – and handed it to him.

'Shine the torch,' he went on, as he inched forward and gently parted the bushes with the barrel. There was no intruder. Lying horribly dead in a pool of blood at his feet was one of the Speke-Johnsons' goats.

'Strewth – thank God for that!' exclaimed the now penitent Arthur.

Morgan was not wholly relieved. To his mind slaughtering one of Speke-Johnsons' pet goats might well bring almost as much retribution as wounding an intruder with mayhem in mind.

'You'd better wait here to explain when they come back,' he said.

'You'll stay as well?' asked Arthur tremulously. 'They'll take more notice of 'ee.'

For the second time that night Morgan succumbed to weakness.

'I can't, Arthur,' he said. 'Mrs Morgan will be wondering where I've got to.'

It was a lame excuse in the circumstances but he had had enought for one night and having to face the wrath of the Speke-Johnsons seemed, at that moment, unbearable.

'You're late,' said Mrs Morgan as he entered the house.

'Sorry,' he said, 'got talking at the pub.'

His mind was racing as her inevitable reproaches swept over him. How would the Speke-Johnsons react? They'd not been too keen on the communal watching scheme in the first place. Worse still, what would Mrs Morgan say when she found out – he would have to tell her sooner or later.

It turned out to be sooner. He suddenly became conscious of what he thought were her continuing censures over his late return, but it was more serious than that.

'Well?' she was saying, 'what do you make of that?'

'Sorry,' he said, 'I was thinking. Make of what?'

'You haven't been listening, have you?' she said reprovingly. 'What I was saying was that I heard what sounded like a shot about half-an-hour ago.'

There was no escape now. The game was up. He had to tell her.

Naturally she was furious. Morgan bore her strictures stoically, barely daring to reply, until her final outburst.

'Well, you'll have to wait up and explain to them,' she said. 'I'm going to bed.'

He had to protest at this. He longed for the oblivion of sleep but it was not to be. He was, of course, on shaky ground. He had started the whole thing off, she reminded him, and he was the one who had to take responsibility. Eventually he capitulated.

Over the next few hours, he spent a solitary vigil, seated at the front window watching for the lights of the Speke-Johnsons' car to signal their return. Now and again he would creep to the front door to catch sight of Arthur perched on a dustbin at the drive entrance, a solitary sentinel, with the offending shotgun cradled in his arms. In the early hours of the morning he gave up. The Speke-Johnsons, unusually for them, were obviously at a very late party on this of all nights. He was beginning to think that the misfortune surrounding the whole affair was unrelenting. He went out to Arthur.

'You go to bed,' he said. 'I'll sort things out with them in the morning.'

Misfortune, however, was to continue to dog him. He overslept. Breakfast was a scrambled affair as Mrs Morgan deprived by his lateness of her early morning cup of tea, strove irritably to get him off to work on time. Inevitably, in the process she was to ask the question he dreaded about the night before.

'Well, how did they take it?' she asked.

There was no hiding place for Morgan.

'I'm afraid they still don't know,' he said tremulously. 'I waited up as long as I could but they still hadn't returned.'

He waited for the explosion. Curiously, when it came it brought him a modicum of relief.

Slamming her fist on the table she said, 'I've had a bellyful of this. I'll have to sort this one out. You'd better be off to work.'

He didn't demur. The sanctuary of his office where he could plan his response looked at that moment a very attractive option.

'Off you go then,' went on Mrs Morgan, studiously offering her cheek rather than her lips for a departing kiss. 'I'll go and talk to Marigold later.' He put on his coat; no-one could have looked more chastened. But Mrs Morgan was not quite finished with him. 'By the way,' she said, taking a glossy brochure from a drawer,' I got this from a burglar alarm company. You'd better read it and get in touch with them.

It was a long day in the office. Not even the pressures of work could take his mind off the problems he had left behind at home. The communal watching scheme was in tatters and doomed to abandonment. The installation of the detested burglar alarm was now inevitable. And there was still the wrath of the Speke-Johnsons to face. Things couldn't be worse, he thought – but they could.

When he arrived home, Mrs Morgan compounded his agony.

'Oliver's been to the police,' she said. 'Sergeant Plomley's coming round to see you shortly.'

About half-an-hour later the sergeant arrived. Mrs Morgan left them alone, possibly to spare Morgan further embarrassment. As the sergeant droned on about the folly of trying to take the law into one's own hands, Morgan sat silent like a schoolboy before his headmaster. Then the time came for him to express humbly his deep regret. He was still doing this when Mrs Morgan returned; strangely Morgan had the feeling she was trying to protect him. Certainly Sergeant Plomley seemed to take it as a sign to bring the ordeal to a close.

'Well, that'll be all, sir,' he said. 'I'll be off to see Mr Potts now.'

'Will you be taking any action against him?' enquired Morgan nervously.

'Not this time, sir,' replied the sergeant, 'but he might have a problem when his shotgun licence needs renewing. Pity about that – he's had it these long years.'

Morgan felt it was not too bad an outcome in the circumstances. Of course, he mused, they're both 'villagers' – but that wouldn't influence Sergeant Plomley – or would it? He would never know.

The sergeant was at the front door putting on his

helmet.

'We just can't have it, sir, you see – not with firearms. It's not the Wild West, you know.'

Surprisingly, Mrs Morgan intervened.

'It is on Saturday nights,' she said, 'and that Maritime is the Last Chance Saloon.'

She deserved to get that one in, thought Morgan. The sergeant's reply was equally surprising.

'Well, you won't have to worry about that much longer, ma'am,' he said, 'they're leaving soon – Sonia and that there Jason – taking a pub in the city, I 'ear.'

Morgan was not to know then that this would be the first of a series of departures which would dramatically change his perception of Gatehaven and seriously jeopardize his ten-year love affair with the place.

26

Departures

The departures from The Maritime of Sonia and Jason, presumably in the company of the sorrowing Dolores – although he never found that out for sure – should not have caused Morgan much regret. After all, he and Mrs Morgan, like countless others, had long ceased to patronize the establishment. Strangely enough though, it did. For a long period, extending well into 1982, no other tenant appeared to be forthcoming and the building remained boarded up, occasionally vandalized, weeds growing in the car park and the surrounding gardens running wild. As he passed by now and then, Morgan could not help reflecting on his earlier years in Gatehaven and the extraordinary events which had taken place in the hotel. Would he ever see such things again?

His growing conviction that he wouldn't was heightened early in 1982 by the news that Father Alphonsus too was leaving. He had grown fond of the priest, more because of than despite his undoubted idiosyncrasies.

'I'm sorry to hear you're going,' he said when he ran across him one evening in the men's bar of the club.

Father Alphonsus put down his snooker cue and laid his hand on Morgan's shoulder.

'Unfortunately, my son,' he said – as if he had practised his response – 'I am a man subject to a vow of obedience. When the powers-that-be say "go" then I go.'

'But you've been here so long, Father,' said Morgan, 'you're a local institution.'

'Maybe too long,' replied Father Alphonsus, 'I've got too comfortable perhaps. It gets in the way of a vocation, you know. There always has to be a new challenge.'

Morgan sensed a mini-sermon coming on. Perhaps it was time to change tack.

'Where are they sending you then?' he enquired.

'Believe it or not – Borneo,' was the reply, 'we're starting a new mission station there. It seems I am the man for the job.'

Morgan could scarce suppress a smile at the thought of Father Alphonsus and his somewhat extrovert brand of Catholicism exploding into the lives of the poor people of that far-off land.

'Anyway,' continued Father Alphonsus, 'why don't you and the missus come up to the presbytery for a farewell drink. I'd like that. Next Wednesday about seven say?'

'We'd be delighted,' replied Morgan.

As it happened Mrs Morgan was not quite so delighted as Morgan. She had never enjoyed quite the same closeness to the priest as Morgan had, probably because in his leisure time Father Alphonsus liked to be among men. His natural habitat was among the pints, the banter and the raucous laughter which abounded in places like the men's bar but rarely elsewhere. She also harboured the gravest suspicions about any function which he organized. Nevertheless, her upbringing had taught her to regard a request from the clergy more as a summons and – albeit none too enthusiastically – she agreed to come.

When they arrived at the presbytery, Bridie answered the door as usual – perhaps not quite as usual since there was a glass in her hand and the suspicion of a tear in her eye.

'Come in both,' she said, 'we're in the common room.' At least that must be better than the kitchen, thought Morgan, with Mrs Morgan's sensibilities in mind, and recalling his last visit.

It was a curious gathering even by Gatehaven standards. Seated around the sides of the room in non-matching armchairs – no doubt donated by various parishioners over the years whenever they re-furbished their homes – were the three curates and Sister Katherine with the young nun of Knock fame. Bridie hovered near the sideboard on which were assorted bottles from which she was to proffer glasses at frequent intervals throughout the evening. Facing the guests in one corner of the room Father Alphonsus sat in a battered black leather swivel chair on which he swung gently from side to side as he addressed them.

'Ah, come in and sit down now,' he said as the Morgans arrived, 'you know everyone I expect' – his eyes twinkled – 'including my little partner in crime from Knock.'

The young nun giggled. Sister Katherine looked at her reprovingly at first, but then her face creased into an unexpected smile.

'Sure that must have been a great trip, Father,' she said. 'I'm sorry I missed it.'

That was the cue for Father Alphonsus to launch into a succession of anecdotes about his years in the parish, each becoming, as Morgan could recall, slightly more embroidered and distant from the truth as Bridie refilled his glass from time to time. The guests could do little but nod or titter at appropriate intervals. The three curates said nothing at all, no doubt innured by years of enforced silence when the great man was in full flow. Time passed quickly. No other parishioners arrived, which Morgan found strange, and eventually, Sister Katherine broke the sequence by signalling her intention to leave. The young nun, of course, had no choice but to follow suit. Father Alphonsus levered himself from his chair and extinguished his cigarette in a saucer on the table beside him.

'Well, Sister,' he said, 'this is it then.'

She wiped a tear from her eye as he suddenly grasped her by the shoulder and planted a resounding kiss on her cheek.

'God go with you, old friend,' she said.

'And with you, my dear,' was the reply.

Morgan was astonished. After all the starchy stand-offs he had witnessed between them could it be that they liked and respected one another after all? Admirable as that thought was, it was another nail in the coffin of his perception of the old ambience of Gatehaven which had beguiled him over the years.

Mrs Morgan took her cue from the departure of Sister Katherine.

'We had better be off, too, Father,' she said, 'it's getting late.'

It wasn't, but Morgan guessed she was anxious not to become involved in what she termed a 'session'.

As they took their leave, Morgan, still curious about the absence of other parisioners, enquired, 'We'll see you again, Father. The parish will be putting on a bit of a farewell do, won't they?'

'Ah,' replied Father Alphonsus, 'some of them think they are but they'll by lucky. I've had a drink in various places' – he tapped the side of his nose conspiratorially –

'with those I wanted to and I'll be slipping away early in the morning.'

Perverse to the end, thought Morgan. He was both sad and pleased. At least he had qualified for a farewell drink.

'So this is really goodbye,' he said.

'Yes, my son,' replied Father Alphonsus, 'now you get the new feller sorted out with club membership and all that and you'll hardly notice the difference. God bless now and take care.'

That was the last they saw of him.

Morgan had cause to mourn the departure of Father Alphonsus. The new parish priest was austere and authoritarian and would no more think of joining the social club than he would the Salvation Army. The social life of the parish, including the parish parties, all so vibrant under the enthusiastic guidance of Father Alphonsus, withered and died. Mrs Morgan drifted back to her weekly bingo sessions at the club, in the company of Bridie, as she used to before her brief flirtation with local politics. As a result Morgan found himself more and more in the company of Arthur in the men's bar, but even that didn't seem the same without the loud infectious presence of Father Alphonsus.

In the summer of 1982, fate was to deal him an even more devastating blow. Arthur died suddenly of a heart attack. The celebration – for that's what it seemed to Morgan to be – of Arthur's passing was to be the last great 'villager' occasion he would participate in for a very long time. He was conscious of preparations for the event being discussed in the men's bar, but without the protecting presence of Arthur – his long-time guide and mentor in that company – he found himself excluded from them. He began to think that he was not quite as much a 'villager' as he had thought and hoped, despite all his efforts over the years to distance himself from the 'newcomers'. Nevertheless, he was determined to attend the funeral.

It was, of course, a 'men only' affair. Sergeant Plomley had been persuaded to close a section of the High Street to traffic for a short time while Arthur's coffin was borne from his house to the old parish church. About two hundred 'villagers' followed, ill-at-ease in old-fashioned dark suits, poorly fitting collars and shiny black boots. In the church, Morgan hovered at the back, resting his elbow on the font as the vicar delivered a long eulogy. Morgan learnt things about Arthur that he had never heard before. He had, it seemed, a distinguished war record. Over all their pints of scrumpy together in the club, he had never mentioned it.

As the coffin was carried from the church for burial in the adjacent graveyard – a spot which by accident or design seemed to be reserved as a last resting-place for 'villagers' only – Morgan was buttonholed by Sid, the steward from the club.

'You'll be coming back to the club for the wake,' he said.

Morgan was surprised and pleased. Perhaps he was more of a 'villager' than he had thought.

The wake was a boozy rumbustious affair with each successive intake of scrumpy loudly dedicated to Arthur amid claims that this was just how he would have wanted them to mark his passing. No doubt it was; Morgan savoured the occasion despite the sadness of the event which had precipitated it. Eventually he extricated himself from the mêlée around the bar which showed no signs of evaporating, and made his way home – it has to be said a trifle unsteadily. Naturally Mrs Morgan was not impressed with his claims about what Arthur would have wanted. To her, funerals were meant to be altogether more sober affairs. But even her temporary disaffection with him could not dissipate the sense of satisfaction he felt at just having been there.

That sense of satisfaction, of course, could not last for long and in the following months Morgan's life settled into a pattern which, deprived of so many of its main characters, bore little resemblance to what it had been a year or two earlier. His long enchantment with Gatehaven and its people seemed finally to be drawing to a close.

Then, in the latter part of 1982, just coming up to ten years since the Morgan family arrived in Gatehaven, something occurred which was to change the direction of his life dramatically. He lost his job.

To say that he lost it is perhaps misleading; it was more that he relinquished it, after much thought and a future in mind that was very different from the one he was actually to experience. The screws were tightening on public expenditure and Morgan's department was offering everyone over fifty the option of early retirement with full pension benefits. Saddened by the virtual disappearance of the Gatehaven he loved, he saw this as an opportunity to cut his ties and start afresh somewhere else. But, as so often in his life, he failed to take into account the reaction of Mrs Morgan.

She was adamant. She liked Gatehaven, she was settled in Gatehaven, their youngest child was still at school in Gatehaven. the people who had departed were not her closest friends in any case, whatever Morgan's relationship with them had been. Besides he was over-pessimistic about the future in the town. New characters would emerge, they always did. In her view these things went in cycles. Not that she minded him retiring. There was plenty to do about the garden – and the house for that matter – she reminded him ominously.

Poor Morgan. He still wanted to retire – his career urge had gone – but his intention to search for some other Avalon seemed to be doomed too. If he was to believe Mrs Morgan only gardening and housework beckoned. How could he face a future like that?

The answer came to him suddenly. It was another departure of a kind which would take him down a road which in his wildest dreams he would never have expected to tread. When he was ready he confronted her.

'I've decided to go ahead with the early retirement,' he said.

'Good,' she replied, 'but we're not moving from here – you understand that.'

'Yes, I understand that,' he said quietly.

She looked at him quizzically. Her curiosity was aroused.

'You're happy to stay here?' she enquired, 'even though you'll be hankering after how it all used to be.'

'Yes,' he said, still strangely quiet but firm, 'and I shall still hanker for it but,' he paused for effect, 'I am going to recreate it.'

That puzzled her – even alarmed her.

'Recreate it?' she asked, 'whatever do you mean?'

For Morgan this was the crunch – the watershed in his life.

'I am going,' he said in the most measured tones he could muster, 'I am going to write a book about it.'

And so Morgan arrived at his vision of the future. Not for him an unwilling consignment to the role of domestic assistant to Mrs Morgan, but something creative and inspiring to give him purpose, direction and satisfaction in the use of his new-found leisure time. Well, that was the vision. Inevitably, he being Morgan and the place being Gatehaven, things were not to turn out in quite that way; but that's another story!